"Are you having second thoughts about our marriage?"

The eyes Hannah lifted to his might not look like those of an excited bride, but they were steely with determination. "Marriage is what I want. Are you changing your mind?"

"No, ma'am." Matt grinned. "I'm corralled and ready for branding. Thing is, which brand will I wear?"

"The Lazy P, what else."

"And you're just the woman to get the job done."

Hannah grinned back at him. "Never doubt that, cowboy."

Good to see her feisty side back. A man didn't hanker to be led around by his nose, but if pretending Hannah was boss would put a smile on her face, that's what he'd do.

But he couldn't help wondering at what point a marriage based on pretense would blow up in his face?

Books by Janet Dean

Love Inspired Historical

Courting Miss Adelaide
Courting the Doctor's Daughter
The Substitute Bride
Wanted: A Family
An Inconvenient Match
The Bride Wore Spurs

JANET DEAN

grew up in a family that cherished the past and had a strong creative streak. Her father recounted wonderful stories, like his father before him. The tales they told instilled in Janet a love of history and the desire to write. She married her college sweetheart and taught first grade before leaving to rear two daughters. As her daughters grew, they watched *Little House on the Prairie,* reawakening Janet's love of American history and the stories of strong men and women of faith who built this country. Janet eagerly turned to inspirational historical romance, and she loves spinning stories for Love Inspired Historical. When she isn't writing, Janet stamps greeting cards, plays golf and bridge, and is never without a book to read. The Deans love to travel and to spend time with family.

The Bride
Wore Spurs

JANET DEAN

✦ **HARLEQUIN**® LOVE INSPIRED® HISTORICAL
™

Recycling programs
for this product may
not exist in your area.

 ™ LOVE INSPIRED BOOKS

ISBN-13: 978-0-373-82962-0

THE BRIDE WORE SPURS

www.LoveInspiredBooks.com

Printed in U.S.A.

My grace is sufficient for thee:
for my strength is made perfect in weakness.
—*2 Corinthians* 12:9

To my friends and family who believed
I'd achieve my dream. Your support means everything,
then and now. Thank you.

Acknowledgments

A huge, heartfelt thank-you to Mary Connealy
and Becke Turner for their invaluable help with
researching this story. Their expertise enabled this
greenhorn to ride into the Old West largely unscathed.
Any errors are my own.

Chapter One

Bliss, Texas
Spring, 1888

The wrong man showed up to collect Hannah Parrish at the train station. And he was late.

Matt Walker.

Hannah bit back a groan. Of all the people in Bliss, why him? Matt never saw her as grown-up and capable. Instead he still treated her like a child, like the young girl he'd teased.

The man was too sure of himself. Tall, broad-shouldered, long legs encased in denim, his suntanned face hidden by the wide brim of a black Stetson, Matt's every inch oozed cowboy. And every one of those inches oozed irksome.

He came to a halt in front of her, boots planted in a wide stance as if buffeted by the winds that blew across the open range. With a smile, Matt doffed his hat, the late afternoon sun gleaming in his dark wavy hair. The man was good-looking, she'd give him that, but the only man she ached to see was Papa.

"Welcome back," he said. His Texas drawl was polite, yet the pucker between his brows was far from friendly.

"Good to be back." She scanned the crowd milling about the depot platform, retrieving baggage and greeting family. "Have you seen my father?"

Matt plopped his hat in place, throwing his chocolate-brown eyes in shadow. "Martin asked me to pick you up."

Surely after being apart for a year, Papa wouldn't miss meeting her train unless...

Was something wrong? She swallowed against the sudden knot in her throat. "Why didn't he come himself?"

"Didn't say. Better not keep him waiting."

Before she could question him further, Matt took her by the elbow and guided her across the wooden platform, dodging two rambunctious youngsters running through the throng.

Was it only four years ago she'd tagged after Zack, Matt's youngest brother? At the time, Matt had been married to Amy, his high school sweetheart, and had reveled in teasing Hannah at every opportunity. That had been before Amy's horse threw her and she died from a broken neck, when Matt's laugh came easy.

Now, he looked tense. Did he resent picking her up? Well, she wasn't any happier about the switch.

Still, to be fair, she should ease her attitude toward the man, give him the benefit of the doubt. From what Papa had told her, he'd closed himself off after his wife's death.

They stopped before the baggage cart's perspiring attendant. Hannah pointed out her bags and large camel back trunk.

The porter surveyed her luggage, mumbling an oath under his breath.

Heat flushed her cheeks. If she'd had a choice, she would've left every dress behind in Charleston. But, Papa had tired of seeing her in denim and had insisted she return with a new wardrobe. Aunt Mary Esther had made his wishes her mission.

Matt slipped the attendant a tip. "I'll take it from here."

With a snaggletooth smile, the porter doffed his hat, then turned to the next traveler.

Matt hefted the trunk onto his shoulder, letting out a grunt. "A man could bust a gut toting this load. Must've brought the entire state of South Carolina back with you."

"That's not my fault, I—"

"If you packed them, I'd say that makes them yours," he said before she could explain the large number of cases weren't her idea.

He balanced the trunk then grabbed a valise's leather handle, straining muscles that pulled his shirt tight over powerful shoulders and arms, producing an odd flutter in the pit of her stomach.

"Stay put," he said. "I'll only be a minute."

"I'm perfectly capable of carrying…" Her voice faded as he swaggered off. How dare he treat her like a hot-house flower.

She grabbed the three remaining cases and marched after him, the sun glaring on her back, her lungs heaving against her cast-iron corset. The ostrich plume on her gray felt hat drooped into view, tickling her nose. Her aunt would say the hat made fashion sense. More like fashion insanity.

Papa had sent her away to gain grace and style and all those put-on manners the finishing school had drummed into her. Now she supposed she was indeed finished.

But not as Papa intended.

Her aunt's aimless life had made Hannah all the more determined to remain a rancher. What she did on the Lazy P had significance, and gave her satisfaction.

Without a free hand to swat at the tormenting feather,

she blew a puff of air. The feather fluttered, then came to rest against her nose.

Matt stopped, turned back. His gaze settled on the feather. He gave a smirk. "I'd prefer you'd wait until I can return for the rest."

"I prefer doing my part."

Surly eyes gave her a cursory glance. "In that?"

Hannah's gaze swept her traveling dress, all flounce and ruffle, as uncomfortable as armor thanks to the torturous corset. "Don't judge me on my attire."

He harrumphed. "Like Charleston hasn't changed you."

She jerked up her chin. "It hasn't. At all." Another breath lifted up the feather. This time it stayed put.

"Whatever you say, Miss Parrish."

He headed down the boardwalk. She followed, perspiration beading on her forehead. At the wagon, she dropped the load with a clatter at Matt's feet—feet clad in cowboy boots, high quality, Texas made. And he accused her of being a clotheshorse.

Matt leaned against the wagon, apparently untouched by the heat. "Didn't that fancy finishing school teach you to allow a man to give you a hand?" he drawled.

"It taught me to take care of myself."

Not exactly the truth. The headmistress's main message was a proper lady relies on a man for everything, not merely heavy lifting. Well, Hannah tried to never rely on anyone for anything.

His amused expression disputed her claim. "Course you can."

She slapped her arms across her chest, arms that ached from carrying that load, but she'd never admit as much by rubbing them. "Are you questioning that?"

"All right, then. Go ahead. Take care of yourself." He gestured toward the trunk.

On the ground. Six feet below the bed of the wagon.

"You mean put that…in there?"

"You said you could take care of yourself."

To admit she needed help would mean admitting defeat. She bent, the feather quivering in front of her eyes, then gripped the leather handles and heaved with all her might, releasing a decidedly unladylike grunt. And managed to budge the trunk three whole inches before she let it drop. A year in Charleston had made her soft.

"Give up?" Matt asked.

"Never." Heat flooding her cheeks, she gritted her teeth and tried again.

"We'll be here all day while you try to prove your point." He bent down, grabbed the trunk as if it weighed less than the obnoxious feather on her hat and shoved it into the wagon, then stowed the rest of her bags.

"I could have done that." She met his amused gaze. "Eventually."

"Next time the trunk is all yours." With a chuckle, he rounded the wagon and gave her a hand up.

His touch trapped the air in her lungs. Since when did Matt Walker affect her this way? Exhaustion had muddled her mind into mush.

He climbed up beside her. His fluid movements revealed how comfortable he was, how completely at ease. Whereas she felt thrown off balance, as if she'd stepped into somebody else's skin with a whole set of reactions she didn't understand. Or appreciate.

She wanted to go home, to see her father, to soak in the tub until not one speck of travel dust remained.

Home. To the cattle, to the land she loved, the limitless expanse under the Texas sky. Home. Where she'd shuck her frills and finery and don her usual garb and favorite Stetson, clothes she could move and breathe in. Home. To Papa.

With large, capable hands, Matt took the reins, then clicked to the horses. The wagon jerked forward as the horses pulled away.

Beyond the depot lay the bustling town with wagons, buggies and horses jamming the streets. After a year in Charleston, returning home was like easing into comfy boots.

Hannah removed her hat, her gaze caressing each edifice they passed. The courthouse dominated Main Street, teeming with storefronts, saloons, Bliss State Bank, Bailey's Dry Goods, The James Hotel, the post office, the office of *The Banner Weekly* newspaper and two groceries. They passed the blacksmith shop, O'Hara's livery stable, the sheriff's office and the Calico Café, owned by the widow Shields with two rooms to let upstairs if boarders met her strict standards.

At the outskirts of town, they headed toward the ranch. No longer distracted by the racket and dust of Bliss, she turned to Matt. "Is my father well?"

Matt glanced at her, then away, staring at the horses' rumps. Just as she decided he wouldn't speak, he cleared his throat. "Martin's had a rough few months. When I stopped in last night to check on him, he asked me to meet your train."

"Check on him? Why? Isn't Rosa there?"

"Yes, of course." Matt shifted on the seat. "Wait to talk to him."

"I need to know what's wrong before I arrive."

"He's facing…some challenges." He met her gaze. "Having you home will lift his spirits."

And lift a load from Papa's shoulders. If he was sick, she could run the ranch. Oversee the foreman while Papa recovered. If only she'd known he needed help. "Why didn't he send for me?" A rut in the road sent Hannah's hat tumbling to the floorboards. She retrieved it, then whacked the crown against her knee, raising a puff of dust. "I didn't want to go to Charleston in the first place."

He shot an amused glance at the mound of baggage in the wagon bed. Proof he didn't believe a word. What did she care?

She'd take the focus off her. "How's Zack? Is he out of school?"

"My little brother graduated and joined a law firm in Dallas." He arched an eyebrow. "He's still single."

"I'm surprised he hasn't met someone."

"Figured he was waiting on you. Or you on him."

"You figured wrong. I'm in no hurry to get married."

Dark eyes bored into hers with the force of an auger. "From what I've seen, most women are downright desperate to get hitched."

Desperate to get hitched, my eye.

The claim didn't deserve a retort. From what Hannah had seen, a wife was either a household drudge or an ornamental knickknack. Determined to ignore him, Hannah kept her gaze on the road, away from the vexing man at her side.

At last they drove onto Parrish land, passing a field of bluebonnets carpeting the earth to the horizon. A sense of serenity absent in Charleston seeped into her spirit. But then her mind niggled, filling her with troubling disquiet.

Matt had danced around her questions about Papa. What wasn't he telling her?

Matt eased back on the reins, slowing the horses to pass through the Lazy P gate. At his side, Hannah soaked up the terrain. Barely nineteen, yet certain she had her future mapped out. The set of her shoulders, her ramrod back, the tilt of her jaw, all pointed to one determined woman.

He swallowed hard. One determined, beautiful woman.

The skinny tomboy in baggy clothes, who sometimes could outride, outshoot and outrope Zack, had grown up. He forced his eyes away from the pretty woman at his side and onto the Parrish house up ahead.

The past year, he'd fallen into the habit of spending evenings here with Martin, discussing politics or cattle business over a game of checkers. With Hannah away, this ranch had become his refuge, his second home. Here he could unwind, away from haunting memories of Amy in his parents' house, away from the watchful eyes of his loved ones, away from his father's tight control.

As he'd gotten close to Martin, he hadn't seen the signs of his friend's waning health, but when he grew weak, pale, Matt could no longer deny Martin was sick—too sick to run the ranch. Without shirking his responsibilities at the Circle W, Matt had overseen operations of the Lazy P. The additional work pushed him to his limits, but nothing compared to the agony of watching a friend's body deteriorate.

Like a crouching lion, a sense of helplessness, sorrow and anger had sprung up inside him, awakening feelings he'd had when he lost Amy. Feelings he'd tried to bury with endless work, collapsing into bed at night, too drained to feel anything.

He'd seen the flash of fear in Hannah's eyes as he'd spoken of Martin's health. Unless God wrought a miracle for Martin, she'd have her heart broken.

This spitfire in a skirt, about as competent as a man with his hands tied behind his back, could no more handle this ranch than a cowpoke could handle city life. No matter what she said, she'd need to sell the land. Go back to Charleston where she fit, where she could find herself a husband.

The thought of the anguish awaiting her stung the backs

of his eyes. He blinked, clearing the mist, and strengthened his resolve to stay clear of entanglements. He'd do all he could for Martin. But, the debutante's future wasn't his problem. He'd hold himself apart, keep that armor in place. The only way he could be of use to anyone.

He halted the horses in front of the Parrish house, a low-slung solid structure with an inviting shady porch sheltering a cluster of twig furniture. A quiet spot where a man could catch a sunset. Catch his breath. Catch a moment with God.

He climbed down and headed toward Hannah. Before he reached her, she'd grabbed a fistful of skirts, jumped down and dashed up the steps. No doubt impatient to see her father.

The door swung open. Rosa, the Parrish housekeeper, stepped out, plump arms thrown as wide as the welcoming smile on her face. "Hannah!"

Rosa had to be around Matt's parents' age, yet her dark hair held only an occasional strand of silver and not a single wrinkle creased her round face. With one eye on the happy reunion, Matt unloaded and lugged the baggage to the porch.

Before he toted them to Hannah's room, he'd check on Martin, see that he was prepared to greet his daughter. The man couldn't stomach appearing weak, looking like an invalid.

Across the way, Rosa cradled Hannah's face in work-worn hands and kissed her on both cheeks. "You left a girl and came back a woman. You favor your mama more and more."

Tears running down her cheeks, Hannah hugged the older woman. "I've missed you, Rosa."

Why women cried at happy occasions baffled Matt. At least they weren't weeping in his arms.

Rosa smiled at him. "Hello, Señor Matt."

"How's the finest cook in the county?"

Rosy-cheeked and beaming, the housekeeper giggled. "You try for cookie. They cool in kitchen." She tucked an arm around Hannah. "Come. I help you unpack."

"I want to see Papa first."

"Hannah, I'd like a minute with Martin. Why don't you take a second to…" He glanced at Rosa for help.

"*Si,* wash face, hands." The housekeeper led the way inside.

"I'll only be a few minutes," Hannah said, pleasant enough, but her pointed stare warned him not overstay his welcome.

With a nod, Matt rounded the corner and strode down the hall to Martin's room. He rapped on his door then poked his head in. As he suspected, Martin was stretched out on the bed fully dressed, but from his bleary eyes, he'd been dozing.

A smile lit his face as he struggled to rise. "She's home."

"Yes, freshening up." Matt helped Martin stand. Once he was steady on his feet, they walked the short distance to the office. Martin dropped into his chair behind his desk, his back to the window.

Matt sat in a chair across from him. "You sure you're up to dinner guests tonight?"

"I'm fine."

Those words belied Martin's appearance. Yet Matt understood the need to save face, to ignore what was plain to see.

"My illness is going to flip Hannah's world upside down. She can't keep the ranch," Martin said, his tone weary. "I've got to make her understand that her future is in Charleston."

Martin spoke the truth. Yet that truth hurt Martin and would hurt his daughter.

"I let that girl run wild." A smile lifted the grim line of Martin's lips. "Can't wait to see the change in her."

Tomboy turned debutante would please Martin. "If you have everything you need, I'll be on my way."

"Thanks for picking Hannah up at the depot." Martin's gaze dropped to his hands. "Appreciate it if you and your folks kept silent about my troubles. I aim to give my daughter a happy homecoming."

"Of course. You can count on us to—"

The sound of shoes clicking on the floorboards cut off Matt's words, then halted outside the open door.

"Papa!" With a smile riding her face, Hannah rushed to where Martin sat, the late afternoon sunlight putting him in silhouette. As she reached him, her smile vanished. Wide-eyed, she gaped at Martin. Shock was on her face at seeing her once robust father a shell of his former self, a frail man, his face etched with lines, his skin an unhealthy gray.

"Hannah, dear, I've been waiting all afternoon for my daughter's kiss."

She leaned down, kissed his cheek then stepped back, plopping hands on hips. "You're too thin. Are you ill? Are you eating properly?"

"Been ill. Feeling much better now that you're home. You need to change for dinner. The Walkers will be joining us."

Stormy blue eyes flashed Matt's way then turned back to Martin. "Of course. I'll wear one of my new dresses and relay all the news from Charleston."

"That's my girl."

"I'll see you later, Papa. Rest, okay?"

She pressed a kiss to Martin's forehead then strode to the door, grabbing Matt's arm and hauling him with her.

"See you tonight," Matt said over his shoulder.

As the door clicked shut, Hannah whirled on him. "What's going on with my father?" she said in a harsh, hoarse whisper.

"He told you. He's been ill."

"That doesn't tell me anything! Ill with what?"

With a shrug and sealed lips, he met her gaze. He wouldn't betray Martin's confidence.

Her eyes narrowed, latching on to him like a terrier to a bone. "Who's running this ranch?"

"I am."

"The Lazy P belongs to us. You have your own ranch."

"I'm only helping out."

"That was nice of you, but he has me now."

Matt fought to keep a straight face. "You?"

"You think I'm nothing more than a debutante." She poked him in the chest, her dainty forefinger carrying a surprising wallop. "I'm what I've always been, Matt Walker. A rancher."

"That's absurd. The sooner you realize you have no business running the ranch, the better."

"The sooner you realize what I do is none of your business, the better," she said, then stormed off.

A young, inexperienced female boss was about as welcome to cowpokes as a rattler in the bunkhouse. How long before Hannah learned that truth the hard way?

Chapter Two

A nuisance stood on the Parrish threshold. Or so Hannah tried to tell herself. Taller than her by several inches, Matt's dark mesmerizing eyes locked with hers.

"Evening," he said as he stepped inside.

He looked far too appealing, even chivalrous as he swept off his black beaver Stetson, giving access to his features. Pressed flat on the sides from the pressure of the headband, his hair curled around his nape. His full lips and long lashes would make most women envious.

The deep tan of Matt's face and arms were in sharp contrast to the white cotton shirt beneath his leather vest. Open at the neck and rolled up at the sleeves, the snowy fabric revealed dark curly hair on his forearms.

Before she could gather her wits and take his hat, he'd hung his Stetson on the hall tree, obviously very much at home. He'd admitted running the ranch. Give the man his head and he'd encroach on every facet of their lives.

She pasted on a smile, as if she didn't have a care in the world, and glided across the foyer with a ramrod carriage even the persnickety headmistress in Charleston would approve of.

Inside the dining room, candlelight flickered, shimmering in the high gloss of the tabletop. The silver serving pieces, possessions her mother had brought west, looked out of place in the rustic room's whitewashed walls and dark beamed ceiling.

At the table, Matt's parents sat talking to her father. Papa looked even more frail beside the Walkers.

Robert Walker's hair might be streaked with silver, but he possessed the same broad shoulders and dark brown eyes as his son, no doubt the picture of how Matt would look when he aged.

Were father and son preparing to acquire the Lazy P?

Ashamed of her suspicion, Hannah cringed. Just because Matt helped on the ranch, like any good neighbor would, didn't make him underhanded.

Victoria Walker, tall, big-boned and pretty with soft blue eyes and silvery hair, wrapped Hannah in a hug. A strong woman with a contagious laugh and good heart, Victoria could have a sharp tongue. Or so Hannah had heard. A trait that had surely come in handy raising three ornery sons, one son in particular.

Wrapped in a clean apron, Rosa waited, ready to serve from a table laden with steaming platters and bowls emitting enticing aromas. "The food looks and smells wonderful, Rosa. Thank you."

"I cook your favorites, Hannah."

Once they'd taken seats, Papa said grace. Everyone sampled the food—steak, corn pone, mashed potatoes and gravy—and declared every bite delicious. Smiling, Rosa returned to the kitchen.

"A father couldn't be more proud of a daughter than I am of you, Hannah."

"You're a wonderful father."

Papa cleared his throat. "A picture of your mother, you possess not only her beauty but her spirit."

Fleeting flashes of gentle hands, a loving smile, a nine-year-old girl's memories of her mother. The portrait hanging over the fireplace mantel a reminder that Melanie Parrish had been a lovely woman. "Thank you, Papa."

"Martin's right," Victoria declared as she buttered a bite of cornbread. "For an instant earlier, I thought I was seeing Melanie. Gave me quite a start, too."

"Hannah wasn't eager to go to Charleston, but I wanted her to visit the city where her mother and I fell in love." Papa smiled. "High time she got acquainted with her mama's kin, too."

Finishing school wouldn't help her work a ranch, but Papa had been insistent, as unbending as steel.

"Growing up surrounded by cowhands and cattle wasn't fair to you, Daughter. I wanted to give you the social graces your mother would've taught you had she lived."

Etiquette might mend fences, but not the sort made of barbed wire. Still, Papa had good intentions, always thought of her first. Hannah squeezed his hand.

"So, Daughter, tell the Walkers about Charleston."

"The city's beautiful. The grand piazzas and private gardens tucked behind ornate wrought-iron gates are charming."

Victoria put her hand to her chest, feigning horror. "Surely the gardens aren't prettier than our fields of bluebonnets and Indian paintbrush?"

"Nothing is prettier than Texas wildflowers."

"Spoken like a true Texan," Victoria said.

Robert ladled gravy on his potatoes. "South Carolina could never overshadow the great state of Texas."

"True, but with my eight cousins and their friends coming and going, I loved Aunt Mary Esther's garden, the one place I could find solitude."

Matt cut into his steak. "Any damage remaining from the earthquake of '86?"

"The brick buildings that survived have been stabilized with iron bolts. Otherwise I saw few signs of the quake."

Victoria's brow puckered. "Was your aunt's house damaged?"

"Yes, they had to rebuild, as did most people. The city's done an amazing job of restoration."

"After the hectic pace of Charleston, Bliss must seem dull." Matt's tone issued a challenge.

"Hardly." Dull was hours spent practicing stitching, drawing and elocution, but she wouldn't disappoint Papa by saying as much. "I botched needlework and painting. My poor aunt struggled for something charitable to say about my pitiful efforts."

"Your cousins would find working on the Lazy P equally difficult," Victoria said.

Hannah chuckled. "I can't imagine Anna Lee and Betty Jo riding astride, cutting calves or mending barbed wire."

"Do you plan to teach those fancy manners to the young ladies in town?" Robert said. "Maybe start a school?"

"No, I'll work on the ranch as I always have."

Matt turned dark censorious eyes on her. "The work is hard, even dangerous. Not the place for a lady."

Hannah clamped her jaw to keep from sharing a piece of her mind with Matt, a piece that would not fit his image of a lady.

"Matt's right, you're a lady now." Papa patted Hannah's hand. "Nothing would make me happier than to see you marry and settle down with a doctor or lawyer, someone to take care of you, to give you a life of ease."

"Zack's a successful lawyer and single," Matt reminded them, eyes twinkling.

A well-placed heel on his instep would wipe that smirk off his face.

"Zack would make you a fine husband, Daughter."

"I've got two sons needing a wife," Robert said, shooting Matt a pointed look.

Heat flooded Hannah's cheeks. "I'm not looking for a husband." She glared at Matt. "I've never been hurt working on the ranch."

Papa patted her hand. "Wear those dresses you brought back from Charleston. Practice your stitching and painting. Leave the ranch to the men."

The food in Hannah's stomach churned. What had gotten into Papa? Before she'd left, he'd given her free rein. Now he insisted she conform to his image of a lady. Wear clothing that would impede her freedom and make ranch work difficult. She wanted to please him. But the thought of spending hours confined in the garments designed for the "weaker gender"—though any honest woman would admit the clothes took great fortitude to wear—chafed against every nerve.

"I'd like to know what all they taught you at that school."

"I'd be glad to show you, Papa. I brought back paintings, needlework…"

"I heard from Mary Esther that you're a master at elocution." Papa's gaze traveled the table. "Who'd like my daughter to recite a poem?"

Victoria smiled. "That would be delightful."

"Oh, ah, maybe another night. I'm…tired from the trip."

"I'd love to hear a poem." Matt's grin spread across his face. "Nice and loud."

Hannah arched a brow. "Why don't you sing for us, Matt? You're certainly loud enough in church."

"The evening is in your honor, Hannah, not mine. Besides, I'd enjoy listening to a master at elocution."

"I would, too," Robert said.

Papa slapped his hands together. "That settles it. Before Rosa serves dessert, rise and recite a poem, Hannah."

All eyes turned on her. One pair filled with amusement. She wanted to run, but Papa wore a proud smile she couldn't destroy.

She scrambled for a poem, a short poem. The only verse that came to mind was by Elizabeth Barrett Browning, in Hannah's mind the perfect map of love. How could she recite a love sonnet with Matt nearby, no doubt laughing at her?

With Papa's pat of encouragement, she struggled to her feet, hands cold, cheeks as red-hot as a horseshoe in a blacksmith's forge.

Matt sprang up and pulled out her chair, then returned to his seat, watching her.

She glanced at each guest as she uttered, "How do I love thee?" First Robert, Victoria, then Papa. "Let me count the ways." Her gaze landed on Matt. She jerked it away, focusing on the gilt-framed landscape over the fireplace. "I love thee to the depth and breadth and height my soul can reach…" The words flowed from her. "I love thee freely… I love thee purely…" If she ever fell in love—that *if* towered in her mind—she'd want this sweet, deep, true love. "I love thee with the breadth, smiles, tears, of all my life; and if God choose, I shall love thee better after death."

Robert clapped heartily. "Bravo!"

For a second she'd forgotten the audience. Her legs turned to jelly and she plopped into her chair. If only the floor would open up and drop her clear to China.

"Lovely." Papa's pale face glowed. "Just lovely."

Matt leaned in. "The way you were caught up in that poem, I have to wonder if you're pining for some gangly boy back in Charleston."

"Of course not!"

Rosa's arrival cut off conversation. She carried a tray of delicate, amber flan, the dessert of her homeland and normally Hannah's favorite. But her appetite had vanished.

The others dug in with abandon, discussing the drought and Cattlemen Association business while Hannah picked at the flan.

"This dessert makes me think, Matthew. Jenny Sample brought a cake by this afternoon. Said she had extra eggs and knew angel food was your favorite. That's the second cake this month."

A wide grin spread across Robert's face. "Appears she'd like the job of feeding you permanently. Why, Jenny dangles her baked goods in front of your nose like bait on the end of a line. Fishing for a husband, I reckon." He raised a brow. "You could do worse."

A flush crawled up Matt's neck. Amused at his discomfort, Hannah giggled. "One of those women you spoke of, desperate to marry," she said, her tone as loaded with sugar as the dessert.

Something akin to a growl slid from his lips.

Victoria glanced at Papa, took in his hunched shoulders, then laid her napkin beside her plate. "It's gotten late. We should be going. We've had a lovely evening, Martin. Please express our thanks for the delicious meal to Rosa."

With both hands, her father pushed against the table, half rising to his feet.

Hannah's heart lurched. Why, the evening had tired him. "I'll see our guests out," she said.

Papa flashed a grateful smile. "I'll say good-night, then."

While Matt stayed behind, speaking to her father, Hannah accompanied Robert and Victoria to their carriage and waved as they pulled away.

In the cooler night air, Hannah lingered for a moment, listening to the plaintive sound of a harmonica drifting on the breeze from the bunkhouse. In the moonlight, long pale shadows of outbuildings instilled the ordinary structures with a sense of mystery. She tilted her head back and studied the star-studded sky, bright as diamonds.

God had created this land long before the Parrish family lived upon it. The land would remain long after they were gone. The permanence of the land and of its Creator slid through her, wrapping her in tranquility. In gratitude.

Until Matt loped to her, leading his horse by the reins. From the smirk on his face, he'd come to taunt her. At the end of her rope, she hoped he had the good sense to keep his smart-alecky mouth nailed shut. Nothing would give her more pleasure than showing that naysayer she could run the ranch and run it well.

Matt chucked Hannah under the chin. He'd do what he could to encourage Martin's wish to see his daughter settled in Charleston. "You gave quite a performance earlier. Proof you're well suited for Charleston's social life."

She swatted his hand away. "Stop trying to stuff me into a box labeled debutante. That's not who I am."

"Kind of testy, aren't you?"

"I was enjoying the peace of this beautiful night before you came along."

The glint in those blue eyes gazing up at him had nothing to do with reflected moonlight and everything to do with an urge to wallop him. He had no idea why he'd been hard on her, especially with her concern for Martin. "Look, I'm sorry."

Her eyes widened, as if she couldn't believe her ears, then she gave a brisk nod.

Surely on a night like this they could find a way to get

along. He tilted his head, studying the starry expanse. "When I look up at that sky, at the number of stars and planets, I feel part of something big. Part of God's creation."

"I know. I only caught snippets of the sky in Charleston, but here…" Her voice caught, then trailed off. "I love this land."

It was one thing they had in common. "Who wouldn't?"

Her gaze landed on him, intense, eager. He couldn't tear his eyes away.

"Then you understand how much the ranch means to me. Why I have to take charge until my father's on his feet."

"You'd be wise to set your heart on something else before you get it trampled."

At his words, the accord between them evaporated faster than dew on a hot Texas morning.

Hannah planted her hands on her hips. "You'd be wise to keep your opinions to yourself, Matt Walker."

"I know these cowpokes—"

"I've known most of our cowhands all my life. Why, except for Papa, I'm better suited than anyone to handle the job."

"You can mend a fence, move cattle, muck a barn, I'll give you that, but operating a ranch is more than that."

She harrumphed. "You're exactly like the men in Charleston. They treat women as if we are delicate porcelain or, worse, dim-witted. I can run the ranch as well as anyone."

How could he make her see reason? He doffed his hat and ran his fingers along the brim, gathering his thoughts. "You're not fragile or dim-witted. I don't doubt that you could learn to manage the financial end. But, truth is, cowpokes don't cotton to taking orders from a female, especially one as young as you."

"They will if they want to be paid."

Matt stifled a sigh. How could he make her understand what was at stake? Cowhands saw her as the boss's daughter, more capable than many perhaps, but still young and inexperienced, hardly prepared to run a spread like the Lazy P.

"It's not about money, Hannah. It's about respect. Something that's earned, not bought."

Alarm traveled her face. She sighed, clasping trembling hands in front of her. "You make a point. I'll need to earn their respect and earn it fast."

Respect wasn't earned overnight. Nor were these men eager to give it. But to say more would get her dander up. "Let me handle things for now."

"You're no longer needed here." She pinned him with a fierce, chilling gaze. "I don't want your interference."

If looks could kill, Matt would be a dead man.

How would Martin have managed if Matt hadn't—as she called it—interfered? He'd call it lending a hand, being neighborly. How in tarnation did the dainty debutante think she'd manage roundup?

Not his concern. She'd made that abundantly clear.

He jammed his Stetson on his head and swung into the saddle. Without a backward glance, he nudged Thunder in the flanks and rode in the direction of the Circle W, the peace of the starry night shattered.

Hannah Parrish had no concept of the trouble looming on the horizon. Trouble she'd bring on herself, as if she needed more.

She saw him as an enemy instead of an ally. Any action he took, she'd misconstrue. He'd warned her, it was all he could do. Except for checking on Martin and looking after his needs, Matt would stay clear of the little spitfire.

How long before her plan to run the Lazy P singlehandedly blew up in her face?

A rooster's call pierced the muggy morning air drifting through the open window. Hannah stirred then opened her eyes, stretching languidly, relishing the pleasure of waking in her own bed.

A smile curved her lips. In the dream she'd had, a handsome cowboy, tall, dark, held her in his arms.

She reared upright. All the events of yesterday slid into her sleep-fogged brain, rousing her faster than a cold dip in a horse tank. Her stomach knotted, as she recalled Matt's attitude toward women, and Papa's poor health and sudden determination to make her a lady.

Lady or not, she had work to do. Last night she'd looked the part of debutante. Today she'd show Matt Walker, her father and the Lazy P cowhands she could run this ranch, if need be, wearing skirts. That ought to earn their respect. And wipe that smug smile off Matt's face.

Hannah donned a pair of denims and a shirt, her hands trembling. What if she failed to earn the crew's respect? What if they wouldn't listen to her? What would she do then?

One glance around her room's familiar belongings slowed her breathing. The quilt her mother had stitched, the rocker beside the open window, curtains rustling in the morning breeze. Peaceful, normal.

Her stomach clenched. With Papa ill, normal had fled faster than a calf freed after branding.

At the washstand, she splashed water on her face and brushed her teeth, then ran a fingertip over the chip on the blue-and-white ironstone bowl, the result of a carelessly tossed hairbrush years before.

Her possessions might not be perfect but this room was an oasis in a world flipped upside down. "Oh, please, God, don't let Papa…" Her voice trailed off, the possibility too horrible to speak aloud.

Surely things weren't as dire as they appeared. She took a calming breath. She'd see that Papa ate well and got plenty of rest. Whether Matt believed in her ability or not, she'd run the ranch, gladly taking the burden from her father and returning the operation of the Lazy P to its rightful owners.

She braided her hair, shoved her feet into scuffed boots, grabbed her leather gloves and Stetson, then strode out the door.

In the kitchen, Rosa removed a pan of biscuits from the oven.

"How's Papa this morning?"

"Sleeping. You up with rooster."

"I'm heading out to help with the chores."

"I fix big breakfast when you finish."

"Thanks."

Hannah downed a hot biscuit and coffee, then strode to the stable. A few feet away, the pungent odor of manure and horseflesh teased her nostrils, softened by the sweet smell of hay, a welcome relief from the overpowering scents of potpourri and eau de cologne permeating her aunt's house.

She stepped into the dim interior and a ray of sunlight dancing with dust motes lit a path to Star's stall. As she approached, she spoke the mare's name.

With a nickered greeting, Star poked her bronze head over the stall door, bobbing it in recognition.

Hannah pulled the mare's nose against her shoulder,

rubbing the white irregular shape that earned her name. "Oh, I've missed you," Hannah murmured. "Later today I'll take you out."

Hannah grappled with the feed sack, watching the oats tumble end over end into the feedbox. A sense of peace filled her. Here in the stable, among crusty cowpokes, unpredictable livestock and her steadfast steed, she fit. This life filled her as she'd filled Star's feedbox, to the brim, to overflowing.

Across the way, Jake Hardy lugged two buckets of water into the stable. Stooped and wiry, he'd worked on the Lazy P for as long as Hannah could remember. "Hi, Jake."

"Well, welcome home, Miz Hannah!" Jake entered Star's stall and tipped water into the trough. "Star missed you something fierce. Reckon lots of folks like me are glad you're back, specially your pa."

"Thanks, Jake. How's that back?"

He grinned, revealing the gap between his front teeth. "'Bout what you'd expect for an old coot throwed too many times from breaking broncos."

"Any news from your niece?"

The light in Jake's gray eyes dimmed. "No idea where Lorna's gone off to. I don't mind telling ya, she's got me worried. What kind of a woman leaves her child?"

What else had Papa kept from her? "I'm sorry to hear that."

"My sis is taking care of Lorna's girl, Allie."

Lord, help Lorna do what's right. "I'll pray for her."

A smile crinkled his leathery face. "'Preciate it."

If anything happened to Jake's sister Gertie, Jake would have to take care of Allie. He wouldn't know what to do with a seven-year-old girl any more than Hannah would.

Finished with the morning chores, Hannah glanced outside. "Do you know where I can find Tom?"

"I'll fetch him." Jake hobbled toward the bunkhouse, pitched forward from the waist, his legs curved as if permanently astride. Thanks to multiple injuries, Jake looked older than his years, but he was sinewy, his disabilities didn't slow him down.

While she waited, Hannah checked the tack room. Oiled leather hung on the wall. The horses looked well cared for. Even with Papa's poor health, the ranch appeared to be operating efficiently. How much credit was Matt's? How much was Tom's?

She wandered outside and spied the foreman rounding the corner of the corral, ambling toward her, his frame reed thin, a bandana around his neck, spurs jangling. She raised a hand in greeting.

He touched his hat. "You looking for me, Miss Hannah?"

"I want to thank you for keeping the ranch running smoothly."

"Just doing my job."

"Before I left for Charleston, my father and I discussed the need for a well on the south range. When I arrived yesterday, I noticed nothing had been done. I'd like you to get the digging underway first thing tomorrow. I'll arrange for a windmill."

Tom removed his hat and scratched the back of his head. "The boss didn't mention nothing about another well."

"With his illness, the plan must've slipped his mind." She knew ranching. Soon Tom, the entire crew, would see that too, and give her respect. "Progressive ranchers don't rely on nature to supply water to their herds."

Tom shuffled his feet. "I'll check with the boss."

That was the last thing Papa needed. Hannah bristled. "That won't be necessary."

"Ain't no trouble." The foreman tipped his hat, polite enough, but the sullen look in his eyes said otherwise.

As she watched Tom clomp to the house, an unsettling sense of foreboding gripped her, squeezing against her lungs. What would she do if Tom refused to work for her? How could she run the ranch? From the conversation at the table last night, the cows were dropping calves. That meant roundup was only a few weeks away, which was the reason she'd wanted to get the well dug now. Perhaps she'd been hasty in pushing the issue with the foreman.

Across the way, Matt emerged from the house, swung into the saddle and rode toward the Circle W. No one paid a social call at this hour. She sighed. More likely, he'd helped her father dress and shave. Thoughtful of him and easier on Papa's pride than turning to her or Rosa for assistance.

Had Matt heard Tom question her authority with Papa? Perhaps, if she asked him to intervene, he'd set Tom straight. But she wouldn't ask. She couldn't build respect with the men if she didn't handle things herself.

She strode to the house and met Tom coming out. The smug expression he wore steeled her spine.

"Ain't going to be no well dug," he said.

Was her father too ill to stick to his plan, to stand up to his foreman? "Do you think you're running this ranch?"

"Nope." He guffawed. "Appears you ain't either."

Hannah stepped around him. Inside she found Papa at his desk, dressed and freshly shaven.

"Morning, daughter. Have a seat." He looked at his hands, instead of meeting her gaze. "We need to talk."

With an arrowed spine, she sat across from him, her hands knotted in her lap.

"A company back east is buying up land in the area. No reason they won't buy our spread. Without the responsibility of the Lazy P, you'll be free to return to Charleston."

Never. But she wouldn't upset him with a refusal.

"Papa, can we discuss this later? I just talked to Tom. He claims you don't want a well dug on the south range."

Martin motioned to the books spread in front of him. "That was the plan but we've had a tough year. Last year's low beef prices and high costs have put the ranch in jeopardy."

Why hadn't Papa told her all this? Did he see her as some fragile female unable to face realities?

"I've curtailed expenses. Had to let two hands go."

"If I'd known about our financial trouble, I wouldn't have made a fool of myself in front of Tom."

"What Tom thinks doesn't matter." The steely determination in his eyes, something she rarely saw, stabbed into her. "What I think does. Denims aren't fitting for a lady. Change into one of your dresses. If you want to help, help Rosa in the kitchen."

With roundup a few weeks away, how could Papa relegate her to the kitchen? If this drought didn't end soon, they risked overgrazing the land and would need to thin the herd. That meant punching cattle to Fort Worth right after roundup. With only two drovers and Tom, she'd need to lend a hand.

Besides, what if Rosa resented the interference? Years of managing the house had proved she didn't need help.

Roundup wasn't the huge undertaking it had been when cattle freely roamed the range. Still, how did Papa expect to handle branding the calves without her? Or if rain didn't come, driving cattle to Fort Worth to sell without her?

Her breath caught. Was Papa too ill to grasp the work that loomed? "Papa, with few drovers, what's your plan for handling roundup?"

"Matt and I were talking about that this morning. He'll bring a couple of the Circle W hands. We'll get by."

"Why isn't the Walker ranch struggling, too?"

"Things are tight, sure, but they're a bigger operation. Better set financially."

Were the Walkers hoping to pick up the Lazy P for a song?

She wouldn't sit back and twiddle her thumbs. If dresses pleased her father, she'd work in dresses. She'd ride astride in dresses. She'd run this ranch in dresses. But she wouldn't turn over their ranch to anyone.

In her room, she changed into one of the simple dresses she'd owned before Charleston, then joined her father in the kitchen for breakfast. Rosa had prepared hotcakes, eggs, steak, biscuits and gravy—food to keep a working man and woman going.

Throughout the long day, she tested the corral, the gates, then rode fence, assisting with repairing barbed wire, as she had before she left for Charleston. The cowpokes tipped their hats and spoke politely, treated her like a lady.

But, when she gave instructions, they played deaf or openly rebelled. By the day's end, she'd seen and heard enough to know their hands and foreman were used to taking orders from Matt, but refused to listen to her.

Matt had used the pretense of helping her sick father to worm his way into running the Lazy P. Why would he do that? Did he expect to benefit financially?

She saddled Star and rode for the Circle W, determined to have it out with the man.

Chapter Three

Trouble in a skirt was heading Matt's way. Trouble he'd tried to avoid by doing exactly as Hannah asked. Except for helping Martin dress and shave, he'd kept his distance from the Lazy P. So why the long face?

Unless—

His heart skidded. Had Martin taken a bad turn?

No, by the looks of that ramrod posture, the no-nonsense set of her shoulders and those flashing eyes, the filly was out for blood.

His.

As if she were a bounty hunter and his face topped a Wanted poster, Hannah had tracked him to the far border of the Circle W. Not that she looked like any bounty hunter he'd ever seen. Her feminine dress was hiked to reveal dusty-toed boots in the stirrups. Her black Stetson slung low completed an enticing mix of female and rancher that would've held an appeal, if not for that bloodthirsty look in her eyes.

He removed his hat, swiped the sweat off his brow and then arched his back, stretching achy muscles. With his pa slowing down, Zack a big-city lawyer and Cal overseeing his in-laws' spread, Matt barely kept up with the work. He slapped his hat in place. Now he had to take time to deal with an irate female.

She dismounted, standing there waiting.

He turned to the cowpoke working beside him. "If I'm lucky, I'll only be a minute." He released a gust of air.

"More likely you'll have time for a siesta."

"Sounds good. Looks mighty good, too." He winked. "If you need help, holler."

"I'll manage." Though when it came to women, his past had taught him to curb expectations.

Matt strode to where the feisty female stood. Chin sky high, arms folded across her chest, she started yammering at him before he reached her.

He held up a palm. "Now slow down, little filly."

Hannah stiffened. "Don't call me that."

"What's wrong with filly?"

"I remind you of an awkward young horse?"

"Way back when, you reminded me of a newborn foal, all legs, yet I knew you'd be a beauty."

Who could help noticing the red highlights in her auburn hair shooting sparks in the sunlight. Without thinking he lifted a hand to a tendril coiled along her jaw.

As if his touch branded her, she jerked back, but then gathered her wits and anger and leaned toward him.

You're in for it now, Walker.

"Thanks to your meddling, our drovers are accustomed to taking orders from you and won't listen to me."

"Martin's not up to running the ranch. A foreman needs someone looking over his shoulder, making sure the ranch operates efficiently. I stepped in because I had to."

Those sky-blue eyes of hers narrowed in a vise of disapproval. "Isn't it more that you want to take over the Lazy P?"

He snorted. "Why would I want to do that? I've got more work than I can handle here."

"Good question. The only answer I can come to—you're in it for the financial gain."

Those were fighting words. If she'd been a man, her implications would've raised his fists. "If you knew anything about ranching, you'd know that profits are at a record low. I'm not earning a dime from the Lazy P."

She harrumphed, as if she didn't believe a word.

"Examine the books," he ground out. "You won't see any mysterious loss of funds. Your father is overseeing the accounts. Talk to him."

"I will." She whirled to go.

Why had he said that? "Wait, don't. Leave him be."

"My father has a right to know what's going on."

"Nothing's going on." Matt let out a breath. "He doesn't need the worry. Not now."

Alarm sprang to her eyes. "What aren't you telling me?"

"That you're going to ruin that land you love with your confounded stubbornness," he said, edging away from the truth.

Martin was dying. Nothing she did, nothing Matt did could turn that tide.

The alarm faded, replaced with a stony stare. "I want you to talk to our hands. Tell them I'm in charge of our ranch."

"I told you that cowpokes resent taking orders from a woman, especially one as young as you. That's got nothing to do with me."

"So you say, still I want you to make clear that I'll be giving the orders until my father's health improves."

"Hannah, you need every ranch hand to keep things running. Cowboys are an independent bunch. If you get them riled, they'll quit."

A flash of doubt traveled her face, but then she squared her shoulders. "I'll hire more." She planted gloved hands on her hips. "Set them straight today. If you don't, I'll suspect you of malicious intent."

"Get this straight, Miss Parrish. I'm not your lackey. I've got a ranch to run."

"Then stop trying to run mine!"

He crossed his arms, stepping toward her until the toes of his boots touched her hem. "You're one stubborn woman. I'll enjoy watching you run your ranch into the ground."

She looked stunned, as if he'd slapped her. His stomach gnarled with regret. Before he could apologize, she stomped to where Star grazed. With a swish of skirts, she mounted, then glared his way. "I can't understand how good people like your folks got saddled with a son like you," she said, then rode off.

He couldn't remember the last time he'd been told off by a woman. He wasn't partial to it, especially when he'd spent months slaving for her ranch.

Still, he'd let his temper get away from him.

Hannah might not believe it, but Tom would have no difficulty getting another position if he rebelled against a female boss. He couldn't let her run the Lazy P into the ground. He owed Martin that much.

He'd talk to her. Apologize.

If the words didn't stick in his throat.

Hannah rode hard for the Lazy P, every muscle tighter than a well-strung fence. She could've slapped Matt's face for suggesting she'd run the ranch into the ground. That he'd enjoy seeing her fail. What cruel arrogance.

She'd accused him of swindling.

A sigh slid from her lips. *Forgive me, Lord.*

She didn't really consider Matt a crook. Yet every word out of his mouth raised her hackles. Why, he'd even forbidden her to talk to her father. *He doesn't need the worry. Not now.*

A shiver slid through her. What was Matt keeping from her?

On Parrish land, Hannah hauled on the reins and reversed direction. She'd ride to town. Visit Doc Atkins. Ask him what ailed her father.

The decision made, Hannah's limbs and neck relaxed as she and Star soared over the familiar terrain. Horse and rider blending as one, the miles melted away. The freedom and exhilaration of the ride filled her with hope. Surely, nothing was terribly wrong with Papa.

On Main Street, Hannah tied Star to the hitching post and strode onto the walk, passing the weathered sign, Earl Atkins, M.D.

Inside, she rapped on the open door of the examining room.

"Miss Parrish. Heard you were back. Been expecting you." The doctor motioned to a pressed-back chair across from the examining table. "Have a seat."

Doc's no-nonsense tone carried such authority Hannah dropped into the chair he'd indicated. A short man with white thinning hair and shaggy brows, his faded blue eyes often held a fierce expression, perhaps from handling the harsh realities of life and death. Today his eyes had softened with kindness.

"I'm worried about my father. He avoids talking about his health, but he can't do much. He's lost weight. His skin tone isn't good." The words escaped in a rush. She bit her lip, waiting for Doc to allay her fears.

With a sigh, Doc Atkins leaned against the examining

table. "I'm sorry I don't have better news. Martin's got a cancerous tumor in his abdomen."

Pain exploded in her chest. Tumor? Cancer? Papa? Her trembling fingers found her lips. "Oh, no."

"I'm sorry."

"Isn't there an operation? A medicine?"

He shook his head. "I've done all I can. The specialist in Dallas agreed."

"Papa saw a doctor in Dallas?"

"He treats nothing but cancer. He tried what he knew, but…"

The "but" said it all. She released a shuddering breath. Nothing could be done. "How…how long?"

"Only God knows, but he's…failing fast. All I can do is ease his pain."

Doc turned to an oak cabinet and withdrew a bottle. "I'll send out more pain medication with you." He scribbled the dosage, then handed her the paper and bottle. "Wish I could do more. If we'd found it sooner, he could've gone to St. Mary's, an excellent hospital in Minnesota, but… I'm sorry."

With herculean effort, she rose and walked to the door, her limbs slogging through an invisible thick haze, the shocking verdict vibrating with each step she took.

"See that he takes the medicine." Doc laid a gentle hand on her arm. "I'll be out to see him in a few days."

"Are you sure this isn't some horrible mistake?"

Doc shook his head, his eyes glistening. "I never get used to the losses, especially of someone like Martin."

As if she were a sleepwalker, Hannah found herself outside, dazed and disoriented, her hope shattered. She leaned against the building, shivering in the glaring sunlight, head and heart pounding.

Papa is dying.

A sob tore up her throat. She stuffed a fist to her mouth, biting down on gloved knuckles. What would she do without him? Papa and the ranch were her life. A squeezing fist of fear encircled her neck, closing her throat. She lifted her gaze to heaven. *Lord, help Papa. Help me handle this.*

She breathed slowly. In. Out. In. Out.

As she did, her heart regained its rhythm. She straightened, tamping down the paralyzing panic. Papa needed her. Needed her to be strong. She wouldn't waste precious time she could spend with her father wallowing in despair.

She pushed away from the clapboards, untied Star and rode for home, happy memories with Papa parading through her mind.

In the stable, she met up with Jake. Eyes averted, he toed the ground.

"What's wrong?"

"Tom picked up his back pay, said he don't see a future here."

"He what?"

"Said he wouldn't work for a woman today or tomorrow." Jake sighed. "Our top hand went with him." He huffed. "Was a time when a man took pride in riding for the brand."

The news slammed into her like a stampeding herd. She fought for footing. Matt had been right. What would she do?

"You have a problem working for me, Jake?"

"Nope. Way I see it, money is money no matter who's paying." He met her gaze with moist eyes. "I reckon this here's my home."

"Thank you." She laid a hand on his arm. "The Lazy P is your home and always will be." If the ranch survived. But she wouldn't say that.

"Want me to round up some new hands?"

"I'll take care of it." How, she didn't know. But Jake would have more than enough to do.

Once the last heifer dropped her calf, they needed to drive the cattle into pens, brand and cut the calves. Without a foreman and only two hands, how could she handle roundup? Especially now that she'd told Matt to stay away?

She believed in God's power. With every breath she took, she prayed for a miracle for her father. Without one, Papa wasn't getting better. Tears stung her eyes. Her father had spent his life running the Lazy P. If Papa didn't make it, she wouldn't let the ranch die with him.

Lord, please give me wisdom. Show me how to keep the ranch.

Only yesterday her world seemed secure. Only yesterday her future brimmed with rosy hopes and dreams. Only yesterday she welcomed the challenge of running the ranch.

Today Papa was dying. The foreman had quit. Most of the hands had either been let go or quit. Only two drovers remained.

She took a calming breath, steadying her wobbly emotions, and headed inside the house. Outside her father's room, she pinched color into her cheeks and forced a smile.

Papa was lying down but not asleep. The bed dwarfed him. The pale color of his skin matched the pillowcase beneath his head. Were the lines edged into his face lines of suffering?

"Hi, Papa," she said, then set the pain medicine on his nightstand.

His gaze settled on the bottle. "You know."

"Yes." She dropped onto the bed and clasped one of his hands in both of hers. Tears burned the back of her eyes. She blinked them away.

"I'm sorry, Daughter. I'd hoped to keep it from you a

little longer." He raised his other hand, cupped her jaw. "I'd do anything to change things. To be here for you."

"I know." She sucked in a breath. "Tom and our top hand quit."

As if warding off the bad news, Papa closed his eyes, then met her gaze. "You've got decisions to make. I'm sure Matt will step up and run things until you can sell the spread."

"I won't sell."

"Hannah, you've got no choice. It'll take a while, but we'll manage. I'll hang on as long as I can. When my time comes, I want you to return to Charleston, live with Mary Esther. They'll treat you well, be the family you'll need."

She wouldn't leave the ranch. She couldn't. Never.

With the strength of her will, she squared her shoulders. She and Papa couldn't give up. She moved his blue-veined hand to her lips and kissed it. "You have plenty of time. Let's talk about something else."

"I have to know you'll be taken care of after I'm gone. Please, hear me out on this. You can't stay. This ranch is too much for a lone woman."

Weary lines carving his face, Papa closed his eyes.

She tucked the blanket under his chin. "You're right, Papa. Rest."

"That's my girl." A smile curved his lips, yet his eyes remained closed. The smile eased, his breathing slowed. He slept.

Hannah slipped out of the room and headed for the stable. She had to give her father peace. But how?

Her mind churned with Doc's diagnosis, the approaching roundup and Papa's determination to sell the ranch. She needed the wisdom of God but with everything churning inside of her mind, she couldn't hear His quiet voice.

A ride would clear her head. She threw a blanket and

saddle on Papa's horse. Lightning probably hadn't been ridden much and needed the exercise.

She found Jake in the tack room. "I'm going to ride out to the north range."

"Always do my best cogitatin' on horseback."

"Me, too." She gave him a weak smile then led Lightning from the stable, mounted and headed north.

In her entire life she'd never carried the weight of responsibility she shouldered now. What if she couldn't find the hands she needed? Most honest, hardworking cowpokes were employed. She didn't trust those loafing around town.

She bit her lip. Matt had been right. She couldn't handle things by herself. Not a camel back trunk, not a cattle ranch. Not her father's death.

God, please, help me. Show me what to do.

Near the copse of cottonwoods alongside the creek winding through the Lazy P, Hannah slowed Lightning then stood in the stirrups. Her gaze scanned the herd dotting the landscape, a mix of breeding Hereford and longhorn, evidence of one of the many changes in ranching, along with fenced pastures, wells, windmills, earthen tanks and short drives to railroad heads. By fencing their cattle, they'd protected the land from overgrazing. Or so she hoped. Without rain they still faced that risk. They'd raised hay and saved half of their herd during the harsh winter of '86 and '87. Exactly why she couldn't deplete their supply in spring.

She dismounted and the leather creaked, loud in the stillness. A fly buzzed near Hannah's head then lighted on the horse's flank. Lightning flicked his tail but the fly persisted.

Hannah shooed the pest, then walked the horse to a patch of shade, struggling to gather her thoughts and come up with acceptable options. Each alternative that paraded through her mind was worse than the last.

Her gaze roamed the pastureland she loved, settling on the prairie dogs playing tag across the way. The cattle lowing in the background was a sound she'd heard all her life. A few calves bunting each other brought a smile to her face.

How could she leave the ranch? She'd shrivel up and lose herself in Charleston. To remain on this land and give her father peace, she'd do whatever she had to do.

In the distance she spotted a lone rider. Even from here she could identify him and his horse. Matt. A man who cared about Papa and would understand her grief.

Papa trusted him. Matt had only been helping Papa, not trying for financial gain. He'd been right about the cowhands, but instead of listening to his advice, she'd suspected his motives. She'd misjudged the man. She had nothing to fear from Matt, a man she could lean on.

He loved the land. He'd help her find a way.

Matt had come to apologize. The fire he'd seen in Hannah's eyes earlier had vanished, replaced with a gut-wrenching sorrow that slammed into him.

God help her, she knows.

Huddled on the ground in the shade of a cottonwood, she exhaled a shaky breath, turning her gaze to the pastureland beyond. Her shoulders sagged, as if the starch had left her spine.

"Papa's dying," she said, tugging on a weed that wouldn't budge.

To hear the words from her lips, each word laden with anguish, knotted his throat. He sat back on his heels beside her. "I'm sorry."

She stopped fiddling with the weed and folded her hands on her knees. "Me, too."

"Your father doesn't deserve this." But then, who did?

"How long have you known he has…he was sick?"

"About a month, since I took him to the specialist in Dallas." He took her hand. "What are you going to do?"

"I don't know." She raised determined eyes to his. "But I'll tell you what I'm not going to do. I'm not going to leave this land."

He'd seen Hannah as a nuisance, incapable of facing realities. Yet look at her now. Strong. Not falling apart as most women would've done. He bit back a sigh. Strong or not, she couldn't run this ranch alone.

"Martin needs the peace of knowing you're with family, back in Charleston. Best thing you can do for him is sell the ranch."

"I'd do anything to please him." Her voice broke. "Anything but that." She rose and turned her back to him, swiping at her eyes. Yet that ramrod spine spoke of spirit and strength. Silhouetted against the horizon, small and alone, she had no one to turn to for comfort.

Except him.

Matt crossed the distance in two strides and gathered her into his arms. Something he'd do for anyone struggling with sorrow, for any one of his brother's friends.

She laid her face against his chest, her tears dampening his shirt. He cradled her close, his heart pounding like the hooves of a herd of wild mustangs. What was happening to him?

"I can't run the ranch alone," she said, lurching away. "I can't handle the roundup without a crew. I can't make Papa well." She lifted glistening eyes rimmed with spiky lashes, eyes filled with desperation.

"I'll help any way I can." He wanted to ease her burden. Ease her heartache, but he didn't have the power. *God, help her.*

As if deep in thought, she stepped away, eyes fixed on the horizon, filled with a faraway look. What was she thinking?

She turned to him, resolve on her face. "You'd help me even after the way I treated you earlier?"

"Yes, of course. I care about Martin. About what will happen to you. I'll do whatever I can to help."

She gave a nod, resolute blue eyes nailing him with the force of a blacksmith's hammer shoeing a horse.

Something in her gaze made him take a step back, unsure he wanted to hear what was coming.

"If you mean that, marry me."

Chapter Four

Matt held up his palms and took another step back, tripping over a tree root, but managed to stay on his feet. Barely. What the tarnation had just happened?

Assistance with the coming roundup he'd expected.

A helping hand on the Lazy P, sure.

But marriage?

Nothing could've been further from his mind. Hannah Parrish, that gangly girl from the neighboring ranch, his kid brother Zack's tagalong, had proposed?

To him?

"Did you just say...marriage?"

"I did," she said.

His gaze swept over her slender yet curvy frame, wide blue eyes, wind tossed red-brown hair. That gangly girl had grown into a fine-looking woman. Still, the idea of marriage was crazy. Why, Hannah could barely tolerate him.

Not that he hadn't been at fault for raising her hackles. Since he'd laid eyes on her at the depot, he'd teased her about her finery, her debutante days in Charleston, her elocution. He'd done it to keep her attention on him and off her father.

He bit back a sigh. Why not be honest? He'd become

an expert at holding women at arm's length. He had no intention of falling for a woman, especially a female with an iron will.

A scowl on her face, Hannah folded her arms across her chest. "You look like a man sentenced to hang."

An apt description considering his throat had constricted with the pressure of a squeezing noose. He took a step closer. Lifted a hand toward her. "I'm sorry, I…ah, you surprised me."

She whirled out of his reach. "Forget it!"

"Wait." He shot after her, taking her by the arm. "You can't blame a man for being taken aback. A request for help doesn't usually include a marriage proposal."

"These aren't usual circumstances."

He released a gust of air. "No, they're not."

"I don't want marriage any more than you do." Her eyes flared. Then drifted in the direction of her house where disease and worry dwelled. "I don't see another option."

"Reckon marriage to me means you get help with your pa, an experienced cowhand and a husband all rolled into one."

"Husband?"

"That is what you call the groom once you tie the knot."

"I…" Her cheeks bloomed. "I hadn't thought about a husband."

"A husband does come with the wedding band," he ground out.

That chin of hers shot up. He hadn't meant to sound testy, but matrimony was sacred, not to be entered lightly. If they wed, they'd be hitched for life. With that stubborn streak of hers, marriage would feel like a life sentence, too.

Her gaze dropped away. She fiddled with the sleeve of her dress. "We're not in love so we'd, ah…well…"

"Have no proper marital…union, is that what you're trying to say?"

"Yes."

Why didn't he feel relieved by her answer? If he married, a marriage without love was what he'd want. Even four years later, Amy's death haunted him. He clamped his jaw. He'd never again risk that kind of anguish.

Tears brimmed in Hannah's eyes. Eyes filled with desperation. Disquiet. A host of emotions he couldn't handle. A damsel in distress. How could a man look into those eyes without wanting to save her?

But, at what cost? "What do I get out of this marriage?"

Her eyes widened. Like the question surprised her. "You?"

"Yes, me. I'd be half of the man and wife." He didn't mention her opposition to a proper man and wife relationship, but the arrangement hung over them just the same.

"Well, you'd, ah, get a home. Good food. Rosa's an excellent cook. And—" she wrinkled her nose that cute way she had "—you wouldn't have to ride to the Lazy P twice a day to help Papa and…." Her words trailed off. "That's not much."

Without a doubt, Hannah wouldn't have turned to him if she'd had another candidate for the position of husband. "What I'd get is another ranch to run." He removed his Stetson and slapped it against his thigh, raising dust and his ire with each whack. "You've resented what you called my interference. Now you're asking for it?"

She straightened her shoulders, but didn't look him in the eye. "I'd prefer you not interfere. I'd make the decisions on how to run the Lazy P. I will work on my ranch. None of that nonsense about leaving the job to the men."

Mercy, if he married her, he'd have to put up regularly with this spitfire. One thing he'd give Hannah, she had bravado, more like audacity, considering her lack of alternatives.

"All I need a husband for is…" Her brow furrowed, groping for the word.

"Respect," he finished for her.

She nodded. "I'm seen as an upstart, not a boss. With a husband—" She shot him a defiant stare. "In name only, well…if you showed your support, the hands would listen to me, figure the instructions came from you."

That much was true.

"Well, will you marry me or not?" She crossed her arms over her bosom, trying to look in control, but her lips trembled like a terrified toddler.

As long as he'd peered into those pretty, haunted eyes, how could he expect to make an intelligent decision? Could any decision be called intelligent that involved marrying a woman he didn't love? And who didn't love him?

Lord, I need the wisdom You gave Solomon.

"I'll think about it. Pray about it. This isn't an agreement a man enters into lightly."

With that assertion, he plopped his Stetson on his head, strode to his horse and rode for the Circle W, leaving Hannah behind, from what he'd heard, sputtering. Had she expected his answer on the spot?

He needed time to wrap his mind around her proposal. He supposed marriage to Hannah would mean no risk of entangling his heart and no more of Jenny Sample's cakes. And, marrying Hannah would allow him to care for a dying man he saw as a second father.

Amy's death had killed his capacity to risk his heart. A marriage of convenience would work for him, but didn't seem fair to Hannah. She deserved love. Even if he could love again, he didn't deserve her, any woman.

If only—

He refused to let his mind travel to the day of Amy's death. As much as he lived with regrets, nothing could change the past.

A bright, sunny morning didn't fit Hannah's mood. As she and Jake finished the last of the chores, she'd prayed for an answer to her dilemma. Never thinking God would put words in her mouth, she'd never have spoken if she hadn't been desperate to give Papa peace. *Marry me, Matt,* she'd blurted out. Yet marriage was the last thing she wanted. If Matt agreed, would the solution bring even bigger problems? If he refused, she'd have no recourse but to sell.

She felt out of control, swept along like the cattle she'd often witnessed in Fort Worth, driven through narrow chutes and onto waiting railroad boxcars that would deliver them to their final destination.

Annihilation.

She shivered. Surely marriage wouldn't be that bad. She knew little about wedded life, had no more than an outsider's view. Would a husband want to herd her into the narrow shoot of his will and destroy the freedom she held dear, freedom to work, freedom to run the ranch? To have purpose and meaning, be part of something bigger than her?

Across the way, Matt emerged from the back door, no doubt finished helping Papa shave and dress, the actions of a thoughtful, caring man. Why had she thought he had ulterior motives for his kindness?

With a strong, hardworking, no-nonsense air about him, Matt's long legs gobbled up the distance as he strode to his horse. Where was he headed?

She caught up with him just as he took Thunder's reins. "Heading back to the Circle W?" she said, trying to sound casual, when every muscle tensed with wondering if he'd come to a decision about marrying her.

He turned to her, a smile on his lips. The sight of that dimple winking at her and his dark eyes, soft, kind, whooshed the breath out of her lungs. Why couldn't she stop reacting to the man? He saw her as a gangly kid to be teased, barely tolerated.

"Several of your cows will be dropping calves. Thought I'd ride out to check on them."

Here was an opportunity to take back the reins of her life. "If you can wait while I change out of this dress and saddle Star, I'll ride along. See for myself how the herd looks."

And along the way ask a few questions about the ranch. Make sure he saw her as being in charge. Prove she wasn't the debutante he believed her to be.

"I'll saddle Star for you," he said, then disappeared into the stable.

Within minutes, she'd told Papa her whereabouts, changed into denims and returned just as Matt emerged leading Star.

"That was quick," he said, his gaze sliding over her.

"Papa's determined to see me in a dress. I'll change back before he sees me."

With an impish grin on his face, Matt gave her a hand up. "I don't understand Martin's position. You look mighty good in pants."

Her cheeks heated and the smile wobbled on her lips. At least Matt wouldn't insist on her wearing dresses if they married, but would she lose the freedom she cherished?

Lose her identity like Belle, her married friend? Once she and Belle had shared the thrill of riding, of lassoing calves, of shooting tin cans off fence posts. Now Belle had turned into a lady, answering to her full name Marybelle, spending her days cooking and cleaning, washing and ironing, mending and gardening. Not that Hannah shunned hard work, but she'd find such confinement suffocating.

With maids and a cook to do the work, Aunt Mary Esther spent her days socializing and didn't appear to have an independent thought from Uncle Clyde. That existence would be even more unbearable.

In comparison with the alternatives, marriage to Matt looked tolerable.

They rode out toward the north range, the view from horseback exhilarating. But then the realities of life invaded her mind, dashing her pleasure like a deluge doused in hot coals.

"How does Papa seem to you?" Hannah asked.

"Having you home has lifted his spirits."

If Matt agreed, Hannah knew their marriage would give Papa peace. And her the certainty of staying on the land she loved. He hadn't broached the topic, probably still praying about his answer. She wouldn't press for his decision, for fear that pushing him would raise his ire and he'd give a hasty no.

Instead she'd focus the conversation on the ranch and look for ways to resolve the problems. "Did we lose many cattle last winter?"

"Nope. Mild winter. Another year or two like that and the herd will come close to its size before the winter of '86–'87."

That was a terrible winter and spring. Cattle that survived the blizzard were swept away in floods. They'd lost half the herd, more fortunate than some, but still they'd taken a serious punch in the pocketbook.

Ahead of her, the cattle dotted the fenced pasture, their large frames of every imaginable color. Their horned white faces bent toward the grass. "Crossbreeding longhorns with Herefords makes an interesting herd."

"Yep, the offspring are the best of both breeds, even-tempered, early maturing and mighty fine eating. They fatten up fast and handle drought. The cows make excellent mothers."

At the entrance to the north pasture, Matt guided Thunder alongside the fence, opening the gate from horseback, letting her ride through before closing it behind them.

Up ahead two calves bunted each other, then stopped to stare as they rode slowly through the herd, counting calves. A few of the babies were overcome with fear and rushed to their mamas to nurse and be comforted.

Hannah grinned at Matt. "Aren't they cute?"

"Yep, better yet, they're profit on legs. I—"

He rose in the saddle, then with a nudge of his knees, urged his horse forward. Hannah followed. Up ahead, away from the herd, a cow lay on the ground. At their approach, she staggered to her feet, took a few steps then lay down again.

Matt frowned. "She's calving and in distress."

When they were a few yards from the animal, the cow rose, scrambling away from them, revealing the emerging calf's snout.

The first time Hannah witnessed the birth of a calf she'd been a tyke riding in front of her father. She knew the front legs should appear before the head. Head first meant trouble.

Matt grabbed the lasso draped on his saddle horn, twirled it overhead, then released the line. The loop settled around the cow's neck. He tightened the hoop, then hauled the cow toward a fence post. She trotted a few steps, then lurched to the side, attempting to get away, but rider and horse cut off her escape.

At the post, Matt dismounted, heaved the lariat around the wood and, using the leverage, pulled the animal closer, then knotted it, holding her in place.

Breath coming fast and shallow, the cow bellowed as a contraction slithered through her. Matt strode to her hindquarters. "Front legs are folded back."

Hannah tethered the horses, then moved to Matt's side. "Poor thing."

"I've got to fish for the front legs." He didn't look up, merely unbuttoned his cuff, then jerked his head toward the horses. "Stand by Star. Turn your back. Can't have you fainting on me."

"I've seen calves born countless times." She jerked up her chin. "Besides, I'm not the fainting type."

One arched brow said he doubted her claim. "Suit yourself, but don't say I didn't warn you."

Hannah may have seen calves born, but had no idea what to do in this situation. She bit her lip, grateful Matt didn't hold back, and took fast action. He tried to slide his hand past the calf's head. Once. Twice. A third time. "My hand's too big."

"I'll try. What should I do?"

Matt's eyes lit with something akin to admiration. "See if you can find a small flat surface right below the jaw. That's the calf's knee."

Lord, help me. She slipped her hand in. "Found it."

"Follow it back till you find the hoof. Bring it forward."

"Oh, no, the calf pulled his leg away." Perspiration beaded her brow. "Wait, the legs are straight now. Got 'em. Slippery."

The sweet scent of amniotic fluid filling her nostrils, she hung on, guiding first one leg, then the other, producing the calf's fully extended front legs and head. With the next contraction the body followed in a whoosh of fluid and slid out onto the grass, a slick dark speckled lump.

A motionless lump.

Holding her breath, Hannah slid away the sack, waiting for the calf's chest to rise, fall. Nothing. She ran to Star, jerked her bedroll from behind her saddle and wrapped the blanket around the glistening calf, rubbing the fibers over its hide.

"Come on, baby. Breathe," she said, warming the calf.

The calf jerked and sucked in air. Its eyes opened and stared up at her. Hannah peered into those dark eyes. "Well, hello there, little guy."

The cow lunged against the rope, determined to reach her calf. Matt grabbed Hannah's hand, pulled her out of harm's way, then untied the rope and removed the lariat. The cow paid them no mind, merely circled to the now bawling calf and proceeded to lick every inch of him. Within minutes the calf staggered to his feet, swaying against the pressure of his mother's tongue, keeping his balance, barely. A quick maneuver by the mother and he found nourishment.

His grin as wide as the outdoors, Matt met her gaze. "Looks like they'll both make it, thanks to you."

"And you. You told me what to do. If you hadn't decided to ride out here and check on the cows dropping calves…"

"Most likely they'd have both died. We'll head to the south range." He winked. "Maybe next time, you'll help birth twins."

"I've had enough excitement for one day."

With a chuckle, he swept a hand toward her. "No debutante would be caught looking like that."

Hannah glanced at the damp smears streaking her shirt and denims. "I'm no debutante, remember?"

"I'm starting to believe it. You and I make a good team."

The mischief left his gaze. A gaze that suddenly turned tender. "You love this land, the ranch, the cattle. Everything."

"I do."

"I do, too." He touched her hand. "Reckon with all those I dos, we'd better get hitched and keep you here."

Her gaze locked with his. She lost herself in his eyes, dark, mysterious, full of life and offering marriage.

"See something you like?" he said, dimple twinkling.

Heat surged to her cheeks. Nothing about the man met her disapproval. "No, nothing much."

When had she uttered a bigger lie?

Matt's self-assured, relaxed posture said he was sure of himself—and of her, most likely. Why wouldn't he be? She'd done the proposing. First.

"With the six-year difference in our ages and your year away, we don't know each other all that well. But, we're alike in our bond with this land." Expression earnest, Matt leaned toward her. "I can think of far worse reasons to marry."

Just like that, with few words, the bargain was sealed.

"We need to do this right," he said, taking her hand and sending a shiver along her spine. He moved as if to get down on one knee.

With a gasp of protest, she snatched her hand away. "This marriage is business only. No need for a proper proposal."

"Is it really? Just business for you?"

Her gaze settled on those eyes searching hers, as if peering into her soul. She wouldn't get swept up by a handsome face and fall for a man. Not even a man with a dazzling smile and a dimple begging for her touch.

At her silence, he took a step back, erect, formal. "Hannah Parrish, will you marry me?"

A lump rose in her throat. Once she agreed, there'd be no turning back. Yet what choice did she have? "Yes, I'll marry you."

"We'll need to marry soon."

Hannah stiffened. "How soon?"

"Today's Monday. Can we get it done by Thursday?"

Get it done. As if marriage was on his list of chores. Her stomach clenched. How could she be ready in three days?

"Martin's a very sick man," he reminded her. "He'd want to see you wed."

For Papa she could do anything. "Yes," she said in a voice that wobbled.

"I'll do my best to be a good husband." His soft tone matched the kindness in his eyes.

She had no idea what constituted a good husband…or for that matter, a good wife. Could she fit into a husband's expectations? Especially a mature man like Matt?

One thing Hannah knew, she could never abide a bossy spouse. Papa seldom gave her orders. Until now. She'd grown up making her own decisions and had felt stifled under Aunt Mary Esther's thumb. She couldn't imagine a lifetime of being dictated to by a man. Would Matt allow her the freedom she needed?

Her gaze swept the land. To remain on the ranch, to keep her way of life and to give her father peace, she'd marry.

If only they had more time.

If only Papa wasn't dying.

If only they were in love.

She thought of the tenderness that had fleetingly appeared in Matt's eyes. Perhaps love was possible…eventually.

No, that expectation was a foolish peg to hang her heart on. A fairy-tale ending wasn't what she wanted. She would deal with the real world. Papa was dying. To run the ranch and remain on the land she loved, she'd marry a man she didn't.

Chapter Five

Wound tighter than a coiled spring, Matt rode into the Circle W stable, stripped leather, then brushed Thunder's coat. As Matt led the stallion to his stall, fed and watered him, large, wide-set eyes alert with intelligence gazed back at him. Quick, smart and high-spirited, much like his future wife.

But Hannah was a woman, not trained to bridle and bit. Truth was, she held the reins, using him to keep her ranch. Not that he didn't want the same.

At the pump, he scrubbed his hands and doused his face and neck. Had his admiration for Hannah's coolheaded competence during a calf's difficult birth triggered his proposal?

No, he had prayed for wisdom. Felt a deep certainty he'd been led by God and had done the right thing. He wanted to give Martin peace. He wanted to help Hannah. He didn't want love. The lack of expectations in this marriage fit him perfectly.

Cal and his family were joining them for supper. Normally a good time, but with the task of telling his family the news, his steps lagged. No doubt they'd question his sanity.

He found his mother and Cal's wife, Susannah, in the kitchen preparing the evening meal. "Smells good, Ma," he said, letting the screen door slap behind him. "Hi, Susannah."

Blond silky hair swept into a sleek bun, Susannah looked up from laying plates on the table and smiled. Fair and blue-eyed, Cal's petite wife had an innocent, delicate quality about her, yet had a mind of her own if the occasion warranted.

Victoria turned from the stove. "Hoped you'd get here in time for supper."

He hung his Stetson on a peg beside the door, then walked to his ma. "Let me help with that." He took the potato masher from her hand and battled lumps in the potatoes. An easy skirmish compared to what lay ahead.

As if led by their noses, Cal with his son, Robbie, tucked in his arms, and Pa trooped into the kitchen. Matt greeted them, then turned the pot over to his mother, who scooped the creamy potatoes into a large crock.

"Hey," Cal said, clapping Matt on the shoulder, "you look down in the mouth."

"Hush," Victoria scolded. "Your brother's been over to the Parrish ranch. You know Martin's poorly."

Cal's gaze clouded. "Sorry. Martin's a good guy."

At the moment, Matt's disquiet involved the task at hand, not merely Martin's health. He'd like his family's blessing, and would get it…in time.

They gathered at the table, Robbie tucked in his high chair between Susannah and Cal. Pa offered grace, thanking God for the food and asking His mercy on Martin. After a hearty amen, Robert nabbed a piece of fried chicken, then passed the platter on.

Susannah tied a bib around Robbie's neck. "Hannah has no family in these parts. What will happen to her?"

"She should sell the ranch and go back to Charleston," Robert said. "Running a ranch isn't a woman's place."

"The Parrish family has endured a lot. First losing both Melanie and the baby in childbirth, now Martin." Ma's voice caught. "Poor Hannah. Makes me want to weep."

Susannah handed Robbie a spoon. The boy promptly dug into the potatoes and managed to get a spoonful into his mouth. "Hannah loves the ranch. I can't believe she'd leave willingly."

Appetite gone, Matt moved his potatoes around his plate with a fork. Might as well get it said. "I asked her to marry me."

Stunned silence followed his declaration. All eyes turned on him, while the startling news sank in.

"So when is the wedding taking place?" Susannah asked.

Martin was dying. They had no time to cement their relationship. "If Pastor Cummings agrees, Thursday at the Lazy P."

Ma gasped. "Mercy, that's fast. Are you sure about this?" she said, searching his face.

Matt had seen that look before. Knew Ma was trying to read his thoughts, zipping him back to when he was ten and had played hooky from school. Ma had been judge and jury, meting out justice. As he recalled, he'd had to muck out the barn every night for a week.

He glanced away from those perceptive eyes. "I'm sure."

Ma didn't smile, merely nodded instead. "I'll drive over to see how we can help."

"You can't possibly love the girl," Cal said. "Why, you barely know her." He plopped his elbows on the table, his expression aghast, as if Matt had grown two heads. "Hannah's a great kid. One thing to feel sorry for her, and I do, but quite another to marry her."

"Obviously, Cal, you haven't seen Hannah since her return," Pa declared. "She's all grown-up."

Cal plopped tiny bites of chicken on Robbie's tray. "There's always been pretty women around. Why the sudden decision to marry this one, big brother?"

Matt would never reveal that Hannah had proposed first. He couldn't explain their decision to marry without revealing the personal details of the agreement, something he'd never do.

"May be overstepping," Cal went on, "but I trust grief over Amy isn't making you settle for a loveless marriage."

Hands balled into rock-hard fists alongside his plate, Matt glared at Cal. "Keep Amy out of this."

As if held at gunpoint, Cal raised his arms, palms out. "Whoa, brother. I want you to have what Susannah and I share. I'm just saying—"

"Saying what? That I don't have the sense to know my own mind?"

"Matthew! Calvin! You're behaving like bullheaded toddlers," Robert said. Then he nodded his head, a smile forming on his lips. "A merger with the Lazy P makes sense. By pooling our resources, both ranches might survive dropping cattle prices and the bad economy."

Leave it to his father to see marriage as a business opportunity. "Hannah hasn't agreed to a merger," Matt said.

"See that she does." Robert glanced around the table, at the untouched food. "Enough of this talk. Eat."

"Eat!" the food-smeared toddler ordered with pride, then stuck a gooey spoon in his hair and grinned.

Everyone laughed, easing the tension at the table.

Matt settled back in his chair, taking a deep breath, trying to slow his breathing. His father tried to run every facet of his sons' lives. It was the reason Zack had turned to the law. And Cal spent most of his time at Susannah's folks' spread.

Still, the ongoing strain between Matt and his father didn't explain Matt's reaction to Cal's concern. He'd thought he had peace about the decision to marry Hannah, but in truth, he was entering uncharted territory.

One grim possibility after another marched through Matt's mind. Without the benefit of a loving relationship, he and Hannah would deal with Martin's illness and without a miracle, his death. This marriage could backfire in a myriad of ways.

Matt had grown comfortable with the emptiness of the past four years. Each day had held a blessed sameness, with neither highs nor lows, just a flat, hollow monotony. He had filled those days with work. The highlight of his week were evenings spent with Martin, another lonely man fighting his own demons. Martin's waning health triggered painful memories of Amy's death.

Still, none of this excused his treatment of Cal. "I'm sorry for overreacting, Cal."

His brother met his gaze, an apology in his eyes. "Me, too."

"To see Hannah wed will give Martin peace," Ma said. "Hannah's a lovely young woman, a rancher at heart. A good match for you."

Robert gave a nod. "Marriage to Hannah is a solution for everyone."

Cal looked pained, as if he'd taken a bite of cactus.

At her husband's silence, Susannah frowned at Cal. "Hope you and Hannah will be very happy," she said, then reported Robbie's latest humorous antic and conversation resumed as usual.

Matt's mind wandered back to how all this started. During his visits to the Lazy P, Martin spoke often of Hannah, the daughter he obviously adored. The day Martin was diagnosed with cancer, he'd shared his heavy burden for his only child's welfare. Matt shared that concern. Hannah was in a tough spot.

Yet, to wed a nineteen-year-old without love scared him silly. Marriage might be a solution for her, but marriage would also create new problems.

Unlike Cal, Matt knew why he'd proposed. He couldn't risk love, but at twenty-five, he wanted a new beginning. He'd settle for companionship, settle for a woman to share his dreams and goals, settle for a woman who'd share his way of life.

The honest truth was that he was tired. Tired of dodging unsuitable women with matrimony on their minds. Tired of feeling alone in a houseful of people. Tired of fighting his father's control.

By marrying her, Matt would see that Hannah could remain on the land she loved. He hoped that would make her happy. If not happy, at least content. Something he'd come to appreciate.

Matt had come, hoping for his family's support of the marriage. For the most part he'd gotten it. Cal would come around. But Pa…. Would Pa's expectation of a merger between the two ranches wind up causing trouble?

Two days till Hannah lassoed and tied herself to Matt Walker. Married. The word twisted in her stomach. Wedding vows meant until death do us part, faithfulness, respect.

She stiffened. Obedience. She hoped Matt could tolerate giving up one of those promises. If he tried to keep her on a short tether—

She swallowed against the sudden lump in her throat,

shoving down all the misgivings trying to spew out of her mouth and into Papa's ear.

Instead she helped her father to his desk. Last evening Matt had asked for Papa's permission to wed. Papa had clapped Matt on the back, declared he already thought of Matt as a son and nothing could make him happier than seeing Hannah in good hands.

As if she wasn't capable of taking care of herself.

Still the news had eased the tension around Papa's eyes and put a big smile on his face. That was reason enough to bite her tongue.

Hannah glanced out the window. The Walker buggy was coming up the lane. She kissed her father's cheek. "Matt's here."

"While you're in town, spread the word about the wedding. A chat with the town's bench sitters and Pastor Cummings should do the trick."

Hannah dreaded the townsfolk's reaction, but forced a bright smile.

Martin motioned to the package in Hannah's hands. "Is that your mama's dress?"

"It is. I'm taking it to Miss Carmichael's for alterations. Are you sure you'll be all right while I'm gone?"

"You're in more peril in Biddy Carmichael's shop than I could ever be here."

"Papa!" Hannah laughed. No matter how much he suffered, her father made the effort to bring laughter to others. "You know her name is Belinda, not Biddy."

"How could I make such a mistake?" He winked. "Now skedaddle. Don't keep your groom waiting."

She kissed him once more, her heart swelling with love, and then walked as fast as her dress would allow, more tortoise than her usual hare. Who could abide such restriction?

Outside, she popped up her frilly parasol, an accessory

Aunt Mary Esther had insisted upon. On such a sweltering day riding in an open buggy, Hannah welcomed the shade.

Matt rounded the conveyance, his gaze traveling from the hat perched atop her head to the silk toe of her pump. He doffed his Stetson. "The debutante is back."

"You looking for a fight, Walker?"

"No, ma'am, I'm not." He grinned wickedly. "One thing's sure. Whatever garb she's wearing, the filly's a Thoroughbred."

Hannah thrust up her chin. "I'm becoming your wife, not joining your stable."

Obviously not the least bit repentant, his impish smile held. "Kind of fun having two of you, debutante and cowgirl, all wrapped up in one very nice parcel."

At his perusal, butterflies fluttered in her stomach. She corralled her skirts, then allowed him to assist her into the buggy. Whether she would be in good hands as Papa had said, was to be seen, but his grasp was strong, secure.

"You have an admirer in Rosa. She's very excited about our wedding," Hannah told him.

"It pays to be on good terms with the cook. Since I've been made to understand that won't likely be you, I plan on buttering her up."

"So the way to a man's heart is indeed through his stomach."

He cocked a brow. "Are you sure you want to know the way to a man's heart, Hannah?"

A shiver slid along her spine. She quickly looked away from the amusement in those dark, smoldering eyes.

"The filly's a tad skittish," he said. Then with a flick of the reins, they got underway. "Know what kind of a wedding you want?"

"A simple ceremony at the Lazy P, outside if weather permits."

"Sounds good."

She sighed. "Papa insists on inviting half the town and hosting a barbecue afterward."

"He doesn't want his illness to cheat you out of a pretty wedding. Most women want that."

Hannah had been thirteen when she and Papa attended Matt and Amy's wedding, a grand affair. Hannah recalled the glow on their faces as they'd recited their vows. After such a love match, Hannah found Matt's acceptance of a marriage of convenience baffling. Perhaps he'd understood that no one could take Amy's place in his affection and wanted companionship.

She plucked at her skirts. "What he doesn't realize, and I can't tell him, is I can't abide the thought of putting on a charade. We aren't an ordinary couple."

"True, but a private wedding might set tongues a-waggin'."

"I suppose you're right, but a party seems…deceptive."

"People marry for many reasons, Hannah." His gaze locked with hers. "If we're committed to one another, then our wedding won't be a charade. I believe we'll be as happy as we choose to be. That's what I want. Do you?"

As she looked into those dark orbs that penetrated her soul, she vowed to do everything in her power to make the marriage work. "Yes," she said softly.

A smile curved the corners of his mouth. "God will bless us, help us find our way."

He took her hand in his. At that moment, the sense of connection between them felt as meaningful as the vows they'd speak on Thursday.

Matt released her hand. "I told my family our decision to wed."

"What did they say?" Hannah asked, her heart in her throat.

"They were…surprised, at first." He shot her an impish grin. "But then, no more than I was."

"Did you tell them I did the proposing?"

"Nope, that's our little secret."

"What did they say?"

"They think you're a lovely young woman and wish us happiness."

Had Matt omitted much of his family's reaction? What had they really said? Perhaps she was better off not knowing. She'd have to get accustomed to the startled reactions of others, those who'd question their sudden nuptials.

On Main Street, Matt pulled up in front of Miss Carmichael's shop, rounded the buggy, then placed his hands around her waist. As she rested her palms on his shoulders and he lifted her down, she stared into warm cocoa eyes, gentle, kind, appealing. Too appealing. She gathered her package, keeping her eyes anywhere except on him.

"I'll stop at the church and ask Pastor Cummings to perform the ceremony. After that I've got business at the bank. What do you say we meet at the Calico Café at noon?"

"That should give me time to visit Leah."

"We won't leave town until you're ready," he said, then loped up the street to set the wedding plans in motion.

An urge to call him back, to renege on the proposal lurched through her. Foolishness. If she'd had another choice, she'd have taken it.

She threw back her shoulders and stepped inside the shop, in actuality, Miss Carmichael's parlor. Overhead a tiny bell jingled. Cases and tables held gloves, hats, bolts of fabric, and baskets of feathers, silk flowers and papier-mâché fruit, the tools of her trade.

Belinda Carmichael bustled through a curtain separating the shop from her private quarters. Behind wire-rim glasses, the spinster's hazel eyes missed nothing. Nor, for that matter, did her ears. Tall, thin, as prim and proper as a starched collar, Belinda gloried in her role as town gossip. No doubt she would gossip about the suddenness of her and Matt's marriage. Still, Hannah wouldn't trust Mama's dress to anyone else.

"Good morning, Miss Parrish. I heard you were back from Charleston." She glanced at the package in Hannah's hands. "What can I do for you?"

Hannah untied the string and wrapping, revealing her mother's wedding dress, an off-white silk confection with a row of pleats edged with lace at the hem, at the flared sleeves and on the draped overskirt.

"I'd like you to alter this dress to fit me."

Miss Carmichael's fingers skimmed over the bodice that tapered to a point below the waist. "The stitching is impeccable. Let's see what needs to be done."

She guided Hannah behind a screen and helped her change, then turned Hannah around, studying the fit. "I'll need to add length. If I trim the sleeves and hem with the matching lace on this overskirt, no one would suspect the additions aren't part of the original dress."

Hannah agreed the solution would be perfect. She skimmed her palms over the overskirt, proud to wear this lovely dress. If only she were marrying a man she loved. She tamped down the thought. Love didn't matter. The Lazy P did.

The bell over the door danced a cheery tune. A second customer entered the shop. "Be right with you," Miss Carmichael called.

"No hurry." The newcomer removed her hatpins, then her hat, obviously eager to try on one of Miss Carmichael's creations.

Miss Carmichael leaned in. "I'm curious, Miss Parrish. Why are you having this dress altered? Surely your rela-

tions in Charleston didn't give you their hand-me-downs."
Miss Carmichael's tone oozed sympathy. "You might want
to consider having something new made. I have several
beautiful fabrics that would compliment your coloring."

"Thank you, but I came back with a trunk full of
dresses, more than I'll ever wear."

The seamstress's expression soured. "Then why alter
this one?" Her eyes widened. "Unless you intend to wear
it for sentimental reasons, like at your wedding." She
smirked. "How silly of me. You have no beau." She raised
a brow. "Unless you met someone in Charleston."

No point in avoiding the truth. Papa said to spread the
word about the wedding, no better way than to tell the
seamstress. Hannah steeled herself for Miss Carmichael's
reaction. "This is my mother's wedding dress," she said.
"I want to wear it at my wedding Thursday. You won't
have any difficulty getting the alterations finished by then,
will you?"

Hazel eyes gleaming, Miss Carmichael clapped her
hands. "For a wedding, it'll be my priority! Who are you
marrying?"

"Matt Walker."

"Matt Walker! From what I hear, he's a most elusive
catch." Her shrewd beady eyes resembled a predator moving in for the kill. "You've only been home a few days,"
she said. "Isn't this wedding rather sudden?"

Sudden hardly described it.

"To marry that quickly, why, you must've fallen in love
at first sight." She tittered. "Not really first sight, of course,
but first sight since your return." Her hands fluttered like
tiny birds in flight. "How romantic!"

Heat flooded Hannah's cheeks. Love at first sight had
not been the reason for the marriage. More like, at first
sight of her ailing father. At first sight of her foreman's

refusal to follow orders. At first sight of Papa's worry about her future.

Harsh realities had led her to propose, not romance, not affection for the man. Still, she'd play the role of blissful bride. She owed Matt that much. "Isn't it exciting? Matt's a very persuasive man."

Miss Carmichael's gaze sharpened. Perhaps the waver of Hannah's smile or the wobble in her voice had raised the seamstress's suspicions. Thankfully, the older woman didn't pursue the topic, no doubt unwilling to risk a paying customer's ire. After all, the seamstress had to make her own way.

A wave of sympathy for the woman swept through Hannah. Belinda Carmichael carried a load of responsibility and had no one to help share the burden. At least with Matt she'd have a partner.

All business, Miss Carmichael grabbed a tape measure and whipped it from the edge of Hannah's hem to the toe of her shoe, then wrote her findings in a tiny notebook. She did the same for her sleeves. "I have all I need. Let me help you change."

Behind the screen, the seamstress eased the garment over Hannah's head. "I'll have the dress finished by tomorrow afternoon and drive out to the ranch and deliver it personally."

"That's too much trouble."

"Not at all, if you'll show me the fashions you brought back from Charleston," Miss Carmichael said with a smile, then rushed toward the waiting customer.

On the way out of the shop, Hannah passed Miss Carmichael and the shopper, their heads together, their smiles couldn't cover the speculative look in their eyes.

As she escaped into the sunshine, Hannah heaved a

sigh. She'd survived Miss Carmichael's reaction, so surely she could survive anyone's.

Up ahead, Bertram Bailey swept the entrance of Bailey's Dry Goods. Thin as the broom in his hand, and not much taller, Mr. Bailey propped the handle against the building. "Good to have you home, Miss Parrish," he said, then followed her inside.

She handed the proprietor the list. "Rosa needs a great many things to prepare for a barbecue at the Lazy P Thursday."

"Ah, a celebration for your homecoming," he said, scanning the order.

"Actually a celebration of my wedding."

Mr. Bailey blinked. "You don't say. Who are you marrying?"

"Matt Walker."

"Well, if that don't beat all. I waited on Mrs. Victoria Walker a couple days ago. Never said a word about her son marrying. Reckon she's better keeping secrets than most folks."

No need to tell Mr. Bailey that Matt's mother didn't know about their wedding a couple days ago. For that matter neither did she nor Matt. "Since the order is sizable, I'll pick it up this afternoon before we leave town."

"I'd appreciate it. I'll add this to your bill."

Bills got paid when cattle got sold. That's the way things were done in Bliss. "Thank you."

A glance at the clock on the wall revealed she had an hour before she'd meet Matt. Enough time to visit Leah.

Down the street the town's bench sitters watched the comings and goings in town. At her approach, all three doffed their hats, grins wide on their faces, evidence of their bright outlook despite the infirmities of age. The realization that Papa would not be as fortunate slugged her in the belly like a fist.

"Good to have you home, Miss Hannah. How's your pa?" As the oldest at eighty-four, Mr. Cooper acted as spokesman.

"About the same, thank you. How are y'all?"

"Fair to middlin'." Reed thin, his bushy, untamed eyebrows all but hiding his pale blue eyes, Mr. Cooper's knobby hands wrapped around the handle of his cane. "Ben here is a tad riled. The Fowler twins chucked rocks our way and hit him smack-dab on the nose. They hightailed it for home before we could catch 'em!"

The image of these men swinging their canes in hot pursuit of the notorious eight-year-old boys had Hannah stifling a giggle. Until she took a look at the poor man's swollen nose. "Should you have Doc check it, Mr. Seller?"

Two gnarled fingers skimmed his bulbous nose, ruddier than usual. "Had worse. Don't know what the world's coming to when a man ain't safe minding his own business. Little imps hadn't ought to be out amongst decent folks."

Hands looped around his suspenders, Mr. Brand laughed, his belly bobbing with each cackle. "Seller, you oughta see Doc and give Fowler the bill. Why, that'd make him sit up and take notice. Fowler's so tight he'd walk a rotten rail over the Rio Grande to save hisself a nickel."

Mr. Cooper sputtered with laughter that dwindled into a wheeze. "If Fowler kept as tight a rein on them younguns as he does on his wallet, this town would be a whole lot safer."

Three grizzled heads dipped in agreement.

"I want you gentlemen to be among the first to know that Matt Walker and I are getting married. The wedding is Thursday afternoon at the Lazy P, outside, weather permitting."

"Well, ain't that the best news!" Mr. Brand said. "The Circle W and Lazy P are joining forces."

Was a merger the first thing everyone would think of when they heard of their wedding?

Mr. Cooper smiled. "Don't worry none about the weather, Miz Hannah. If rain was coming, my knees would be hollering."

"That's good to hear. I hope you gentlemen will come. We're having a barbecue afterward."

"Jake Hardy making his famous sauce?" Mr. Seller asked.

"We wouldn't serve anything else."

Mr. Fowler grinned, revealing two missing teeth. "Count on me. Ain't missing the chance to see you two hitched. And have a visit with your pa."

"Pass the word along, will you?"

"You can count on us," Mr. Cooper promised, already surveying the block for someone to tell.

Hannah had accomplished what she'd set out to do— pass the word about their wedding. Thus far, she'd dodged a bullet. No one had openly questioned the match.

So why did she feel like she'd taken a slug in the heart?

Chapter Six

Hannah darted across Main Street, then hustled along Oak Avenue, lined with live oaks and large imposing houses. Only an occasional barking dog disturbed the quiet.

Friends since childhood, she and Leah had shared their girlhood dreams of romance and marriage. How naive they'd been. She batted away tears welling in her eyes. She wouldn't confide in Leah that her marriage was one of convenience and crush her friend's fantasy.

At the Montgomery house, Hannah climbed the steps, then lifted the brass door knocker. She studied the fanciful stork standing on one leg amongst cattails etched in the oval glass of the door. The stork seemed appropriate here.

Her gaze swept the planked porch littered with toys left behind by Leah's four younger brothers and sisters, Abe, Anna, Peter and Susie. In the gap between Leah and her twelve-year-old brother Abe, two precious Montgomery children had died. Perhaps that was the reason the parents didn't fret about disorder. The large, rambunctious family thrived in a house where bedlam reigned. Far different from Hannah's quiet, tidy home with only a caring housekeeper and doting father to keep her company.

Hannah's throat knotted. How could she abide losing Papa?

Leah flung open the door. Blond, blue-eyed and prettier than ever. "Hannah! When did you get back?"

They wrapped their arms around one another, then leaned back to inspect the changes a year had brought. Leah had inherited the best qualities of both parents, her mother's fair beauty and openness, balanced with a good measure of her father's steadfastness.

Mrs. Montgomery, blond hair twisted into a chignon, blue eyes harried, dashed out the door, almost colliding with them. She scooped Hannah into an embrace. "Hannah, you've grown up! I'm amazed how much you resemble your sweet mother."

Hannah might look like Mama but she was her father's daughter.

"Keep Leah company while she looks after the rest of my brood. Better yet, stay overnight. I'll drive you home tomorrow."

"Thank you, but I'm expected back."

"Well, another time then. You're always welcome, dear. Please give our best to your father." Mrs. Montgomery gave Hannah's cheek a pat, peering into her eyes. "If you need anything, anything at all, come to me." Hannah nodded, then the older woman spun off with a moan. "I'm late!"

Leah tugged Hannah into the house and up the stairs. "Everybody's in school and I'm not scheduled today to clerk at Bailey's. We can spend the entire afternoon together."

"I can't stay."

In Leah's room, an oasis of tidiness in the disheveled house, they sat on the brass bed facing each other. Leah's eyes welled with tears. "We know how sick your father is. I'm sorry."

As if a dam had broken, words poured out of Hannah—Doc Atkins's dire diagnosis and the foreman and top hands quitting.

Leah listened, never once interrupting, then took Hannah's hands in hers. "I wish your father wasn't sick. But, wishing doesn't make it so. I've been worried about what would happen to you. What are you going to do?"

"I've got...news. Matt Walker and I are getting married."

Leah shrieked and threw her arms around Hannah. "You're getting married! Oh, how exciting!" Her brows puckered. "How did this happen? You've been in Charleston for a year."

"I've never forgotten Matt. We've seen each other at church, at community events, even at the Lazy P when he'd stop by on occasion." Heat bloomed in her cheeks. "When I came back to town, he picked me up at the depot and...sparks flew."

That much was true, though those sparks stemmed from a clash of personalities, not from attraction.

Hannah's breath caught. Why not be honest? Any woman would notice that cowboy physique, that attractive face.

That arrogance.

"You're blushing." Leah's eyes lit. "How romantic. Matt's perfect, a rancher like you, and no one in the county's more handsome. Unless you count his brother, Cal, but you can't because he's married to my cousin Susannah."

Leah raved about the handsome Matt Walker, as if appearance could cement a relationship.

Countless times she and Leah had shared dreams of marrying a prince, a knight in shining armor, depending on the last book they'd read. The one constant in those stories was the couple's unshakable love, the happily-ever-after ending. Not a marriage based on life's harsh realities.

"Marrying Matt must give your father peace of mind."

"Yes." It was the reason Hannah had proposed. She'd swapped that fairy-tale groom she and Leah daydreamed about for survival. Now sitting here with Leah, away from the ranch, away from Papa, that decision seemed hasty.

"Every unmarried woman in town has been after Matt, and he chose you." Leah pulled Hannah to feet and turned her toward her dressing-table mirror. "Any man would be proud to have you for his wife."

The reflection in the mirror might look all grown-up, but Hannah didn't feel ready to marry. Anyone.

With a dreamy look on her face, Leah swayed to some soundless melody. "Matt Walker's not like boys our age, who all but drool when they steal a kiss." She leaned closer. "I'll tell you a secret. I've flirted with Matt's brother Zack." She sighed. "I'm sure he'd make a woman feel things right down to her toes."

"What are you talking about? Do you think you're ready to get married?"

"Oh, yes! I want to have my own home and a man to care for and love." Brow puckered, lips turned down, Leah paced her room. "I'm sick of taking care of my brothers and sisters. I feel more like their mother than Mama."

Not that Leah handled everything. Able to indulge his wife, Mr. Montgomery employed a cook and a laundress to ensure timely meals and starched shirts.

If she married, Leah might not have that luxury. "If you marry, you'll most likely end up with kids. And have to do all those tedious chores that involve looking after children and a home. I much prefer roping cattle and riding herd."

"I love the little kids and don't mind caring for them, not

really. I'm just ready to live *my* life, to have a man to love, to share our home, our thoughts, our children. With Zack's and my blond hair, our children would be towheads." She plopped her arms across her middle. "Why do you prefer hard, dirty jobs on the ranch? Instead of the genteel pastimes of your mother?"

Hannah shrugged. "I'm more like Papa. Strong."

"Well, you look exactly like your mother. You'll be a beautiful bride." Leah's voice dropped to a whisper. "If Matt's kisses are anything like Howard Honeywell's—"

"Who is Howard Honeywell?"

"A college friend my cousin Mark brought home for the Christmas holiday. I met Howard at a party. He asked me to walk outside to get some air. He kissed me, really kissed me."

Speechless, Hannah gaped at her friend. In Charleston, when a boy acted like he wanted to kiss her, she'd had an urge to giggle.

"I'm sorry I didn't write to tell you about Howard, but I only saw him a couple of times." Leah shrugged. "Before Mark left, he admitted Howard has a special girl at school."

Hannah touched Leah's sleeve. "I'm sorry, that must hurt."

"I didn't really know him. Maybe I wouldn't have liked him if I did." She sighed. "But, I'll always remember him."

A knot lodged in Hannah's throat. In three days, she'd marry a man she barely knew. A man she'd never kissed.

"If not for your papa's health, I'd say you're the luckiest girl alive!"

Hannah tried to work up a bright smile but failed.

Leah gaped. "You don't look…happy. Is something wrong?"

"I'm just upset about Papa." Leah gave a sympathetic

nod as the grandfather clock in the hall downstairs struck noon. "I've got to go. I'm meeting Matt at the café."

"Wait, when is the ceremony?"

"Oh, I forgot. Will you stand up with me?"

"Of course. We've always promised to be in each other's weddings. This is so exciting. What time is the wedding?"

"Thursday at three o'clock. At the Lazy P."

"Those must've been some sparks!" Leah said, chuckling.

"We want Papa to see us wed."

Leah absorbed the significance of her words, her eyes softening with compassion.

To avoid that sympathetic gaze, Hannah strode to Leah's wardrobe. "Let's look at your dresses. See what you might wear."

"Miss Carmichael made this for Mark's graduation party," Leah said as she pulled out a frothy dress. "It'll be perfect for an outdoor wedding."

"It's lovely." An image of Leah wearing the pale peach confection as she stood beside Hannah made the wedding all too real.

Leah's eyes widened. "What are you going to wear?"

"Miss Carmichael is altering Mama's wedding dress to fit me."

"Oh, the gown in the portrait. You'll look beautiful."

"Thank you. I've got to go. I'm late."

Arm in arm, they walked to the door, then faced each other.

"Matt's perfect, Hannah. Not a knight, not a prince, but a cowboy groom is the perfect match for a tomboy."

Hannah nodded, then marched to the Calico Café, her clamped jaw shooting pain up her face. Easy for Leah to rhapsodize over Matt Walker. To babble on about stolen kisses. Courting was one thing, marriage quite another.

The grim reality was that Papa was dying, and she'd proposed to Matt. She had no one to blame for this marriage but herself.

Matt fingered the slim gold band in his pocket. To ensure the fit, Rosa had cut a string the size of the ring Martin had given Hannah for her sixteenth birthday.

The door opened, and Hannah crossed the café. Tendrils of her shiny auburn hair had pulled loose, swaying in rhythm with her steps. Any man would be proud to call this lovely woman his.

Yet, one look at the disquiet on her face knotted Matt's gut. Leah must have reacted badly to their upcoming nuptials. During the meal, he'd do what he could to smooth the rough waters he suspected Leah had churned up.

He rose to help Hannah into her chair, then took his seat. Might as well get to what was troubling her. "How did Leah react to news of our marriage?"

Hannah's gaze dropped to her hands clenched in her lap. "She's thrilled."

Unlike the bride.

"She's excited to stand up with me. Has the perfect dress."

"Good. As soon as I got to town, I wired Zack. Already got his acceptance. He'll arrive Thursday morning."

"I told Miss Carmichael, Mr. Bailey and the bench sitters about our wedding."

Matt grinned. "In that case, everyone in town will know by nightfall. I talked to Pastor Cummings. He agreed to marry us."

Finally. No need to tell Hannah that the preacher had cautioned them not to rush into marriage. As if they had the luxury of taking things slow.

"Plans are coming along at home. Rosa's cousin will

help clean and cook. Jake will dig the pit, make the sauce and handle the barbecue."

"We're making progress." Matt took her hand. "I'm sorry we'll have no honeymoon."

A flush rose to her cheeks. "No reason to go anywhere," she said, then snatched her hand from his.

If he hadn't understood the boundaries of their marriage, that said it all. Not that he disagreed. Far better to rely on common sense than on emotion, an unreliable foundation for happiness.

Carolyn Shields, her salt-and-pepper hair swept back in a bun, a crisp white apron over her middle, arrived at the table. "Know what you want?"

They settled on the special, beef and noodles. The widow left to dish up the food.

"You seem upset." Matt glanced around him, then kept his voice low. "Are you having second thoughts about our marriage?"

The eyes she lifted to his might not look like an excited bride, but they were steely with determination. "Marriage is what I want. Are you changing your mind?"

"No, ma'am." He grinned. "I'm corralled and ready for branding. Thing is, which brand will I wear?"

"The Lazy P, what else?"

"And you're just the woman to get the job done."

She grinned back at him. "Never doubt that, cowboy."

Good to see her feisty side back. A man didn't hanker to be led around by his nose, but if pretending Hannah was boss would put a smile on her face, that's what he'd do.

But he couldn't help wondering at what point a marriage based on pretense would blow up in his face?

Chapter Seven

The rooster's crow jolted Hannah awake. For a moment, she lay between sleep and wakefulness, listening to the swelling pitch of the rooster's call. Then the significance of the day slammed into her. She sucked in a breath and shot upright in bed. Today she'd become Mrs. Matthew Walker.

Was she ready? Her stomach tumbled. She'd better be. She had no way to undo this. Not now.

She crawled out of bed, padded barefoot to the window and pulled the curtain aside, revealing the glow of the rising sun in a pink and blue sky dotted with fleecy clouds Papa called featherbeds for weary angels. From the looks of the morning sky, the Lord had blessed their plan for an outdoor ceremony.

Hannah had laid awake most of the night. Too edgy to return to bed, she braided her hair, then pulled on a simple dress to please her father, rather than her usual denims.

She glanced in the mirror, staring into the anxious eyes of a nineteen-year-old on the verge of taking the biggest step of her life. A lump rose in her throat. If only she could turn back the clock. To the time when Papa was healthy and strong and she rode the land with joy in her heart, free and full of confidence. Her life had been simple then.

Since her return from Charleston, she'd felt caught in a maze, bumping into one obstacle after another. She'd chosen a way out. Where would that path lead?

She refused to question an answer God had given her. Her stomach tumbled. Hadn't He?

As she passed the dining room, stacks of dishes, boxes of silverware and glasses they'd borrowed from the Walkers, Montgomerys and Rosa's cousin to supplement their supply, covered the table.

Mingling aromas of breakfast led Hannah to the kitchen where Rosa bustled about, keeping an eye on iron skillets of potatoes and sausage gravy as she popped a pan of biscuits into the oven.

"Morning, Rosa," Hannah said. "Breakfast smells delicious."

"Good morning, Hannah. Beautiful day for a wedding."

"Yes." As Hannah carried three white ironstone plates to the stove, she kept an eye out for Matt. Some claimed if the groom saw the bride before the wedding, they'd have bad luck.

Not that she believed in luck, bad or otherwise. Her hesitancy was cowardice, the fear that Matt would see the jumble of emotions churning inside her. Or worse, that she'd see he was having second thoughts.

She didn't have to wait long. Matt rode up the lane to help Papa start his day.

"I'm going out to do chores. Jake's got his hands full watching over the fire," Hannah said, fleeing the house by the back door.

By the time she'd finished, Matt's horse was gone. She heaved a sigh. He'd returned to the Circle W. At the pump, she washed her hands, then headed for the house.

Papa sat at the kitchen table, pale, thin, but with a twinkle in his eye. "How's the bride feeling on her wedding day?"

"I'm fine, Papa."

"Your groom looked mighty chipper."

Rosa joined them at the table, setting a large vase of roses in the center. The flower's sweet, spicy scent mingled with the aroma of fresh brewed coffee. "Señor Matt cut flowers for the wedding."

"He did?"

"Your mother cherished her roses," Papa said, "and tended them daily."

Exactly as her father had done all these years. No matter how busy life got on the ranch, he'd check the roses for bugs, disease, drought. The roses, a symbol of Mama, of her life in Charleston that Papa would not let die.

"Tell me about Mama," Hannah said, then nibbled on a biscuit.

"She loved you. Beamed with pride as you grew from baby to toddler to little girl."

"Was she disappointed I was a tomboy?"

"She would've never been disappointed in anything about you, sugar. But, it wasn't until after your mama died that you traded dolls for lassos and spurs." He smiled. "I wish she could see you married. See grandchildren."

If only Mama and Papa were both strong and healthy, how different life would be. But grandchildren...

Hannah shifted in her chair, picking at her food. Papa expected her and Matt's marriage to produce children. Not possible with their arrangement. Still, Hannah could barely imagine motherhood.

She scrambled for another topic. "Tell me again how you and Mama met."

"I was in Charleston to buy a stallion. This beautiful young woman and I had our eye on the same horse. Melanie knew horseflesh and prevailed in the bidding. I pestered the stable owner until he introduced us. We fell in love at first sight. A month later, I brought my bride and her stallion home to Texas." He chuckled. "Melanie always claimed I married her to get that horse."

Her parents' marriage was a far cry from her and Matt's marriage of convenience.

"Your mother loved the slower pace of Charleston. Yet, she gave all that up for me."

Life on a Texas ranch must've been as foreign to Mama as Charleston's frantic social scene had been for Hannah. She couldn't imagine giving up the vastness, the wildness, the challenge of this land. "She loved you, Papa."

"Yes, and I her." He toyed with his fork, turning it around and around in his hands, then lifted moist eyes to Hannah. "I've wondered if bringing Melanie here killed her."

"Why? Women die in childbirth in Charleston, too."

"Yes, but this life is hard, especially for a delicate woman like your mama." He took Hannah's hand. "I sent you to finishing school for the social graces, the skills to marry, to run a home. So you wouldn't spend your life battling bad weather, cattle diseases, trying to make a success of the ranch."

"I'm not like Mama."

"I'll admit you're sturdier, stronger than your mother. In many ways you're more like me."

"I love this land, Papa. I'm as connected to it as deep-rooted cottonwoods, as enduring as perennial bluebonnets."

Brow creased, his eyes searched hers. "Enough that you will marry to keep it."

Papa understood that romance had nothing to do with

the decision to marry Matt. Not having to pretend with Papa somehow eased the tightness in Hannah's chest.

"Hannah, if you're marrying Matt for my sake, if this isn't what you want, don't go through with it."

How could she not? Without her parents, without this land, she had nothing. Nothing of the life she knew, the life she loved. By marrying Matt, she'd keep that way of life. She'd keep this land and give her father peace. "I've made my decision, Papa."

"You sure?"

"I'm sure."

He smiled, relief plain on his face. "I can rest easy knowing you'll be looked after when I'm gone. Matt's a good man. You have much in common. He'll make you a good husband."

The prospect of being yoked to a man she didn't love and who didn't love her flopped in her stomach. Yet, she believed Matt was a good man. She could do worse.

"Promise me you'll give Matt a chance. In time, I'm sure love will come."

"I promise."

Papa sucked in air, the sudden grimace on his face a reminder of the pain he endured. "Reckon I'd better take a dose of my medicine."

With a lump in her throat, Hannah helped Papa to his feet. By the time she had settled him in his room, had given him a dose of his pain medication, then helped Rosa with last-minute food preparation, she needed to start getting ready.

As she filled the tub with water, she thought about her conversation with Papa. Deep within her soul, she wanted that true love her parents had, wanted it with a desperation that took her breath away. To have a love so strong that nothing else mattered—not location, not traditions, not a way of life—was implausible. But she'd have all the rest, the things that gave her security, that filled her life with meaning, that gave her purpose. That and God would be enough. Enough for a lifetime.

She bathed and washed her hair, then rinsed it with vinegar for shine. On the porch, she lifted and finger-combed the strands, letting them dry in the gentle breeze.

Strange how the day felt ordinary when she'd soon take the biggest step of her life. Somehow she managed to eat a few bites at noon, then went to her room to dress and finish her hair.

Rosa had laid out Hannah's wedding finery in a fan of silk on the bed. True to her word, Miss Carmichael had brought the dress out yesterday. The alterations done perfectly, the dress was pressed and ready to wear.

"I hope I'm as prepared," Hannah whispered, as she swept her hair onto the top of her head, anchoring it with hairpins and pulling shorter ringlets free around her face.

There was a tap at the door. Forehead beaded with perspiration, the strings of her apron flapping behind her, Rosa barreled into the room, a bouquet of roses in one hand. "Oh, your hair so pretty," she said a she set the flowers aside. "I come help you dress."

Rosa cinched Hannah into her corset, the hated contraption she rarely wore on the ranch, then carefully lifted the dress and slipped the skirt over Hannah's head. With the help of several hairpins, Rosa secured the halo of waxed orange blossoms to Hannah's hair, then smoothed the attached filmy veil that fell almost to the floor.

The mirror reflected an uncanny likeness to her mother's wedding portrait hanging over the mantel in the parlor. Hannah had viewed the painting her entire life, but today she felt as if she had stepped into the portrait...had become Melanie Parrish.

With shaky fingers, Hannah smoothed the gown over her petticoats. The toe of a white satin slipper peeked from beneath the hem. She felt like a princess in the fairy tales she and Leah had read as youngsters.

"The bride is most beautiful in all Texas!" Rosa gushed, then retrieved the roses tied with a silky ribbon and handed the sprig to Hannah.

Hannah blinked back tears and buried her nose in the petals, inhaling the heady scent, the fragrance of Mama.

"You are sad?"

"I miss Mama."

Tears flooded Rosa's eyes. "*Si*, a bride needs her mama on her wedding day." With both hands, Rosa cupped Hannah's face and kissed her on both cheeks, then tapped her heart. "She here. She here for you."

"Thank you, Rosa."

"I go change clothes." She smiled. "Señor Matt helped your papa shave and dress."

A gentle warmth slipped through Hannah. Without fanfare, Matt recognized and quietly met the needs of others. Papa was right when he'd said she was marrying a good man.

As Rosa hurried out the door, Hannah bent over her jewelry case and removed the dainty pearl earrings Mama had worn at her wedding. As she fastened the pearls in front of the mirror, troubled blue eyes looked back at her. Nothing like the smiling eyes in Mama's portrait. This dress, the dress in the wedding portrait, had been worn by a bride deeply in love with her groom. A bride willing to leave everything behind and move across the country to share his life.

If only Hannah felt that deep love that mattered more than anything on this earth. If her mother could see from heaven, would she be disappointed in her daughter? Disapprove of giving up girlhood dreams for grown-up realities?

Determined not to surrender to the sudden tightness in her throat, Hannah took one last look in the mirror. Would Matt think her pretty as he had Amy on their wedding day? Ashamed of such foolishness, Hannah tamped down the thought, eyes misting. The image before her blurred.

The jingle of harnesses, the squeak of a wheel took Hannah to the open window. Buggies were pulling in the lane, parking in the barnyard.

Settled in an armchair in the shade of the pecan tree, Martin greeted their arriving guests.

Please, Lord, help Papa handle the long, tiring day.

Hannah heard a shriek and reeled to the doorway.

"Oh, you're a beautiful bride!" Leah said, charging into the room. "Are you excited?"

"Of course!" Hannah despised the lie but what else could she say? "You look lovely, Leah."

"Thank you." Leah spun in a circle, a wide grin on her face. "I adore this dress."

Leah looked fetching indeed in her delicate peach frock with a modestly scooped neckline and deeper peach sash at the waist. A wide-brimmed straw hat, trimmed with flowers and matching ribbon and white gloves completed her outfit.

"You better hurry. The yard is full of people and the preacher is here," Leah said. "Matt is pacing out front, looking more handsome and nervous than I've ever seen him."

What had happened to the confident cowboy? Was Matt having second thoughts? She tamped down the temptation to look out the window to see for herself, afraid she'd see regret on his face.

"Zack looks gorgeous in his Sunday best," Leah went

on. "If you don't need me for anything, Rosa gave me strict orders to bring you down. It's almost time to begin."

"All I have to do is slip on these gloves."

Leah again clutched Hannah's hands. "I know you'll be happy. Matt's the best catch in the county. He's going to fall even more madly in love with you the minute he sees his beautiful bride."

Nonsense. Leah's head was filled with romance, not reality. Some sentimental part of Hannah wished he would, but love would complicate everything.

"Where will you stay tonight?" Leah said, her blue eyes gleaming.

"What do you mean?"

"You know, where will you…ah, sleep?" Leah's gaze traveled to the full bed.

Tonight. Her wedding night. Perception dawned, trapping the breath in Hannah's lungs. Leah had skirted a subject too personal to broach, even with a best friend. Hannah's stomach knotted. The expectation would be for her and Matt to share a room. The knot cinched tighter. She'd do what she could to hide the truth that Matt would stay in the guest room down the hall.

"We'll stay here," Hannah said. "We don't have to travel far for the honeymoon."

Leah giggled. "That's a surprisingly sensible thought for such an impulsive wedding."

Hannah worked a smile to her face. "I'm almost ready. Go on ahead. I'll be right along."

After Leah left, Hannah battled back tears. Everyone was here, the time had come. A part of her wanted to run. To take off the gown, release her hair, dash to the stable. Let Star take her away from all this.

She walked to the window. Papa sat on the front row of chairs beside Rosa, too weak to walk her down the grassy aisle, but looking happy. Her gaze swept the land, Parrish land all the way to the horizon as far as the eye could see.

For her father and for this ranch, she could marry Matt. She turned to the mirror, pasted on a smile and a brave face that didn't reveal the uncertainty underneath, then before she had second thoughts, grabbed the bouquet of roses and hurried from the room.

In the entry hall, Robert Walker waited, a wide, teasing grin on his face. "Your guests are roasting and need a bride before they're as barbecued as that beef. You look most fetching, Hannah, a stunning bride. My son is a lucky man."

"Thank you. No more than I, to be joining your family."

Wearing a pleased expression, Robert offered his arm. Together they walked out into the sunlight, the scent of roses overridden by the tantalizing aroma of barbecue.

Up ahead Leah sashayed toward the front, serene and in her element, carrying a bouquet of Mama's pink roses.

Under the rose trellis, Matt waited with Zack and Pastor Cummings, looking expectant, nervous and so handsome he took her breath away. Boots planted wide, freshly shaven, his curly dark hair combed into obedience, he wore a dark suit, as befit a proper groom.

His dark eyes focused only on her, filled with unmistakable approval. Her heart leaped, then pounded in her chest. She offered a tentative smile.

He smiled back, the expression on his face content.

With newfound confidence, she proceeded up the aisle, passing their guests. Hannah met Mrs. Montgomery's tear-filled eyes and unwavering smile. Jake gave her a wink and a nod. Matt's mother, Victoria, blew her a kiss. Papa sat beside Rosa, his pale face glowing with pride, with joy.

Robert took a seat beside Victoria. Hannah leaned down and pressed a kiss to her father's cheek. "I love you, Papa."

"I love you, Daughter."

She stepped to Matt's side and accepted the solid warmth of his grasp. Together they faced the preacher as butterflies tap-danced in her belly.

With a smile, Pastor Cummings glanced at those seated before him. "We are here today to witness Hannah Lorraine Parrish and Matthew Aaron Walker united as one in holy matrimony."

Holy matrimony. A permanent union, sanctioned by the church, by God. *Lord, I promise to commit to our vows.*

The ceremony passed in a blur, with Hannah barely aware of the words the preacher uttered. Yet moments of utter clarity branded her brain. The sincerity in Matt's eyes and the strength of his voice when he recited his vows. The warmth of the gold band he slipped on her finger. The scent of roses rising from her bouquet and the trellis.

And then finally, the words she had both dreaded and anticipated. "You may kiss the bride," Pastor Cummings said.

Hannah's heart skipped a beat, fluttering in her chest. A moment passed, then Matt lowered his lips to hers, his gentle, feathery touch tingled through her, trapping the air in her lungs until she had to remind herself to breathe.

He drew back, but her brain lingered on that kiss and on the riot of emotions and reactions churning in her belly. What had just happened? A part of her had been swept away, caught up in some fantasy of happily ever after.

She steeled her spine. He didn't love her. She wouldn't let herself care for him. She wouldn't.

Matt's heart thudded in his chest, as he gazed down at his bride, her lips slightly parted, cheeks rosy—from the heat or from his kiss? Had she been as stunned by the reaction to his lips on hers as he had?

Long dark lashes fluttered as she opened her eyes and stared up at him, looking dazed, vulnerable and oh, so beautiful.

His throat clogged. The responsibility for her that once weighed on Martin's shoulders shifted to his. This time, he would protect his wife from harm.

Within minutes of the ceremony, Pastor Cummings ushered Matt and Hannah into Martin's office to sign the license. Behind them, dapper in a three-piece suit, Zack walked beside a radiant Leah, obviously smitten with Matt's brother. Hannah's signature never wavered, the strokes precise and straightforward much like the woman. Matt added his own signature, then thanked everyone.

"Let's give the newlyweds a moment alone," Zack said, after the preacher took his leave.

"Very considerate of you, little brother." Matt grinned. "Though I suspect your plan is for a moment alone with Leah."

Leah giggled, blushing like a want-to-be bride, then removed Hannah's headpiece and floor-length veil. "Can't have you tripping when you dance."

Once the others left the house, Hannah stopped at the open front door, scanning the yard where their guests milled about, chatting.

Matt took her hands, engulfing them in his own. The delicate bones of her fingers proof that women were fragile and needed protection. "I'll take good care of you, Hannah," he promised.

A flash of disquiet traveled her face. She tugged her hands away. "I'm a big girl. I don't need coddling."

"Is that right? Or is it cuddling you don't need?"

"That, too. Don't let the flowers and my finery fool you." She nailed him with her gaze. "We married for convenience, remember?"

A chuckle rumbled inside of him. "Married only a few minutes and you're already putting me in my place."

Exactly where he wanted to be, a distance from Hannah, in a place of contentment. Not of infatuation or a rush of emotion, as unreliable and perilous as a tattered saddle cinch.

"I'm sorry. I didn't mean to sound harsh."

She laid a gentle hand on his jaw, peering up at him. At her tender touch, his heart tripped. An urge stormed through him to cradle her hand, kiss the palm and each fingertip.

A bright smile on her lips, she removed her hand. "That should pacify our guests," she said.

Tarnation. She'd played the role of blissful bride so perfectly, even he'd fallen for the charade.

With every ounce of his will he tamped down his reaction and turned away. To keep that distance they both wanted would require fortitude and willpower. If all else failed, a reel of barbed wire should blockade his heart. No matter what, he'd not fall again into the trap of impulsiveness and risk another unhappy wife.

"Shall we join our guests?" Hannah said. "I promise they'll never suspect this marriage is a business deal, at least not from watching me."

She had no idea how much she'd affected him. "Of course," he croaked, then cleared his throat. "Everyone is waiting for us to get our food first."

At dinner, he and Hannah smiled into each other's eyes. She touched his arm, a hand, snuggled near. Perhaps that fancy finishing school taught acting classes. Hannah was putting on quite a performance. With each touch, he steeled himself, determined to remain aloof, as they played the game. Yet the dishonesty of feigning love and happiness roiled the food in his stomach.

When their families and guests had eaten their fill, Zack stood, fulfilling his role as best man. "Hannah, you'll need a load of patience to put up with Matt's bossy nature."

"I'm only bossy with those who require direction, Zack." Matt grinned. "Like you, not my wife."

Their guests chuckled at the banter.

"But underneath that, ah, slightly rough surface, Matt's solid, a godly man." Zack raised his glass. "I wish you both every happiness."

Not to be outdone, Cal stood. "Matt and Hannah, may you have a long and happy life together with the blessing of many children. Susannah and I intend to give you a goal to strive for in that department." With a wide grin, he glanced at his wife and small son.

The clink of glasses filled the spring air. Matt pulled his collar from his neck. Children. He adored children. But he and Hannah wouldn't have any. He'd be a good uncle, spend time with Robbie and other babies that arrived. Fill the empty place inside him with Susannah and Cal's offspring.

Eyes aglow, Martin struggled to his feet. "God bless you, my children. I wish you a long and happy life filled with the joy you've given me today."

To see Martin happy, at peace, confirmed he and Hannah had done the right thing.

Tears in her eyes, Hannah rose from his side and embraced her father. Matt and Martin shook hands then clapped their arms around each other.

As Martin took his seat beside Robert, Matt's father stood. "Hannah, welcome to the family. To Hannah and Matt!" he said, lifting his glass.

The wedding guests cheered his toast—no doubt believing he and Hannah were in love.

Matt rose, and cleared his throat. "I'm blessed to have

this special woman as my wife." He stared into Hannah's eyes. "Hannah, I will love you as long as I live," he said, not tripping over the word love, but perspiration beaded his brow.

He leaned down and brushed his lips over hers. Her smile never wavered, even as tears welled in her eyes. He knew full well these were not tears of happiness.

He felt like he'd stepped onstage. He and Hannah were the main actors. He didn't know who'd put on the better performance but the joy on everyone's faces was their applause.

Donned in her best finery, Belinda Carmichael sashayed up and tapped Matt on the arm with her fan. "I'll admit I was suspicious you two had married for reasons other than love. But seeing you together, the looks, the touches." She sighed. "I've never seen a more lovesick couple. I wish you much happiness."

"Thank you, Miss Carmichael. And thank you for altering my wife's wedding dress. I've never seen her look more beautiful."

The rest of the afternoon passed with all the traditions of a wedding. Rosa led them to the tiered cake festooned with white swags and sugary roses and placed a beribboned knife in Hannah's hands.

Then Hannah tossed her bouquet. Leah scrambled to retrieve it and winked at Hannah as she lifted the sprig of roses in victory.

All afternoon Zack had hovered at Leah's side. Both were flirting openly. There was no pretense on Leah's part, but Zack…who knew?

Hannah nudged Matt. "They'd be perfect together."

No doubt their guests thought the same about him and Hannah. "You'd better warn Leah. Zack has broken more than his share of hearts."

"Don't underestimate her. Leah might be the woman to tame him."

"Like you've tamed me?" he said, chuckling.

Head thrown back, eyes twinkling, she laughed. "You're about as tame as a wild mustang, Matt Walker."

"Hardly." He leaned in to her, catching the lingering sweet scent of roses. "But, I must admit, I'm glad you think so, Mrs. Walker."

As much as he wanted a marriage of convenience, a powerful temptation to take his bride into his arms, to hold her close gripped him. This newlywed game they played had undermined his judgment and opened a crevice in the steel casing around his heart.

Where would all this lead?

Chapter Eight

Drained from playing the part of happy husband, Matt saw off their departing guests. Each one expressed appreciation for the delightful evening of barbecue, guitar music and dancing.

Determined not to get close to his wife, who was in the kitchen thanking Rosa and her cousin for all they'd done for the wedding, Matt stowed the bag of toiletries and satchel of his clothes in the foyer. Then he returned to the porch where Martin waited, cane in hand.

He helped Martin down the hall to his room, got him settled for the night, then gave him a dose of pain medicine.

"Thanks, Matt. For everything."

Matt met Martin's eyes, and understood what he'd left unsaid. Martin was thanking him for marrying Hannah. "Thanks for trusting me with your daughter."

"No one I'd trust with Hannah more," Martin said, voice soft and reedy. "No one I'd trust with this ranch more. With only Jake to help, you'll carry a heavy workload."

"I'll see that things get done."

"I won't let you kill yourself handling two spreads."

"Pa is handling the Circle W. Besides, I'm tougher than an overcooked steer."

"I used to be." Face lined with fatigue, Martin chuckled. "Weddings make a man tired."

"That they do."

Behind him, he heard a rap on the doorframe. Hannah entered, still wearing her wedding gown. "Thank you for the lovely wedding and party, Papa. Our friends and neighbors enjoyed themselves."

"Nothing like a wedding to bring folks together for a good time."

She leaned down and kissed Martin's cheek. "I love you. Sleep well."

"I love you, sweet daughter."

Matt laid a hand on Martin's shoulder. "If you need anything, call."

"Hannah, my bit of fatherly advice—look to your husband for leadership."

"I'll…try, Papa."

Martin gave a wan smile. "Reckon that's where you'll need patience, Matt."

"We'll find our way."

Eyes weary, Martin nodded. "Know you will."

He and Hannah left the room, leaving Martin's door ajar and walked to the entry. Matt opened the front door. They stood side by side studying the night sky yet not touching. The awkward silence between them spoke volumes of uncertainty about their new status.

To fill the void, Matt scrambled for a topic. "Looks like we'll have another nice day tomorrow."

As if his words had the power of gale winds, she wobbled and brushed against him, then jerked away, obviously as jumpy as he was. "Yes. Though we could use the rain."

"The water's evaporating from the earthen tanks. The windmill pumps water into the tank in the north pasture. We'll have to move the herd there."

Hannah sighed. "And risk overgrazing."

When had a bride and groom had a more absurd conversation on their wedding night?

He closed the door, then gathered his belongings. They retraced their steps. Hannah's room was directly across from Martin's. Where would he sleep?

She walked past her door, hugging the wall as if she feared they'd touch. At an open door just down from hers, she stopped and faced him. "This is your room."

He met her skittish gaze. "Thanks."

"Well, if you don't need anything…" her voice trailed off "…I'll say good-night."

"Sleep well."

"You, too."

Head held high, back erect, as if she had a broom handle wedged along her spine, Hannah rushed to her room. At her door, she paused and glanced back at him, then ducked inside. The door clicked shut behind her, the sound as clear-cut as a no trespassing sign.

Matt lugged his possessions inside his room, lit the kerosene lamp on the nightstand and surveyed the large space. The windows opened to the back of the house, to the paddock and pasture beyond.

As he put his toiletries on the shelf below the washstand, his thoughts turned to the wedding ceremony. To the moment Pastor Cummings declared him and Hannah husband and wife.

Married. *Again.*

Unlike the first and despite its speedy execution, this marriage was not an impulsive act, far from it. He'd prayed repeatedly about the decision, felt guided by God's wisdom and had been filled with peace when he'd accepted Hannah's proposal. A levelheaded decision motivated by his concern for Martin, his concern for Martin's daughter and his desire to get on with his life in a way that honored God.

Yet right now, that decision felt anything but sensible. He hadn't expected his response to Hannah's touch. He was a red-blooded male. Could he kiss Hannah, hold her hand, touch her soft skin without opening his heart to his wife?

Somehow he would.

He'd treat his wife as he would a good friend. He'd be considerate. Supportive. Share the work. If he kept his distance, kept his focus on the ranch, on Martin, not on the woman down the way, he could carry out their agreement.

As Hannah made preparations for bed, what was going through her mind? Did she regret her insistence on a marriage of convenience? Or did she thank God for a solution to her problem?

He shoved the drawer closed on the last of his belongings, then hung his shirts in the wardrobe and put his Bible on the nightstand by the double bed. A chair across the way would be a likely spot to shove into his boots. The room resembled what he had at the Circle W. Except this room was next door to Hannah.

His wife.

Of its own volition, his mind traveled back to Amy, to the hole her death had left in his life. A hole he'd filled with regret and self-recrimination.

He dropped into the chair and lowered his head to his hands. He'd loved Amy, but their marriage had been far from tranquil. If he hadn't been blinded by attraction, he'd have seen that she cherished activities in town, daily encounters with friends and wouldn't be happy with the life he'd chosen. The life he couldn't give up.

During their courtship, he'd found ways to leave the work and get to town to see her. But once they'd married, he'd expected Amy to enjoy ranch life as much as he did.

To find her own purpose, while he concentrated on proving himself to his father. Yet, she'd resented the hours he spent working on the ranch, claiming the Circle W took him away from her as surely as a mistress.

With time on her hands and little interest in housekeeping, she made frequent trips into Bliss or spent her days moping. During their evenings and Sundays together, her unhappiness with the life he loved chipped away at their relationship until the tension between them was a wall they couldn't penetrate.

He swallowed hard against the lump in his throat. He could've made concessions, could've found a way to spend more time with Amy, but hadn't. Then one horrible day, Amy was thrown from her horse and died.

Too late to make amends. Too late to compromise. Too late to make her happy.

He shed his dress boots, wiped dust from the toes with his handkerchief, restoring the shine. If only he could clean up his past as easily, clean up the mistakes he'd made.

Each day he lived with the knowledge he'd failed his wife. That heartache had taught him a lesson—to never make decisions with anything other than clear logic. To never just fall into a pattern as they had. Months of courting had led to expectations of marriage, as if they traveled a river flowing to a preconceived destination. Instead of scrambling up the bank for a clear view of their prospects for happiness, they'd paddled along with the current, never discussing anything of importance. Making assumptions. How wrong they'd been. How little they knew each other. How little of importance they'd shared. That negligence had cost them a terrible price.

He rose and laid on the bed, staring out at the night sky. He didn't understand the mysteries of the heavens, but he was grateful God was there. God was here. God was inside him. That gave him hope that with Hannah's love of the ranch, her knowledge and appreciation of the life he held dear, they'd have what he and Amy hadn't. Contentment.

Yet this strong attraction to Hannah caught him off guard, put his gut in a twist. If they got close, fell in love, what would happen then? Would her expectations change? Would she want something from him, some level of closeness and awareness he couldn't comprehend, much less give?

And would he fail her, too, as he had Amy?

He rose from the bed and paced the room. He'd share with Hannah a love for Martin, a love for the ranch, a love for their way of life.

That was enough. More than enough.

Tomorrow he'd ride the range, check on the last of the cows dropping calves. Then do the same at the Circle W. Each day he'd work tirelessly until he fell into bed exhausted. Too exhausted to think about his new wife one door down.

As tired as Hannah had been when she'd gone to bed, she'd tossed and turned all night. Finally, toward morning, she'd given up on sleep and sat at the window, soaking up the peace of the sky, of the resting land with only the hoot of a barn owl to disturb the quiet.

Her thumb traced the slender gold band on her finger, for most brides, a symbol of love. Her marriage was a sham. If she wanted proof, she need only acknowledge she'd spent her wedding night alone. Worse, she'd had to go to Rosa's room off the kitchen and ask for help getting out of her wedding gown. And reveal that Mr. and Mrs. Matt Walker were married in name only. Rosa would keep their secret. Still, she'd no doubt grieve that Hannah didn't have the love of her life as Rosa had believed.

The marriage was exactly what she'd wanted, yet beneath the levelheaded reasons for their business deal lay a heavy heart. She'd thought she'd tossed aside her girlhood dreams, but they clung to her still.

Lord, help me handle this loveless marriage. Help me appreciate the answer Matt has provided. Let that be enough.

Matt had agreed to her stipulations and had no idea that she struggled with the cold reality of the life she'd chosen. No matter what, she'd never let him know her misgivings. She'd keep a smile on her face. Work the ranch, learn all she could. The ranch would give her purpose and satisfaction.

She'd learn about the accounting side of ranching. See when to order and pay for supplies at local merchants, learn how to negotiate cattle prices. Last year's books should reveal how things were done.

As the sun rose in the east, she slipped into a skirt and blouse, brushed her hair, then hurried to the kitchen, determined to make this first day of married life productive and peaceful.

Rosa was nowhere in sight. No doubt exhausted from handling the food and cleanup for the barbecue, she'd slept late.

Hannah lit the cookstove, then made a pot of coffee. She was about to pour a cup when Matt appeared in the doorway.

She jumped, slopping coffee. "I didn't hear you coming."

With his boots dangling from one hand, he motioned to his bare feet. "Not trying to sneak up on you."

"Good thing." She grinned. "Men have been shot for less."

His dimple winked. "Guess I should be relieved you're not wearing a gun."

"Sure should." She lifted the pot. "Care for coffee?"

"Please."

With shaky hands, she poured, proud of not spilling a drop, then handed him the cup.

He thanked her, then leaned against the counter and took a sip. "Mmm, good."

Odd to share an early morning cup of coffee with a denim clad, barefoot husband with his shirttail out, hair mussed, the stubble of his beard shadowing his jaw.

A crazy urge to run her fingers through the hair curling at his nape slid through her. Fingers tight on her mug, Hannah took a swig of the steamy brew, then hissed. She grabbed a ladle of water and cooled her burning mouth. It was a painful reminder that focusing on Matt presented a greater risk to her than gulping hot coffee.

"You okay?" Matt stepped closer, invading her space, trapping the air in her lungs.

"Coffee's…ah, hot," she muttered.

"Yep, supposed to be."

"I forgot." Could she sound more stupid?

Truth was, she'd forgotten pretty much everything, where she was, what she was doing. But she wouldn't admit how much his early morning presence unnerved her.

Bloodshot eyes met hers. "Hope you slept well last night."

"Fine. And you?"

"Like a log."

Apparently they were both good at concealing the truth. But what could she say? *I didn't sleep a wink knowing you were next door?*

"I thought you'd sleep in—after the hectic day," Matt said.

"I like rising early. Besides, with morning chores to do, I never had the privilege."

"I figured that fancy finishing school didn't start the day till noon."

She shot him a glare. "I'll have you know that classes started at nine."

"Never thought you were a shirker, Hannah, but for all your lessons on deportment, you're mighty easy to rile."

"You might want to blame yourself for that."

He smirked. "You're fun to tease. Thanks for the coffee." Matt set his cup on the counter. "What time is breakfast?"

"Knowing Rosa, she'll have a hearty breakfast on the table at eight."

"Wouldn't miss it." He stomped into his boots, then grabbed a cold biscuit off the table. "See you then."

This first morning of their marriage she'd make it clear that she wouldn't be confined to the kitchen. "I'm coming."

She grabbed her Stetson and dashed after him. A stiff breeze whipped the brim of her hat and her skirts. She held onto both until she stepped inside the stable, out of the wind.

As they fed and watered the horses and mucked the stalls, Matt whistled a soft tune, as if he were happy, at peace. If only Hannah could capture that tranquility, instead of feeling skittish, like a colt being trained to the bit.

She and Matt tramped from the feed bin and pump to the stalls, hauling feed and water to the horses. Each time they passed, she averted her eyes. As they worked, their movements were awkward, a dance of stops and starts, first sidestepping, then motioning the other to move on ahead. All done clearly to avoid brushing against one another, as if contact were a crime.

The stable had never felt so confining. Or its occupants

so tantalizing. Muscles bulging, Matt insisted on carrying the water, a pail in each hand. As quickly as she scooped up feed, he'd be there to tote the bucket. He was trying to be thoughtful, but she felt restricted, confined, edgy enough to crawl right out of her skin.

How long before she got used to having him around all the time? Until they figured out who did what, without this awkwardness?

Jake entered the stable, a welcome disruption.

"Morning, missus," Jake said.

At the label, heat climbed Hannah's neck. "Morning."

"Not sure she's used to the missus part, Jake," Matt said, then shot Hannah a teasing grin.

Hannah tried to return the smile, but it wobbled on her lips. One glance at the ring on her finger, shiny like a new penny, reminded her of the vows binding her to Matt. This simple gold band was as much a brand of ownership as the Lazy P brand. If only she could leave it in her jewelry box, claiming wearing it was hazardous. But to keep up the charade, she must.

Determined to keep her mind off Matt, Hannah turned to Jake. "Any word from your niece?"

The furrow between the old cowpoke's eyes deepened. "Got a letter from Gertie yesterday. I could throttle Lorna for going off with a no-account man and leaving my sis to clean up the mess."

"Taking care of a child must be hard on Gertie."

Jake bobbed his head. "Gertie loves Allie like any grandma would, but sis ain't no spring chicken. Running after a seven-year-old day in and day out has her plum tuckered out."

"Lorna hasn't contacted Gertie?"

"Nope, too selfish, I reckon. Ain't easy to explain such behavior to a child."

No doubt Jake felt as helpless as Hannah did watching Papa grow weaker every day. At least by marrying Matt she'd given her father peace. Yet, she could barely comprehend life without him.

With a wave, Jake hobbled out the door, heading toward the barn.

Matt shoved his hat back on his head. "Jake looks like he's carrying the weight of the world on his shoulders."

"His niece Lorna's been a worry for years."

"You're the opposite of Lorna. Responsible, considerate of your pa, a daughter he's proud of."

Hannah's throat knotted. What would Matt think if he knew doing the right thing for Papa had cost her peace of mind?

He sent a clod flying from the toe of his boot. "I'm sorry you're going through this. Martin, too. Sometimes life's a kick in the teeth." He cupped her jaw with his hand, and peered down at her. "Just know that I care. I'm here to help."

"Thanks," she said, leaning into the comfort of his palm, if only for a moment before she pulled away.

With the chores in the stable finished, she and Matt washed their hands at the pump, eyes averted as if this ritual was somehow too personal to share. As she scrubbed her nails with a bar of lye soap under the cold blast of water, Hannah shivered. Inches away, water splattered Matt's boots. He was standing so close, she could feel the heat from his body.

She took a step back, wiped her hands on her skirt. "The water's cold this morning," she said. Ridiculous thing to say on a warm Texas morning in May.

He took her hands and rubbed them between his.

She jerked them away. "While you're warming my

hands, our breakfast's getting cold," she said then strode for the house.

In a few steps he caught up with her. "Happy to warm you up, anytime you say," he said, then gave her a wink.

Heat climbed her neck, flooded her checks. Though she wouldn't admit he already had, the blush she wore surely did.

They entered the cozy kitchen. As always, wonderful aromas of Rosa's home cooking filled her nostrils.

While Hannah and Rosa dished up the food, Matt helped Papa to the table. He slumped forward, resting his elbows on the wood as they all took seats. Lines of pain etched Papa's eyes and mouth. The backs of Hannah's eyes stung. She blinked, warding off tears. Yesterday had been one of his good days, but the wedding and party had worn him out.

As Martin murmured a blessing for the food, Hannah silently formed a prayer of her own.

Lord, please heal Papa, let him live. I need him, God. I promise I'll work hard. Even listen to Matt, if you'll save Papa. I'll do anything You ask. Anything.

No matter how often she'd prayed for healing, her father grew weaker. God could heal with a spoken word. Yet Scripture didn't promise healing or a trouble-free life. Only that God would walk with them through those troubles.

As her husband, Matt would also share those troubles, a thought she found oddly comforting. Losing Papa would hurt Matt, too. Just watching the two of them revealed the respect and trust they had for each other. And for God.

If only she could trust like that. But every time she thought about life without her father, her veins flamed, her throat went dry, her heart rattled in her chest.

Fear. Fear had her by the nape. She wouldn't let fear win.

"You planning on bringing Tom back," Papa asked, his gaze on Matt.

"No, your foreman didn't exactly endear himself to Hannah. Your two drovers along with me, Pa and Cal can manage both roundups."

"Good to hear." Papa laid down his fork, having eaten only a couple of bites. "Want to let you all know where I stand on a few things."

Face grave, Matt nodded. Hannah took her father's hand.

"Jake's an old codger like me. He's worked here since I brought Melanie here as a new bride." He smiled at Rosa across the way. "He and Rosa are family and will always have a home here. Take care of them."

"Consider it done. Anything else?" Matt said.

Hannah's hands went cold. Papa was making arrangements. He wanted to ensure Matt understood people mattered more than money. People mattered more than productivity. She'd never loved her father more. "We'll take care of everything."

He gave Hannah's hand a squeeze, then glanced at Matt. "Sorry to ask, but I'd like to lie down."

As Matt helped her father to his room, Hannah glanced at his full plate, then met Rosa's troubled gaze. "The barbecue tired him," she said. "He'll be stronger tomorrow."

"*Si.*" Rosa turned her back, fussing with the stove.

Rosa couldn't admit the truth, anymore than Hannah could. Each day Papa grew weaker. Yet, Hannah wouldn't lose hope. Hope for more time with Papa.

She'd see that he ate better. Got his rest, didn't overdo. She would never stop praying for a miracle.

Chapter Nine

Matt found Hannah in the office hunched over the Parrish account book, her pen hovered over a sheet of paper scribbled with notes. No doubt trying to understand the particulars of the ranch's finances. From that pucker between her brows, she was losing the battle. A ride would do her good.

"Having fun?" he said.

She jumped, then set down her pen with a sigh. "Not at all. All I'm sure of is we owe a pile of money due upon the sale of our cattle."

"That's how things work."

"If we have to cull the herd early, I have no idea who to contact."

"We'll need to wire ahead to make sure a cattle buyer will be in Fort Worth. We drive the cattle, corral them, agree on the tally, then make a deal."

"That's it?"

"Well, in a nutshell." He smiled. "I'm riding out to the north range. Want to ride along?"

"I'll change." She popped to her feet, heading out the door before he'd gotten the invitation out of his mouth.

"Meet you outside."

In the stable, Matt slapped leather on the horses. By the time he'd finished, Hannah appeared clad in denims, hair loose under her Stetson, eyes smiling. His wife loved nothing more than a ride, the outdoors. Already the tension he'd seen in her shoulders had eased, which was the reason he'd suggested she accompany him. Not that this hardworking tomboy would be left behind.

She must've found that year in Charleston stifling. He'd find being cooped up in an office just as suffocating.

"Well, Mrs. Walker," Matt said, glancing at the gold band on her hand. "Ready to deliver a calf or two?"

"Nothing to it," she said, shooting him a saucy grin.

They rode side by side to the north pasture and stopped their horses to survey the cattle cropping grass, quiet and peaceful.

Hannah shifted in the saddle. "The outstanding bills on the books and that loan payment due in September make me uneasy."

"If you studied last year's numbers, you know the herd's growing. The Lazy P should show a profit this year. The price in the spring may be lower, but the sale of your cattle should make more than enough to handle the bills."

"Good to hear."

"Too pretty of a day to talk invoices." On their own volition, his eyes sought her lips. "Too pretty of a woman to talk business," he said, then raised his gaze to hers.

Their gazes locked and heated, the pull between them a powerful living thing.

"Not talk business?" she repeated, a dazed look in her eyes. "Can't think of anything more important."

"Your peace of mind is more important."

"Hard to have peace with Papa so sick. With all those perplexing numbers to wade through."

Much troubled her. How could he bring her comfort?

"Try to live one day at a time." He took her hand. "Enjoy the good. Trust God for the rest."

She glanced at his hand, then lifted her eyes to his. "You're kind," she said. "I'm grateful you're helping me run this ranch. Helping me with my father."

His gaze lingered on her lips. One hand gripping the saddle horn, he leaned toward her, cupping her jaw with the other. "I want to make your life easier."

Matt nudged Thunder closer until their knees touched, gazing at her upturned face. The dreamy look in her eyes, those parted lips beckoned. Surely she wanted his kiss. The insight trapped the air in his lungs. He leaned toward her. Lowered his head.

Her eyes went wide, she reared back, then kneed Star. The horse leaped forward. "Race you to the creek!" she hollered. "The loser mucks the barn. Yeehaw!"

Bent forward in the saddle, hat dangling, her hair flying out behind her, horse and rider devoured ground.

With the force of a right hook to the gut, memories assaulted him. As the horror played out in his mind, he broke out in a cold sweat. Amy. Racing her horse toward the creek. Her mare stepping into a prairie dog hole, stumbling, falling, throwing Amy to the ground. He'd reached her in seconds, cradling her limp body in his arms, willing her to breathe.

Too late.

She was already dead from a broken neck.

With a shake of his head, Matt cleared the image, kneed Thunder into action, racing to intercept Star before Hannah met the same fate. A larger animal with a longer stride, Thunder's pounding hooves pulled him closer. Then Star and Thunder raced neck and neck.

Her eyes dancing, Hannah slapped the reins, urging Star on.

Thunder inched ahead. Matt leaned out, grabbed Star's bridle and tugged back, slowing the mare's pace from a gallop to a canter to a walk. Soon both horses stood muzzle to muzzle, lathered and heaving.

Hannah slapped at his hand. "What are you doing?" she demanded, eyes blasting like a six-shooter.

"Saving your pretty little neck."

"I ride as well as any man."

"That may be, but racing Star with the huge prairie dog colony between here and the creek is insanity," he shot back.

"I'm careful."

"Careful? At that speed you can't see the tunnels."

She slammed her Stetson in place. "When did you become a fraidycat, Matthew Walker?"

Her words cut off his air. Once, he had been a risk taker, even toyed with danger. Life had changed him.

Hannah's expression softened, her eyes filled with regret. "I'm sorry, that was thoughtless of me. I forgot about Amy's accident. But, I know this land. I know every tree, every gully, every blade of grass."

"You've been away for a year. The terrain is constantly changing."

Eyes downcast, she sighed. "You're right. I should be more cautious." She patted her mount's neck. "But, Star and I love the thrill of a race, don't we, girl?" Star bobbed her head up and down, slinging lather, as if taking her mistress' side.

Matt motioned to the trees. "Let's give the horses a breather." And give his stomach time to move from his throat to its rightful location.

Shoulders squared, Hannah rode alongside him to the creek and the canopy of cottonwoods at the water's edge.

They swung out of the saddle, then walked the horses under the trees, letting them cool down.

At the creek, Matt filled his hands and offered a gulp to both horses, careful not to give them too much and risk colic.

Once they'd settled the horses in the shade, Matt doffed his Stetson, wiping his forehead on his sleeve, then plopped the hat in place.

One glance at those pursed lips of Hannah's told him plenty. Had he overreacted?

"I understand what happened back there and I'm sorry for scaring you. But a ring on my finger doesn't give you the right to tell me what to do. I'll be careful, but ultimately, I decide what's risky for me and what's not."

He released a gust of air. "I can see keeping you alive will be a full-time job."

"If I listened to you, I'd be sitting in the corner like little Jack Horner, twiddling my thumbs."

"Jack didn't just twiddle those thumbs. He put one into a Christmas pie, pulled out a plum and said what a good boy am I."

Her jaw dropped. "How did you know that?"

"I have a nephew who's fond of nursery rhythms."

"Don't expect me to say you're a good boy for stopping the race." She snorted. "I suspect you were afraid of losing."

He chuffed. "Didn't you notice you had a head start yet I still caught up with you?"

"Well…yes. The point is, you have no confidence in me or my abilities. I thought you were different than Tom and the others. That you believed I could carry my weight."

"I'm not saying you aren't capable or a hard worker. You're all those things, but I won't let you risk your life.

Ranch work is dangerous. Spend every minute you can with your pa. Allow me to shoulder the load."

A flash of pain crossed her face. "Papa sleeps more than he's awake. I need to—" she bit her lip "—keep busy."

"Do some of that painting, stitching that Martin admires. Stay close to the house in case—"

"What? In case I hurt myself? That's no way to live."

"Can't say I have a yen for a strong-willed wife, but that's what I got. And I'd like to keep her safe."

"I know you loved Amy. I can understand that her death makes you cautious, affects you still."

Matt stared at the water flowing serenely between the banks, picking up sticks and leaves, moving the debris along until the creek rounded the bend and disappeared from view. Like that stream, he needed to move on, to hang on to the good and let go of the heartache, the bad times.

He turned back to Hannah. "Amy's gone. I'll always care, but that doesn't mean I don't care about you. As a friend, I can't allow you to risk harming yourself to prove some fool point." He leaned closer. "Like you tried to do at the depot."

"Lifting that trunk risked nothing, except maybe a toe."

Laughter burst out of him. "You're not an easy woman to tame, Little Filly."

"Stop calling me that." She doffed her hat, then shook her head, the mane of her wind-tossed hair settled along her shoulders in waves of umber. "I'm all grown up and no filly."

"I'm not sure I'd want to tame you if I could."

"Good thing," she said, then plopped her hat on her head and strode to the horses. She grabbed the reins then swung into the saddle and nudged Star into a quick getaway. Back ramrod-straight, her chin lifted skyward. He should recognize those feisty gestures. He'd seen them often enough.

He'd nicknamed her Filly, but the pet name in no way described the woman she'd become. Truth was, he hadn't thought of her as a child since she'd helped deliver that calf.

Hannah was a flesh and blood woman, a powerful temptation to let go of the reins of his heart and take a risk.

Not that he would.

He'd once walked the fine line between fearless and wayward. He'd prized challenges, pitted himself against nature, against man and beast, pushing his limits and beyond. He'd lost the yen for that boldness the day Amy died.

Since then, he'd tamped down his penchant for danger, the carefree cowboy part of him. Yet the decision to play it safe warred within, in constant battle with his temperament, leaving him in turmoil. Sometimes the tight grip on his reckless side chafed like too many hours in the saddle, but that's what he'd do. Nothing was worth the penalty of his impetuous nature.

Nothing.

No matter how lovely Hannah was, if they got close and fell in love, he could end up making her miserable.

Icy fear twisted inside his gut. Or worse, he could lose her, too. He'd hold his new wife at arm's length.

It was all he could do.

All during supper, Hannah struggled to keep her eyes on her plate and off Matt. She wouldn't behave like a woman enthralled with her husband. Not when her husband had called her a friend.

A friend watched out for a friend. Gave a helping hand, even a shoulder to lean on. To have a friend was nice. Especially now, with Papa sick, and the Lazy P to run.

A friend did not ogle the other, did not come close to kissing either. Yet wasn't that exactly what Matt had been about to do? Worse, wasn't that exactly what she'd wanted?

Shaken by her reaction and to put distance between them, she'd challenged him to that race. Protective of her safety, he'd stopped the race and started an argument, shriveling the connection between them.

If some vague discontent churned inside her, she'd ignore it and focus on learning more about running the ranch.

Finished with supper, Rosa had insisted on cleaning up the kitchen alone. Hannah, Papa and Matt retired to the porch. Soon Jake ambled over from the bunkhouse.

A breeze had kicked up, stirring the unusually hot night air. Beyond the porch, birds flitted about, darting in and out of bushes and trees. Hannah loved spring, the time of new beginnings, of birth, rebirth.

Even Papa seemed stronger. He sat on the settee, reminiscing of the days of long cattle drives. She sat beside him and held his hand in hers.

"When I was young, Daughter, we'd trail our cattle north to the railhead in Abilene where our longhorns were shipped to stockyards in Chicago," he said. "Nowadays, with windmills pumping water into earthen tanks, and the range divided by barbed wire, we're ranchers, not cowboys."

Jake chuckled. "Cowpokes once raised Cain. Nowadays we're raising hay."

With the loose swagger and lean frame of a cowboy, Matt ambled to the porch railing, leaning against it. He was better looking than a man had a right to be.

Hannah struggled to turn her attention to the conversation. She treasured these times with Papa and wanted to absorb every word, learn everything she could about ranching. Then and now.

"Tell us more about those drives," she said.

"Martin was trail boss," Jake said. "He assigned duties, scouted for water, kept an eye out for trouble. Us drovers punched cattle. Nothing purty about heat and dust and risky river crossings. But a man likes a challenge."

What role would Hannah take? When she knew so little, the men wouldn't see her as trail boss. Was there enough water for the herd between here and Fort Worth?

"Challenges were the norm," Papa said. "On almost every drive a thunderstorm spooked the longhorns into stampeding. Getting the beeves under control made for a rough night. Every drive we'd lose several head. Sometimes a man."

If the herd spooked, Hannah knew how to get a mill going, until the herd formed a tight circle and wore down. But they couldn't afford to lose one animal. The weight of the responsibility rested heavy on her shoulders.

As the men talked, bringing to life the hardships of the two or three months on the trail, heat lightning flashed around them, but giving no promise of much-needed rain.

One of the brief flashes illuminated the porch. Hannah's gaze slid to Matt's. His dark eyes locked with hers, a silent connection she didn't want. Matt was a friend, nothing more. She quickly looked away.

"'Tweren't nothing to move two, three thousand head with only ten men. We took turns night herding." Jake shook his grizzled head. "Seen men rub tobacco juice in their eyes to stay awake."

"Rough life," Matt said. "When I was twelve, I yearned to go. My pa wouldn't hear of it."

"Probably trying to protect you from a rough bunch, especially once the drive reached Abilene. Most cowpokes spent every dime they earned on gambling and…" He glanced at Hannah and cleared his throat. "Whatever."

Heat climbed Hannah's neck. She scrambled for a change of subject. "How much did you earn?"

"Twenty-five, thirty dollars a month. Forty dollars tops. Not much, but trailing cattle gets into the blood."

"After I married your mother," Papa said, turning his head toward Hannah, "I never went on another drive."

"Why not?"

"Didn't like the idea of leaving her."

Papa loved her mother with every ounce of his being. How hard to lose her in childbirth, along with his son. Hannah would've liked to ask him more about those days, but not in front of the others.

Martin looked at Matt. "I may sound like a sentimental fool, but once you've been married a while, Matt, you'll feel the same."

"You know your daughter better than that, Martin. She's not one to be left behind."

"Reckon I do." Papa chuckled, giving Hannah's hand a squeeze.

Good, at least Matt understood she wouldn't be denied the right to make her own decisions.

"All this reminiscing has made me bone tired. Will you help me into the house, Matt?"

"Reckon I'll turn in, too." Jake bid everyone good-night and ambled toward the bunkhouse.

Matt helped Martin to his feet and offered his arm. "Are you hurting bad?"

"Won't turn down a dose of that medicine."

"First thing," Matt promised.

Hannah's heart swelled with gratitude for Matt's affection and concern for her father.

"I'll check on you later, Papa."

Hannah laid her head against the back of the chair and closed her eyes. Her father's talk of earlier days connected her to their heritage, to a time when cattle drives tested man and beast. She treasured every minute, a sweet interlude in a day with more ups and downs than a bucking bronco ride.

In the quiet, Hannah drifted off toward sleep. The screen door squeaked. Her head popped up. Matt joined her on the settee, laying his arm across the back.

She gave him a smile. "Thanks for your help with my father."

"Glad to do it. Couldn't be easier now that I'm living here."

A reminder that no matter what Matt had said, he was her husband, not merely a friend. A husband who might get amorous thoughts on such a beautiful night. She rose to her feet, intent on escape. "I'm going for a walk."

He took her arm. "I'll go with you."

Not what she planned, but what could she say? *I'm afraid you've got kisses on your mind, like we came close to sharing on horseback?*

They left the porch, walked to the rose trellis where they'd recited their vows. The air was filled with the heady, sweet fragrance of the roses hidden among the shadows.

"My mother brought these climbing roses with her from Charleston. Other plants, too. Papa favors the red, but I prefer the pink. The scent is more vibrant. The blooms are larger. When they unfurl, they have the prettiest centers." Her voice trailed off. Mercy, she'd been chattering like a magpie, trying to conceal her awareness of the man at her side.

The moon appeared from behind the clouds, lighting his face. A rugged, strong face. Deep-set eyes. Full lips that smiled at her. She swallowed hard.

"When I was a little kid," Matt said, "I picked all the lilacs off the bush, at least the ones I could reach, and presented them to my mother, proud of the gift." He chuckled. "Well, Ma had planned to use those lilacs for some fancy function at church, a week off. That incident taught me not to come between a woman and her flowers."

"Aw, you must've been a sweet little boy."

"Sure was," he said, a grin wide on his face. "Never deserved a single one of her reprimands."

The impish look in his eye said otherwise. "Hmm, from what I've heard you and your brothers were a handful," she said, smiling up at him.

As he stared into her eyes, the smile slipped from his face, as if mesmerized by what he saw. "You got me pegged," he said softly.

Lost in those dark depths, Hannah couldn't turn away. Could barely think. What had he said?

Strong hands slid around her waist, pulling her to him. The solid strength of his chest beneath her palms and the thundering beat of his heart beneath his shirt trapped the air in her lungs. She lifted her face and looked into his hooded eyes, heavy with longing. Time stood still, wiping everything from her mind but the two of them.

He lowered his head, brought his lips inches from hers, close enough to kiss. With a soft sigh, Hannah closed her eyes, slid her arms around his neck, teasing the hair at his nape with her fingers. Her heart pounded in her chest as he brushed his lips over hers, sending a shiver along her spine.

His hands fell away and he jerked back, rubbing the back of his neck. "I…ah." He cleared his throat. "I'd better get you inside," he said, then stepped away.

Dazed, Hannah groped for her bearings, for footing in a relationship with ever-changing rules. The truth slammed into her. What a fool she'd been. *Friend.* He'd called her *friend.* Yet she'd all but invited his kiss.

She stumbled toward the porch, Matt at her heels. At the

door, he reached around her and opened the screen door. "See you in the morning," he said as she walked inside.

"Aren't you coming?"

"In a minute."

He was avoiding that awkward walk down the bedroom hall, then separating, Matt to his room, she to hers.

Why had she asked if he was coming inside? She sounded needy, dependent on him, when that's the last thing she wanted.

Outside Papa's open door, she heard his soft snore, his even breathing. *Thank you, Lord, that Papa is having a good night.*

Inside her room, she changed into nightclothes, brushed her teeth, then took down her hair, reliving those moments in the rose garden. The way she'd reacted to him, his charm. He appeared to care, then stepped away, remote. She wouldn't fall for his antics again.

Finished with the hundred strokes, she laid her brush aside and climbed into bed, stretching out her weary body with a sigh.

Down the hall, a door closed. Matt had come inside.

He appeared in control, strong and caring. He did everything he could for her father. In many ways, he was an admirable man. A man she could care for, if she dared. But his words and actions conveyed contradictory messages. One moment he called her friend. The next he came close to kissing her. Was he toying with her emotions like a cat with his prey?

Tonight's discussion on the porch had proven she needed Matt's help on the cattle drive. If only she didn't have to rely on a taciturn cowboy claiming to be a friend, then behaving like a husband. Matt couldn't have it both ways.

Why not be honest? She had conflicting emotions,

too. For both their sakes, she'd keep her distance. No point ruining a practical agreement. She needed Matt to help her manage the ranch. But she wouldn't let him manage her heart.

Chapter Ten

Matt, as fireman in charge of the fire and the irons, swiped the sweat out of his eyes, stinging from hours spent hovering over a red-hot fire. The iron in his hand had the Lazy P mark, a P laying on its back. The brand had been approved by the Cattlemen's Association and registered in the courthouse. Brands were meant to impede cattle rustling, not much of an issue these days with the demise of the open range, but even so, the brand proved ownership.

Finished with roundup at the Circle W, his father and Cal had joined him and the remnant of the Parrish crew, to round up and sort the Lazy P cattle, then brand and cut two hundred and fifty spring calves.

Across the way, Hannah rode Star, singling out a calf, her long braid under her Stetson swinging with the peg pony's movements. A bandanna over her nose and mouth kept out dust. Denim pants and a long-sleeved shirt protected her skin in the blistering sun.

At first, whenever his wife chased down calves, Matt's heart spent more time in his throat than in his chest, ready at a moment's notice to protect her. She soon impressed him with her ability with the lasso, the ease with which she rode her horse.

Even the drovers respected Hannah's skill with a lariat, but still looked to him for instructions. He didn't need to be a mind reader to see that stuck in Hannah's craw like a chicken bone. Something he understood, having lived with a father who usurped Matt's authority at every turn. Matt had harped at the men, reminding them Hannah was boss and insisted they look to her for orders. He'd even walked away when asked for direction.

Yet, the men refused to change. Change had turned cowboys into farmhands. They'd lost the open range, the long cattle drives, their way of life. He suspected Hannah paid the penalty for pent-up resentment.

She deserved their respect, having handled the long hours in the saddle and the hard work as well as any man. With each passing hour, admiration for his cowgirl wife grew.

Hannah and the cow pony knew exactly what to do. As he watched, Star changed course with the elusive calf, giving Hannah access to her target. She swung the lasso, the rope snaked through the air, the noose settling over the calf's neck.

With the press of her knees, Hannah directed Star to back off, taking up the slack in the rope tied to the saddle horn, bringing the calf to the ground.

Two cowpokes wrestled the animal on its side, wielding a knife, while Matt pressed the Lazy P brand into the hide, barely aware of the stench of singed hair and the raucous bawling. As the men stepped away, the calf scrambled to his feet. Familiar with his mother's voice, he trotted straight to her.

Hannah appeared at his side. "That's the last."

"Thanks to your skill with a lasso, we got it done in record time."

"Thanks, but Star deserves the praise."

"You and Star make a good team." He chucked Hannah under the chin. "So do we," he said, his gaze capturing hers.

"Spoken like a true friend."

She'd thrown his words back at him. Not that he blamed her. He didn't understand his behavior any more than she did.

Hannah motioned to the spring calves. "A year with their mamas and they'll be chubby as butterballs."

"Yep, two years from now, half the spring babies will be full-grown heifers, ready to breed. The other half, full-grown steers, ready to sell."

"I'd like to see the heifers bred to the best of the Walker bulls. I want to strengthen the herd."

Matt nodded. "That's understood."

Without a drop of rain, both ranches had made the decision to drive the cattle to Fort Worth. He directed Hannah's attention to the penned steers and aging cows. "You've got three hundred head set aside to sell." He grabbed his bandanna and swiped the grime from his face. "We'll join your cattle with Pa's four hundred. Unless we encounter trouble we should reach Fort Worth in two days. Without cattle, one day back here."

Martin's words came back to him. *One day, Matt, you'll feel the same and not want to leave your wife.*

Matt looked forward to having three days away from Hannah. With every passing day, he found it more and more difficult to think of her as a friend, no matter what he'd claimed. A few days of separation should ease the pull.

"Well, if I'm not needed here," Hannah said. "I'm going to groom Star." She looked down at her smudged, sweaty shirt, the dusty toes of her boots. "Then clean up myself."

He watched her go, her steps slow, no doubt painful

after days in the saddle. Grubby as a cowpoke or fresh as a debutante, either way, Hannah looked fine.

With effort, he tore his gaze away and swung into the saddle, moving the cows and their calves toward pasture. The sun eased to the horizon as the calves frolicked at their mothers' sides, none the worse for wear after their ordeal.

Once the herd had gotten underway, the drovers took over and Matt returned to the stable. He found Jake grooming Star in her stall. "Where's Hannah?"

"She's gone in to clean up and spend time with her pa. Told her I'd see to Star."

Matt released a weary sigh and peeled off his gloves, then rubbed his forearm across his face. "The men will be back soon, hungry and tired."

"Vittles are ready soon as they are."

"Knew I could count on you," Matt said, slapping Jake on the back.

Matt saw to his horse, then joined Cal and his father at the pump. Wearing tired but satisfied grins, they scrubbed off grime and sweat, dousing their heads under the cold stream, rising up and slinging water like drenched dogs.

Pa pulled a clean bandanna from his hip pocket and wiped his face, yet his eyes stayed on Matt. Matt recognized the look. His pa had something on his mind.

"I'll handle the sale in Fort Worth while you young pups see to separating the herds. While I'm at it, might as well handle the transaction for Martin."

"Martin asked me to handle the sale of his cattle. I intend to carry out his wishes."

His father flapped a hand, as if Martin's request was of no consequence. "No point splitting hairs. See you at sunup."

He and Cal sauntered to their waiting horses, mounted

up and rode toward the Circle W, the horses' hooves kicking up dust.

Matt slapped his hat against his thigh. He was a grown man, yet Pa didn't trust him to close a simple deal. He'd foolishly believed that moving out of the Walker homestead would give him breathing room. But no, his father oversaw everything down to the smallest detail.

Scripture demanded children honor their parents, something Matt had tried to do, to the point that he'd let Robert take over his life. The time had come to stand his ground. The cattle drive to Fort Worth presented the perfect opportunity. He intended to take it.

Hannah walked outside, letting the screen door slap closed behind her. Exhausted from days in the saddle, she looked forward to a quiet evening, then planned to get to bed early. They'd leave for Fort Worth at first light.

Overhead the sky glittered with stars, barely diminished by the light from a full moon. As she ambled toward Matt, she glanced at the moon. *See the man in the moon?* Mama used to say. *He's always got a smile.*

Unlike the man standing across from her.

"You look troubled," she said. "Something the matter?"

"I…." His voice trailed off, then he cleared his throat. "Just planning the particulars for tomorrow. On a short drive like this, all we'll need is a canteen of water and a couple days rations in our saddlebags. I'll pack a gun, makings for coffee, a tin of matches, medical kit."

"Doesn't sound like much to worry about."

"Nope, just the usual. Most likely the hands won't be coming back with us."

"Why not?"

"They'll spend a month's pay in Fort Worth carousing."

"Apparently cowboys haven't changed much since those

long trail drives Jake talked about. Oh, that reminds me, Rosa will serve breakfast at five-thirty so we can get an early start."

He frowned. "We?"

"Well, yes, I'm going." She drew herself up and met his gaze. "Of course."

Before she'd gotten the words out, Matt was shaking his head. "No need for that. We have ample drovers. You can stay here, spend those three days with Martin."

"Part of that herd is Parrish cattle. That makes the drive and sale my responsibility."

"You have enough to handle." He chuffed. "Martin asked me to handle the sale. My pa is claiming the responsibility, but I intend to follow Martin's directive and negotiate the price." He took a step closer. "Or don't you trust me?"

Her breath caught. Did she trust him? The question alluded to far more than handling the sale, at least for her. "You'd never cheat us, but you're trying to cheat me out of an opportunity to learn. If I'm to run this ranch, you said I need to earn respect. The best way to earn the respect of the hands, the buyers, even the men running the Cattlemen's Association is to prove myself by moving the cattle, negotiating the deal, handling the paperwork. That's what I intend to do."

"Hannah, I'm your husband. I'm supposed to ease your burden. Not to ask you to take on another one."

"We had a deal, Matt. A deal that enables me to run my ranch, to make decisions." Her chin shot up. "I'll be riding with you."

"Do you realize we'll sleep under the stars? With only enough food to get by?" He let out a gust. "This is no picnic or society ball."

She bristled at the implications. Did he still see her as

the debutante? Not as a woman who could handle a horse, a ranch, a cattle drive? "I've gathered a bedroll, canteens of water, jerky, dried apples and hardtack, everything I'll need, my gun." She ticked the items off on her fingers. "When I was young, Papa used to take me out on overnight jaunts to mend fence. We slept under the stars. I've had experience camping out."

Matt ran a hand over his chin, shadowed with the day's growth of his beard. He met her gaze. "Are you prepared to handle acting like newlyweds?"

"What?"

"How will it look if we don't…" His voice trailed off. He took a step closer, until the toes of his boots touched her hem. "Sleep close?"

Heat flushed her face then slid through her limbs. With his father, brother and the Lazy P hands looking on, they'd have to play the part of a recently married couple. "Well, I don't have a problem with it if you don't."

The expression on his face said he did. Did he find the idea repulsive? Or did the idea make him edgy?

"I agree we'll have to…stay close. But no more than a friend keeping an eye on a friend."

The grating sound she heard—was that Matt gnashing his teeth?

He stepped even closer. Within kissing distance. "Are you challenging me, *wife?*"

The way he said the word sent a shiver down her spine. Wife implied everything they had agreed they would never have, such as tender kisses. "I'm just saying I can sleep near you. Well, unless you snore."

"Maybe you're the one who snores." He gave a smug grin.

She raised her chin. "Never."

He trailed a finger down her cheek and over her lips.

Her heart thudded in her chest. Lost in his eyes that held not one morsel of humor. Lost in his eyes that looked tormented, revealed a man at the end of his rope.

"We'll have plenty of time to find out the truth, won't we?" he said, his dimple winking with his lopsided grin.

She gulped. Nodded.

"I will be a perfect gentleman. So you have no worries I might…take advantage of the situation." He took a step back, breaking the connection, severing the magnetic pull between them. "Be ready at first light, prepared to ride," he said, then without a backward glance, he clomped off the porch, heading toward the stable.

With Hannah's heart banging inside her chest like a barn door with a broken hinge, she sucked in a breath. Then another, until she'd shoved all these reactions deep down inside of her.

Those moments on the porch with Matt were fantasy, here today, gone tomorrow. She had no patience with such silliness. She had a job to do.

In the next two days, she would once again play the biggest make-believe role of her life, that of the blissful bride. This time, in front of a handful of drovers and Matt's father and brother.

With a husband who appeared to want to change the rules.

Or perhaps he was trying to scare her off from going on the drive to Fort Worth. If so, he'd soon learn she didn't scare easily.

With the sun below the horizon, Hannah led Star out of the stable, spurs jangling, her saddlebags loaded with provisions for the trip, determined to use this opportunity to prove herself. To prove herself, she'd ride drag at the rear of the herd. To prove herself, she'd not lose a single straggler. To prove herself, she'd handle the sale of Lazy P cattle in Fort Worth.

Robert and Cal Walker sat on horseback, talking to Matt.

"Morning, Hannah," Robert said. "Going for a morning ride?"

Matt looked up from checking Thunder's saddlebags. "Hannah will be riding with us."

"No reason for her to do that." Robert frowned, his eyes black as coal. "We're not shorthanded. A woman will add complications."

"Believe I said she's going."

Hannah's breath caught. Matt was actually standing up for her right to go, when she knew he'd prefer she stayed behind.

The pucker between Robert's brow smoothed. "Reckon that's newlyweds for you. Can't stomach being apart."

"Not for a second," Matt said, then strode to Hannah's side, lowered his head and swept his lips across her cheek.

At the husband-like act, heat flooded her face and sent a shiver snaking along her spine. She forced a smile, then allowed him to give her a hand up.

He patted her knee, searching her eyes. "You all set?"

"Yes." With Cal and Robert's scrutiny, the sooner they got underway the better.

"Looking forward to sharing the day with my pretty wife." He plopped his Stetson in place, then leaned closer. "And the night," he whispered.

Heart pounding, Hannah turned away, then searched the horizon. "Where are the Circle W beeves?"

Cal shifted in the saddle to the sound of creaking leather and pointed west. "Our drovers are holding them about a mile from here with a good stand of grass. We'll join up with them there."

"Cal and I will work as pointers near the head of the line. You and Hannah work the flank," Robert said. "Can't have this young lady eating dust." He motioned to the two Lazy P drovers on horseback inside the corral. "Your cow punchers will bring up the rear, make sure cattle don't wander off."

Hannah understood Robert's desire to lead. But, to act as if she couldn't handle the cattle rankled. "I'd prefer to take the drag position. Star and I enjoy rounding up stragglers."

"Then it's settled. We'll take the rear," Matt said.

As if he'd argue the point, Robert's lips flattened, then he chuckled. "Sounds more like you and your wife want privacy."

Hannah looked away from Robert's amused eyes.

"Ready to move?" Jake hollered, hand at the gate.

Matt said a prayer for safety and a successful drive, then glanced at Hannah. At her nod, he raised an arm. "Let 'em loose."

As Jake opened the gate, two drovers on horseback rode behind the milling cattle, punching them out of the pen. They came slowly, plodding along in the dim light. Soon, a few steers took the lead, the aging cows falling back. Robert and Cal rode off to take positions on opposite sides of the herd that now strung out in a long irregular line.

Matt guided Thunder to Hannah's side. Close enough their horses rubbed noses. Mercy, even Star and Thunder feigned romance.

Last night, when Hannah had agreed to behave like newlyweds, to give the little gazes and touches that spoke of love, she hadn't understood the cost.

She'd never felt more devious.

Nor more attracted to the man.

Surely, her reaction stemmed from Matt's support of

her right to join the drive. Once again she was beholden to him. How long before he'd insist on changing the rules of this game they played—and expect a real relationship?

Her thoughts were muddled from Matt's kiss last night and his peck on the cheek earlier, Hannah hoisted the bandanna over her mouth and nose. She hoped this scrap of cloth would protect her from dust, and from Matt's teasing mouth.

She wouldn't get near enough to give him an opportunity. She'd see that there would be no dawdlers—not cattle, not she and Matt. Her heart thudded in her chest. The trek had only begun but couldn't be over soon enough to suit her.

Matt kept an eye on Hannah as they punched cattle along the trail. Drag riders had the most difficult position on the drive. No doubt Hannah had chosen the position for that very reason, trying to prove herself. Drag riders dealt with the herd's most uncooperative varmints that often hung back and tried to make a run for it.

All morning, Hannah and Star, an agile cutting horse, one of the best, had done an admirable job. Still, cattle were dangerous. Only one of many hazards on the trail that included flooded river crossings, stampedes and rustlers. The list was long. Not likely to happen on this trip, still Matt didn't ride easy.

A man never knew when a mean steer would swing its big, long horns at a horse with the aim of killing. Or when a cow would turn on a drover unexpectedly and charge, spooking the horse into rearing and throwing the rider. He'd seen a drover trampled by milling cattle.

He'd keep a sharp eye on his wife. An easy task. He couldn't keep his eyes off her. Even with her Stetson tugged low, a bandanna across her face and her long tresses worn in a braid down her back, he could picture her vibrant blue eyes, those full lips, the red in her brown hair sparkling in the sunlight.

Keep your mind off your wife and concentrate on the job.

Distraction got people hurt. He wouldn't focus on his wife, no matter how much he found her appealing, no matter how much he felt connected to her, no matter how much he cared about her safety.

Toward noon, Matt unearthed a string of jerky from his saddlebags and gnawed on it, then washed it down with a long swig from his canteen. On such a short drive, they managed without a chuck wagon, but he'd worked up an appetite. Already he looked forward to Rosa's cooking.

He'd ride over to make sure Hannah took a drink, got a bite to eat. He grinned, then tugged on the reins. Who was he kidding? All he could think about was getting near his wife.

Across the way, Hannah and Star cut right, chasing down a cow. Within minutes they'd returned the straggler. A few feet from the herd, they passed an outcropping of rocks. Suddenly Star reared without warning.

Matt kicked Thunder and they raced toward Hannah as she fought to keep her seat. He closed the gap—twenty feet, ten feet, five feet. And then he saw the trouble.

Rattlesnake. The lethal creature had coiled into a tight spiral, tail rattling, forked tongue darting, head still, waiting to strike. Star snorted, prepared to rear again. Hannah held tight to the reins, speaking softly to her horse, but her face had paled and he saw fear in the tight set of her shoulders. He pulled his .45 Colt from his holster, cocked the gun, ready to fire.

Star reared again. Hannah lost her grip, falling to the ground not far from the snake.

"Don't move! I'll shoot it," Matt shouted.

In a flash, she rolled to her hip, metal flashed in the sunlight as she yanked out her pistol, took aim and fired. The snake writhed, then lay motionless. Star shied, but held her position.

As Matt swung from the saddle, his gaze scanned the herd. A few cattle bellowed but they kept moving forward in a wide column. He helped Hannah to her feet. They inspected the snake to make sure it was dead. "That was an amazing shot."

"That one even surprised me," she said, giving a weak grin.

A cowpoke galloped their way, no doubt checking on the gunfire he'd heard. Matt waved his hat, signaling all was well.

He put his hands on her shoulders, felt the tremor running through her. For all her bravado, in her eyes he saw fear. "You okay?"

She reached a trembling hand toward him. It was all the invitation he needed to tug her into his arms. She flattened against him, her hand on his chest. Surely she could feel his heart beating beneath his shirt, racing with an erratic rhythm.

"I think so," she said, taking a step back, staring up at him.

He dipped his head and kissed her full on the lips, slow and easy as sensations of longing flooded him from head to toe.

Hannah pulled away. "We've got cattle to tend."

"This promises to be a very long day, Mrs. Walker," Matt whispered near her ear.

They swung into the saddle and rode toward the herd, separating on either side of the moving column.

She'd scared him silly, but she'd handled things fine. Hannah Parrish Walker was no debutante. No filly. No tomboy.

His wife was all woman.

Chapter Eleven

Matt's awareness of Hannah had him tighter than a water-soaked peg. That moment of closeness after the scare with the snake had him longing for more. To make matters worse, the entire day they'd played the role of newlyweds. The attraction between them palpable.

Why had he suggested such a foolish thing?

To appease his family's expectations?

He heaved a sigh. Be honest. Underneath he wanted that closeness to his wife. When he'd accepted Hannah's terms for their marriage, he hadn't realized the difficulty of keeping her at arm's length. With each passing day, his feelings for her grew. Not part of the plan. The plan was sensible, far safer than giving in to feelings. Feelings changed.

Dusk had fallen, they'd bedded the cattle down for the night and had eaten cold rations and had drank hot coffee by the light of the campfire.

Under the cottonwoods alongside the creek, Matt ducked beneath the ropes corralling the horses, carrying feed and water. With a night to rest, the cow ponies would be champing at the bit to get underway tomorrow.

Not that he'd sleep a wink with Hannah curled up nearby. Still, a man never knew what wild animals, snakes, even bad hombres might roam these parts. He wouldn't let his wife out of his sight. To protect her. To keep her safe. Nothing more.

One glance at their camp across the way, at Hannah's perky profile as she sat by the fire confirmed what he knew—looking out for this woman was a privilege, not a chore. He admired her spunk, her appreciation of the life he prized, her devotion to her dying father, a man more father to him than his own. She could've whined about life's unfairness. Instead she faced each day with faith, with courage, with determination to learn everything about ranching.

So she wouldn't need him?

The thought cooled his mood faster than a tumble into an ice-crusted trough. No matter how much he was drawn to his wife, he wouldn't act on those emotions.

Not that she'd allow it if he tried.

If upon occasion her breath caught at his touch, that didn't mean she welcomed the contact or the reaction. More likely, she'd been caught off guard.

A shape moved out of the shadows. Pa. "We need to talk."

With Pa, talk inevitably led to a lecture. Matt squared his shoulders. "What about?"

"You need to get your wife under control."

From this distance Hannah wouldn't overhear, still Pa's censure fisted Matt's hands at his sides. "Hannah's not out of control. Today and during both roundups, she did the work of a man and then some."

"I'll give you that." Pa folded beefy arms across his chest. "But when a woman tells a man what to do, she needs a firm hand."

"Hannah wasn't telling you what to do. She merely stated she'd prefer the drag rider spot, which is her right.

Half this herd is hers. Isn't it more that you resent anyone but you making decisions?"

"Nonsense. Victoria runs the house as she sees fit. But she doesn't give me orders on how I'm to run the ranch or handle a drive." He shook his head. "Can't imagine what's gotten hold of Hannah. She was the sweetest gal."

"Hannah's an owner, same as you. She has a right to make decisions."

Robert harrumphed. "I'm not against considering another way, but she's giving orders, telling *me* what *she'll* do. And telling you, too. A husband shouldn't stand for that."

"Be honest." Matt plowed his fingers through his hair. "No one can take the lead, have an independent thought without raising your ire. No matter what you believe, your way isn't the only way."

"My way has made the Circle W a success. But do you thank me for that? No!"

"I am grateful and respect what you've accomplished. But—"

Robert raised a hand. "Quit your yapping. See that your woman doesn't wear the pants in Fort Worth and disgrace us all."

Pa strode off. No doubt confident of Matt's compliance. And why not?

For years, Matt had taken the backseat to his father, a decent God-fearing man, but a man unable to give up one smidgeon of control. Pa never sought his and Cal's opinions. Even overrode Matt's instructions, humiliating him in front of the hands.

Hannah carried his name. If she wanted to negotiate the sale of her cattle, he'd support her right. She had plenty to learn, but he'd be there to help if she needed him. He wouldn't rule his wife like Pa tried to rule him.

A glance at the horses satisfied him that all was well. He ambled along the creek in the direction of their camp, giving himself a few moments to rein in his temper. As Hannah's husband, he would put her welfare first, ahead of his father.

In the clearing, he found his wife alone staring into the fire, her face relaxed, at peace. If only he felt the same.

On the other side of the campfire, Pa had stretched out on his bedroll, his back to the fire, already snoring. Cal had ridden out to stand first watch with two of the Walker drovers. The two Parrish hands slept nearer the herd. Around two o'clock, Cal would return and shake Matt awake for his shift. He was tired, but with the encounter with his father churning inside him, not ready to sleep, not yet.

He sat beside his wife. "Star's dozing on her feet," he said. "You should get some sleep, too."

Hannah leaned back on her palms, surveying the sky, the twinkling stars overhead, the sliver of the new moon, looking happy, content, beautiful. "I'm soaking up the serenity of just…being," she said softly. "Out here, with only God and His creation."

And him.

In the light from the fire, the dancing flames flickered on her features, the contented smile on her face. That smile towed him to her like a well-thrown lasso. On such a night as this, a man could get accustomed to huddling close to his wife, could visualize many such nights. With everything in him, he resisted the pretty picture he painted, the happily ever after. Nothing was that simple.

Even if wedded bliss were possible, he didn't deserve happiness, a second chance.

In the distance, a coyote howled. The notes of a plaintive melody drifted to them on the breeze. One of the hands soothing the cattle, or perhaps himself, with a song.

"Except for that rattler, we didn't have a single problem today," Hannah said, her tone filled with elation. "The cattle behaved themselves, as if they've taken this trek before."

"They haven't, but we have. More times than I can count. We know the watering holes, the available stands of grass along the way."

"Like I know the Lazy P."

"You said Martin took you camping. Tell me about it."

"After Mama died, Papa would take me along to ride fence, looking for breaks in the barbed wire. At dusk, we'd make a fire, eat beans, boiled eggs and cornbread." She grinned. "And those sugar cookies of Rosa's you're fond of. As we ate, we'd talk and take swigs out of the same canteen. I'd swipe the dribbles of water running down my chin in the crook of my arm, just like Papa." She chuckled. "No wonder he sent me to finishing school."

"What did you and Martin talk about?"

"Oh, lots of things. The stars, school, Mama." Her voice caught. "Heaven. The gold streets, the jewels, the light of God."

Matt couldn't remember sharing anything personal with his father. Robert lectured better than he listened.

She met his gaze. "As the fire would die down, I'd fall asleep cuddled against Papa. Come morning, I'd awaken tucked into a bedroll. Never figured out how I got there without waking. He said us ranchers sleep best under the stars." Tears glistened in her eyes. "Those memories are precious, especially now."

With an urge to comfort her, to give her what Martin always had, Matt tugged her close. "Martin's a wise man. He understood the importance of giving you his time. Time to remember your mother. Time to heal from her loss. Time for the two of you to grow closer."

In the circle of his arms, Hannah swiped at her eyes. "Did you and your pa camp?"

"If the work kept us away from the house, we'd bunk in a line shack, not under the stars."

"What's your favorite memory from your childhood?"

"That's easy." He smiled at the memory that popped into his head. "The day I turned six and got my first pony. Having a horse of my own changed my life, gave me the freedom to come and go. On horseback I was king of everything I surveyed. The land, the cattle, God's creatures—the jackrabbits, lizards, prairie dogs, buzzards circling overhead. I felt as much a part of the land as those cottonwoods growing along the creek." He motioned toward the trees. "As any living thing that grew here."

"If you were king, then I was queen." Hannah chuckled. "Your childhood must've been fun."

"I had chores, but lots of free time, too. By the age of nine, I was a pint-size ranch hand. I found work satisfying and my efforts pleased my father."

"Any special memories after that?"

"Oh, yes. On my tenth birthday, Pa gave me my first handgun and taught me to shoot. I practiced every chance I got, determined to make Pa proud."

And Matt had. Pa had once been generous with his praise, but something had changed. Now, a man in his own right, competent and skilled, he rarely got his father's approval. Instead Pa hammered him, an attempt to keep him under his thumb.

"Horse and gun, a Texan's path to manhood." Hannah smiled. "Things weren't so different in Charleston."

He cocked a brow. "Are you comparing me to those dandies?"

Eyes locked with his, she sobered. "I'd never make that mistake."

Her answer warmed him more than the heat from the fire.

"You want your father's approval as much as I want Papa's." She sighed. "Papa once approved of my tomboy ways. No longer."

Matt knew better. "No father could approve of his child more."

Hannah lifted troubled eyes to his. "You two are close. Do you understand why he wants me to wear dresses? To behave like a debutante when he knows that's not who I am?"

"I suspect he thought your only option was to return to Charleston so he probably wanted you to embrace that life."

"But we're married so why does he encourage me to take the role of a homemaker instead of running the ranch?"

"I'm not sure. Maybe he believes if your mother had lived, you'd desire a more traditional role."

She sighed. "Running a house could never give me the satisfaction of running a ranch."

He cupped her jaw. "You're fine, Hannah, just the way you are."

Tears filled her eyes. "Thank you." She laid her hand over his. "That means a lot."

Those tears would be his undoing. He cradled her hand in his own, then raised her hand to his lips and kissed her palm and each fingertip.

The sharp intake of her breath said his touch affected her all right. As much as hers did him. Where would this connection lead?

Cal would be rousting him out soon enough. "We'd better get some sleep."

He helped Hannah to her feet. She strode to the spot

where they'd stowed their saddles and saddlebags and unfurled her bedroll. He did the same.

"Don't hesitate to wake me if you need anything," he
said.

"I'll be fine." In a flash of moving arms and legs, she
shucked her boots and burrowed into her nest, putting her
back to him.

He doused the flames, kicked dirt onto the ashes, then
yanked off his boots, stretching out on his blanket beside
hers, close enough to touch. An urge to pull her to him,
to hold her in the crook of his arm and cuddle her close
roared to life inside him like a raging bull. He wouldn't
give in to the impulse. He wouldn't let emotion override
common sense. He wouldn't love her.

To keep from reaching for her, he clasped his hands
over his chest, lacing his fingers so tightly his bones hurt.

"Comfy?" she asked.

With Hannah within reach, yet off-limits, he was about
as comfy as a man clinging to a prickly cactus. "Uh-huh.
You?"

Another howl of a coyote.

Hannah jerked upright. "That sounds close," she whispered.

Though tempted to offer his protection, Matt knew the
coyote presented no threat. "Naw." Her only threat was
her husband, a man yearning to hold her.

But he wouldn't. Not when he knew that opening his
heart could destroy the one thing he had. Contentment.

When had he told himself a bigger lie? Contentment
didn't describe his state of mind. At all. Not when the
prospect of a lifetime of celibacy twisted inside him, rising up like a coiled rattler, fangs bared, ready to destroy
all his well-laid plans.

He wouldn't give in to these impulses. And risk another

discontented wife. Not when it appeared he and Hannah had forged a kind of truce. To keep that peace, he'd see that she got to handle the sale of her herd. Even if supporting her meant earning more of his father's disapproval.

At the rear of the herd, Hannah rode on the right, Matt on the left, as they punched the cattle into the untamed town of Fort Worth. Corrals teemed with milling, bawling cattle. Hollering cowpunchers prodded steers through shoots, their hooves stomping up ramps into railroad cars ready to haul them to slaughterhouses and meatpackers in Chicago. Dust and noise everywhere. Obviously with the drought, most of the area cattlemen had decided to sell.

Alert for any sign of stampede, Hannah sat tall in the saddle, scanning the herd, moving Star with quiet commands. A steer dodged right, attempting a getaway. A tug on a rein, her right knee pressed into Star's side, the cow pony wheeled, outdistanced and cut off the animal's escape, then returned the renegade to the herd.

Robert had ridden ahead with documentation of the Circle W and Lazy P brands and the number of cattle in each herd. With a wave of his hat, he directed them to empty corrals. As the lead animals entered the pen, men were perched on the fence, counting each brand. Hopefully their number would agree with Hannah's tally.

The chaos before her was a huge contrast to the peace of the previous night and the quiet interlude between her and Matt. In that one evening, they'd shared more about themselves than in all the years of their acquaintance.

Yet the peace and quiet didn't mean Hannah had been serene. With Matt lying so close, she'd had difficulty falling asleep. When Cal had shaken Matt awake, she'd also awakened. To avoid more connection to her husband, she'd feigned sleep.

And knew the moment Matt had pressed his lips to her cheek.

No matter how much she tried not to think about that husbandly act, the gentle sweetness of that kiss lingered. With a sigh, she laid a palm on her cheek. Had he kissed her in case Cal was watching? Or was a taciturn cowboy transforming into a tender companion?

If so, dare she trust the change in him? Or was this side of him temporary? Part of the pretense of wedded bliss? A romantic night under the stars?

With the last of the cattle corralled, Hannah and Matt leaned against the pen, inspecting the herd, waiting for the tally. On the trek home, without cattle to punch, they'd make good time. Wouldn't need to set up camp. That meant the closeness of the trail, the closeness to Matt would end. Inside her a battle waged. Part of her ached with disappointment, the other part heaved a sigh of relief. She didn't know how to handle all these contradictory feelings.

At last, she and Matt stood inside the sales office while Robert confirmed the number of head of Circle W cattle and negotiated his price.

Hannah was next in line. She strode toward the counter.

Robert stepped in front of her, blocking her way. "I'll take care of this. No need to worry your pretty head with all these figures."

"This is Lazy P business," she said, holding her ground.

His mouth set in a grim line, Robert bent toward her. "I'll get you as good a price as I got for my herd," he said, voice low. "Leave this to the men."

In two long strides, Matt stepped between his wife and his disgruntled father. "You can handle the sale, Hannah. Do you know what your cattle are worth?"

Papa had told her what she should expect to get for the steers and older cows. Besides talking to Papa, she'd studied past sales figures, had soaked up every bit of information.

Ignoring Robert, she leaned toward Matt and recited the number she'd worked out in her head during the drive.

With a nod and a smile, Matt motioned toward the waiting buyer. "Go on and get your price, Mrs. Walker," he said, then took his sputtering father by the arm and led him outside.

Hannah emerged from the office with a smile on her face and joined Matt. "I did it!" she said, her tone light with satisfaction.

"Knew you could." Matt's dark brown eyes softened. "I'm proud of you, Hannah. Proud of how you've handled the deal and the herd. You're becoming a capable rancher."

His approval slid through her, as warm and soothing as hot milk and honey to a sore throat. "Your confidence in me means more than I can say."

She'd negotiated her first deal, had trailed her first drive. Inside, she bubbled with confidence. She could handle anything. Anything, that is, except her marriage.

Her marriage wasn't real, a proper relationship. All that talk about how proud he was of her—why wouldn't he be? As business partners, he wanted her to be capable. He saw her as a rancher, nothing more. Perhaps he'd used her desire for independence more as an excuse to stand up to his father more than to confirm his confidence in her.

In an instant, her elation fizzled like thunder without the promised rain. Truth was, she and Matt might be attracted to each other, but something held them apart.

The more she got what she wanted, the more she realized having this deal they called a marriage wasn't all that wonderful.

Chapter Twelve

At dusk, Hannah rode into the Lazy P with Matt at her side. She hoped Papa was still awake so she could celebrate handling her first cattle sale with him.

A glimpse of the horse and buggy hitched at the rail trapped the air in Hannah's lungs. Pastor Cummings. He wouldn't pay a call this late, unless…

Heart in her throat, she dismounted, telling herself that at least, Doc Atkins's buggy wasn't waiting outside.

One look at her face and Matt took the reins from her hands. "Go on in. I'll see to the horses."

Weak-kneed and wobbly on her feet, Hannah lurched to the house. She met Pastor Cummings coming out the door. Brown hair threaded with gray, his eyes soft and serene, Pastor Cummings tugged his waistcoat over the bulge of his belly.

"Is Papa…all right?"

"He's weaker, but awake and eager to hear how things went in Fort Worth."

A sigh heaved out of her. "Thanks for coming. I know he appreciates your visits."

"Martin's ready, Hannah. Let that be a comfort to you."

He laid a hand on her shoulder. "Give him permission to go."

In those gentle eyes, Hannah read his message. For her sake, Papa was hanging on. Suffering. Hot tears pricked the back of her eyes. Unable to speak, she clamped her lips together, gave a nod.

Inside, Rosa exited Papa's room, dark eyes filled with sorrow, the plate of food in her hand untouched. "He not take medicine before he see you."

Hannah glanced at her grimy garb. She'd give Papa his debutante daughter. "I'll only be a minute." She raced to her room, changed into a simple dress, grabbed the proof of the sale, then smile firmly in place, sped to Papa's room.

Breathing hard, her father lay propped against the pillows, pale, his skin almost translucent. He lifted his hand. "Hannah, my beautiful daughter, so like her mama."

Her smile quivered, but held. "I'm trail dusty, Papa, but I put on this dress for you."

"I was wrong to keep you in dresses. You wear what's comfortable." He patted the bed. "Now, tell me all about the cattle drive and the sale."

She settled on the bed, facing her father, and handed over the receipt for three hundred head of cattle. The paper quivered in his unsteady hands.

"I remembered everything you said, Papa, and negotiated the sale myself."

"You did good, Daughter. I'm proud of you."

His approval slid through her. She took his hand. "Thank you, Papa."

A sigh slid out of him. "I'm surprised Robert didn't interfere." No need to tell Papa that he had. "He needs to ease his hold on the reins and give Matt his head."

Perhaps the tension between father and son explained Matt's fondness for Martin.

Papa looked exhausted from his effort to talk. "I rest easy knowing with God at the helm and Matt at your side, you'll be fine."

Tears welling in her eyes, she kissed his cheek. "I will be fine, Papa."

A soft moan on his lips, Papa squeezed his eyes shut and sucked in a breath, his face carved with pain. He groped for the medication beside the bed.

"I'll get it." She loved him for attempting to smooth the signs of pain from his face. He only thought of her, always trying to protect her. After giving him a dose, she sat stroking his hand, to touch this loving man who'd always put her welfare before his own.

How could she bear to lose him? Her heart plummeted. How could she want him to suffer more?

Once a vital, active man, Papa would loathe being bedridden, unable to participate in the life of the ranch. Was she holding on to him, keeping him here when he wanted only to go to a better place? To join her mother and brother? The thought of losing him burned inside her, yet how much harder to watch him endure this relentless pain. She had to relinquish him into God's care. To do otherwise would be the worst kind of selfishness. But how?

Lord, I love him. Help me release him to You.

A calmness Hannah couldn't explain enveloped her. She bent over her father, felt his breath upon her face. "Papa, can you hear me?" He squeezed her hand.

Matt entered the room and stood behind her, his hand on her shoulder.

Her father opened his eyes. "Matt."

"Yes, Martin. I'm here."

Their eyes held in silent communication. "Take care of her."

"I will."

A smile, then Papa looked into her eyes, his gaze soft, tender. "I love you, Hannah."

"I love you, Papa." Her chest squeezed until she felt she couldn't breathe. "Go in peace."

The tension in his face, in his brow eased. "To your mama and brother."

"Rest, Papa," Hannah said, rubbing his hand. Within minutes the fingers under hers relaxed. She laid her head on the bed, listening to him draw each ragged breath.

Throughout the night, Matt sat beside her, held her close, while Hannah spoke words of love to her father, sang his favorite hymns, watched the struggle in the rise and fall of his chest.

Matt's strong arms made her feel safe and secure. Just for tonight she'd pretend she was in love with her husband. Just for tonight she'd pretend he loved her in return.

Toward morning, the time between Papa's breaths lengthened, each one more shallow than the last.

Hannah laid her palms on either side of his face, then leaned close to his ear. "Goodbye, Papa. Godspeed."

As the sun was rising, streaking the heavens with rosy light, Martin Parrish stopped breathing.

Hannah turned and stumbled into Matt's arms.

He gathered her close. "I'm sorry," he whispered.

She choked back a sob, looking into her husband's kind eyes, grateful that she had Matt to lean on. "Our marriage gave him peace," she said, her lips trembling.

"Hannah, you don't always have to be strong. It's all right to cry."

Pulling her close, Matt nudged her head against his broad chest. Wrapped in his strong arms, she wept.

Matt knew where he'd find Hannah. At the family burial plot, making her daily visit to Martin's grave. Where he'd found her every day since her father's death. His gut tightened. He'd never felt more helpless.

Martin Parrish had been a man respected and mourned by all who knew him. Upon his death, neighbors, parishioners and friends rallied around his daughter, bringing food, attending the wake and funeral, offering sympathy and support.

As they'd uttered condolences, many spoke of the blessing of Hannah and Matt's love, that they had each other in this time of grief. The comments were meant to comfort, but Matt suspected the assumption made Hannah feel all the more alone.

Yet, that outpouring of love had gotten Hannah through those first days. But now, three weeks after the funeral, she merely went through the motions of living, barely eating, steps lagging, devoid of energy and unable to make the simplest decisions. He missed his feisty wife.

Inside the fenced enclosure, Hannah stood beside her father's grave, head bowed, hair swept up, a few tendrils curling along her slender neck, full skirt billowing in the breeze. She placed three red roses at the base of the headstone. The third rose for her baby brother buried with her mother. Each day Hannah exchanged the withered blooms with fresh cut flowers. The ritual seemed to bring her comfort.

Yet, Matt knew the futility of this daily pilgrimage. Undergirded with guilt, he'd wallowed in his grief for Amy. Only to learn that his only hope for survival was to get back to living. At first that meant merely going through the motions, but over time, he'd found his salvation in work, in his friends, in the Psalms.

For three weeks now, each evening on the porch Matt had held Hannah, listened to her memories of Martin, offered comfort, but the time had come for her to move forward.

He squatted beside her, his boots mashing the tall grass alongside the mound of earth. She lifted her face to his. The lost expression in her bleak blue eyes snared his heart.

Matt reached for her hand. Her hand fit his perfectly. In many ways they were well suited. They both grieved Martin and shared their sorrow, yet the time had come to be direct. "Your father would want you to get on with living, not come here every day and put flowers on his grave. In fact, knowing Martin, he'd have a stern word for you about now."

"I'm…trying."

That sorrow-laced claim tore at him. He remembered the sorrow of losing Amy. Even with the issues between them, he'd loved his wife. He hadn't known how to fix those problems, any more than he'd known how to ease his sorrow over Amy's death. But he'd had a mother with a will of iron and friends who wouldn't take no for an answer.

She needed a diversion to pull her out of her despondency. "I have an idea. Let's go on a picnic."

"A picnic?"

He swept a hand. "The day's too fine to waste working. What do you say?"

"It's kind of you to offer, but—"

"You think I'm kind for wanting to spend time with my wife? Truth is, I like seeing her have some fun." He slid a finger across her lips. "I've missed that smile."

A weak smile formed on her lips, as if her mouth had forgotten how.

Still, that smile was a start. "Ah, there it is."

He offered his arm and she slipped her hand through the crook. They left the plot, closed the gate behind them, then strolled to the house.

One word to Rosa and she set to work making sandwiches while Hannah poked around in the icebox looking for leftovers.

In a matter of minutes, Matt had hitched Lightning to the buggy and helped Hannah onto the seat, then climbed up beside her, depositing the basket and blanket at his feet.

As they followed the trampled path toward the creek, he glanced at his wife's profile. The broad-brimmed straw hat she wore shaded her face, hiding her expression. Still, with the slump of her shoulders, her gaze focused on the hands in her lap, she looked sad.

"Spring is my favorite time of year," Matt said. When she didn't reply, he went on, "The grass is green. Calves are born. We're not sweltering. Yet."

Apparently caught in her grief, she didn't respond. They passed a field of bluebonnets. Women liked flowers. He pulled the buggy over.

"Why are we stopping?"

"You'll see." He helped her down and then took her hand and practically towed her into the middle of the field.

She stood amidst the flowers, gazing around her. "I love bluebonnets."

He released her hand, then stooped, gathering flowers fast and furious. With a bewildered expression on her face, she stared at him, as if he'd lost his mind.

"Hold out your arms."

She complied and he piled them with bluebonnets. Dozens and dozens and dozens of bluebonnets.

"Stop!" Laughing, she gazed down at her loaded arms. "Any more and I won't be able to carry them all."

He cupped her jaw with both palms and gazed into the prettiest blue eyes he'd ever seen. "They match your eyes."

As if uneasy under his scrutiny, her gaze shifted. Then she shoved the flowers at him. "Race you to the buggy!"

She gathered her skirts and sprinted across the field, her laughter trailing behind her.

The blooms tumbling out of his arms, he sped after her, his heart all but bursting with joy. He had his feisty wife back.

With a smug grin on her face, her eyes twinkling like the North Star, Hannah leaned against the buggy.

He skidded to a stop in front of her.

"I won," she said.

"I let you win." He knew full well his claim was ridiculous, but he couldn't resist teasing her.

"Did not."

"Okay, maybe not, but admit it. You had a head start and I had to run with my arms full."

"Not full for long." She pointed to the trail of flowers he'd left behind.

He stared at his empty arms. "I wanted to give you a field of posies," he said, his voice laden with regret.

"Oh, but you did," she murmured, then turned to him, smiling, truly smiling. "Thank you."

The radiance of that smile smacked him in the gut. When he'd said he missed her smile, he hadn't realized how much. To see the numbness and pain replaced, even temporarily, by playfulness, lifted an enormous weight from his shoulders. He knew then that Hannah would be all right. He'd see that she kept smiling, even if it meant losing a race every day of his life.

Tranquility transformed her features as her gaze traveled the horizon, scanning each field, the grove of pecan trees up ahead. "What you said about spring, the green grass, the birth of the calves—made me realize how thankful I am for Papa's new life in heaven."

"He will dwell in the house of the Lord forever."

"The twenty-third Psalm," she said. "One of my favorites."

"As a rancher, I'm not much for sheep, but I find the message of the Good Shepherd protecting His flock reassuring."

He took her hand and helped her into the buggy. As they drove beneath the canopy of the pecan grove, not far from the creek, he tethered the horse, then wrapped his hands around her waist and lifted her to the ground.

Had she lost weight? If so, he'd see that she ate. The picnic was the perfect place to start. He grabbed the basket and they strolled through the trees toward the creek, the branches swaying in a windy dance.

At the water's edge, he set down the split oak basket and unfurled the blanket that flapped in the breeze, then fluttered to the ground. Then anchored it with the basket.

A gust of wind caught the wide brim of Hannah's straw hat, sailing it through the air toward the water. Matt chased after it and grabbed the brim, then returned it to her. "At least your hat didn't beat me in a race."

She giggled. "My hat had a head start, too. But this time, you didn't whine about that."

"It would've been a whole lot less embarrassing to be beaten by the wind, than by my wife."

Their laughter carried on the breeze, chasing away the shadows of Martin's death. Leaving only the two of them. She met his gaze, her blue eyes wide, filled with uncertainty.

He touched the lock of hair that had fallen from its moorings and tucked it behind her ear. Soft, silky. A temptation to unpin her hair left him gulping. He sucked in a steadying breath. Then her lips parted, sweet, enticing, ripe for kissing. The need to kiss her exploded within him. *Sweet Hannah.*

A pang of uneasiness niggled in his muddled mind. *Careful, Walker. You've walked this road before.*

He turned away. He knew where this intimacy would lead. To a true relationship.

Memories of Amy's dissatisfaction and his resentment, of bickering, then silence as the gaping wound of their marriage scabbed with apathy.

He wouldn't let attraction spur him to an impulsive decision, as he had with Amy. Better to focus on the picnic, on giving Hannah a fun day, and leave well enough alone.

In the cool, dim interior of the stable, Hannah brushed Lightning's coat, her mind replaying the playful moments in the field of bluebonnets, the relaxed picnic by the creek, all the things Matt had done to get her mind on other things, to lift her out from that dark cloud she'd been living under.

All those good things made her feel closer to him, made her think they were turning a corner in their relationship. But then he'd turned away from that almost kiss, making it clear he didn't want anything more.

A sigh escaped her lips as she watched the dust from Lightning's coat drift to the floor. She carried Matt's name. Might even be attracted to him. Might respect and admire much about him. Might share work on the ranch and grief for Papa. But her husband had no intention of cleaving to her.

With Papa gone, she missed the love he gave her, so badly she hurt. Hurt or not, she'd live with her agreement. She couldn't expect more from herself and from Matt than they could give. They both were wounded by deaths of loved ones.

As unfair as the feeling was, when Mama died, she'd felt abandoned. Lost. She could no more risk that pain again, than she could walk on water. Even reckless Peter had sunk.

"Hannah."

Matt stood in the open doorway, framed by the sun; tall, lean and tanned, every inch the cowboy. He doffed his hat, uncertainty in his eyes, and held out a bunch of bedraggled bluebonnets. "I want you to have these." He strode toward her, stopped inches away, then pressed the bluebonnets into her hand. "They're not much, but they're a part of Texas, a part of this land, something you and I treasure."

The stems in her hands were drooping but not severed. Like herself, bent but not broken. "Thank you."

The gaze he turned on her held tenderness. They might not be in love but they were committed. "I'm glad you're my wife, Hannah."

The statement rocked her. She swayed on her feet. "Why? Now that Papa's gone and you no longer need to be here to help him, why are you glad you married me?"

"We share a commitment to each other, to the land. During the weeks since we married, my respect and admiration for you has grown."

"What do you admire about me?" Hannah wanted—no, *needed*—to know.

"I admire you in that dress, though no more than I do in denims." He let his gaze roam over her. "You're a lovely woman."

The sweet words and the gesture of the flowers captured her heart as surely as if he'd used a lariat.

Not that she'd let him know. Hannah harrumphed. "A sound basis for respect, Mr. Walker."

"I've heard of worse." Matt grinned down at her.

She noticed the lighter lines around his eyes from squinting into the sun. As he pushed a shock of hair off his brow, a band of paler skin on his forehead revealed where his hatband rested and that work ethic she admired.

"What else? What else do you admire?" she asked, gazing into his dark eyes.

"Apparently my wife craves compliments." He smiled. "That being the case, I'll list your many admirable qualities." He touched her hair. "You have beautiful hair that sends off sparks in the sunlight." His fingers slid to her brows. "Eyes that change hue at whim." Then traveled her cheek to her lips. "A smile that would light the darkest night."

Laughing, Hannah covered her ears with her hands, the bluebonnets waving wildly above her head. He was teasing her. "This is a business alliance. You don't have to woo me."

With a nod, he took a step away, giving her room to breathe. There were needs and goals she and Matt could meet for one another. They were friends united in a business cause. In many ways they were well suited, giving her hope they'd find a way to travel the uncharted waters of a marriage based on convenience. That they'd find contentment in companionship.

"Thank you for taking me on the picnic," she said. "It's time to get back to work. Tomorrow I'll go to town, deposit the money from the sale, pay the Parrish bills and order supplies. Then go over the Lazy P accounts until I'm as savvy with running the ranch as any man."

He studied her face, then with a brisk nod, ambled out of the stable.

She glanced at the bluebonnets in her hand. She would put them in a vase. Not that the flowers represented anything more to Matt than his love for all things Texan. For the land. For the way of life. Not that they implied Matt loved her.

That honor belonged to Amy, the young woman buried in the church cemetery.

Chapter Thirteen

Hannah sat at an enormous desk in the president's office of Bliss State Bank, a desk that confirmed his position but failed to hide Mr. Thomas's wide girth, and signed her name.

Across from her, Mr. Thomas shoved his spectacles up his nose and craned his neck toward the form. "Ah, I need to remind you that you're Hannah Parrish *Walker.*"

Cheeks aflame, Hannah stared at her signature, barely able to believe she'd signed her maiden name. "Oh, I'm sorry."

Below his neatly trimmed mustache, Mr. Thomas's mouth twitched in an effort to contain a smile. "No problem. Plenty of room to add your married name."

With a nod, Hannah lowered the nib to the paper, then paused. The Walker name affirmed her wedded status. But, what would a real marriage be like? A marriage in more than name only? She bit back the sigh trying to shove up her throat, tightened her grip on the pen and scrawled Walker.

The last of her errands completed, Hannah emerged into the sunshine and turned toward Leah's. She'd end the hectic afternoon with a visit to her friend.

As she passed the Western Union office, Mr. Katter sped out the door, hatless and huffing for breath. "Miss Parr—Ah, Mrs. Walker, mighty glad I saw you. We just received a telegram for Jake Hardy. If you'd take it to him, that would save our delivery boy a trip out."

"Happy to." Hannah tucked the envelope in her purse.

Mr. Katter's face hadn't revealed anything about the contents, but a telegram rarely brought good news. The visit to Leah would have to wait.

On the drive to the Lazy P, Hannah soaked up the peaceful pastureland, the cattle grazing in the fields. As she neared the stable, she slowed Lightning, then stopped the buggy. A few yards away, Matt and Jake leaned against the corral fence. Matt waved a hand, then ambled over, a welcoming grin on his face.

"Hello," he said, gazing up at her.

The warmth in his dark eyes slid through her, left her unsteady on her feet. With strong hands, he clasped her waist, then lifted her down. Her heart thudded in her chest. This marriage might not be real, but the man most certainly was.

Odd as she'd felt signing Hannah Parrish Walker, for the briefest moment in town, she'd wished for a real marriage. Now gazing into Matt's eyes, hunger for that closeness rose inside her.

"Everything go okay in town?" Matt asked.

Had her expression revealed the turmoil inside her?

"I opened an account in my name at the bank and deposited the profit from the cattle sale. Paid the bills at Bailey's and the feed store and ordered supplies. Our attorney verified Papa's last will and testament. Shouldn't take long for probate to confirm the will is valid."

"Knew you could handle things."

"Thank you." Matt's confidence in her soothed like

butter on a burn. "Some people underestimate me. Papa's lawyer and the bank president both expressed surprise I'd come without you."

"You're smart, capable. You don't need me holding your hand." He arched a brow. "Though I'd be happy to oblige."

Their eyes locked, tugging her closer. "I'll keep that in mind."

Jake ambled over to where they stood. "How are things in Bliss? Any news?"

Mercy, she'd been so caught up in Matt, she'd forgotten the telegram. She reached into her purse and handed Jake the envelope. "I was asked to give this to you."

With trembling hands, Jake tore open the envelope, then read the telegram. He lifted tear-filled eyes to hers.

"What's wrong, Jake?"

"Gertie fell. Broke her back." He sucked in a breath. "No idea how long my sister will be laid up, probably all summer."

"Oh, I'm sorry." Poor Allie. Her mother had deserted her, now her grandmother was bedridden. At Gertie's age, recovery would be slow.

"Not sure how to help, what with my job here." Jake sighed. "Suppose Allie could go from neighbor to neighbor."

To leave the ranch had been hard, but at least Hannah had the support of family in Charleston. Allie needed that too. "Bring Allie here."

Jake rubbed his forehead. "Is that too much, so soon after losing yer pa? With the ranch to run and all?"

Hannah knew the pain of being motherless. "She'll be happier here than shifted from pillar to post. On the ranch, she'll have room to run, animals galore, fresh air. That should help take her mind off her troubles."

"You sure?" Jake asked.

"I'm sure."

Matt nodded. "I agree. Bring Allie here."

"If it's all right, I can leave tomorrow. A train runs to Amarillo on Fridays."

"Tomorrow is fine," Hannah said.

"I should be back to work by Monday. Allie can stay in the bunkhouse—"

"The bunkhouse is no place for a child. Allie will stay in the main house." Hannah touched Jake's sleeve. "I'll do all I can to help her adjust."

"'Preciate it. She needs a woman's touch."

Hannah gulped. Emotion had overpowered her common sense and she'd invited the girl on impulse. She'd make a mess of mothering a child. What did she know about kids? About this child, a girl she'd never even met?

She tamped down the panic rising inside her and took a calming breath. When she'd lost her mother, Rosa had provided a warm lap, fresh baked cookies and gentle ways. Hannah wasn't a cook, but surely she could read to Allie, hug her, tuck her into bed. But what if Allie wouldn't allow that?

"Losing your folks, Miz Hannah, you'll understand if Allie misses Gertie, misses her mom."

Hannah's heart lurched. Allie's parents had deserted her willingly. Abandonment she couldn't imagine. "I'll do my best."

Tears welled in Jake's eyes. "Can't thank you enough. Reckon I'd better pack." On bowed legs, Jake trudged toward the bunkhouse.

On their way to the house, Hannah turned to Matt. "Jake expects me to comfort Allie, but what if I say or do something to make things worse?"

"It'll work out. I'll do what I can to help." He rubbed

his jaw. "Maybe you and Allie can connect over a favor-ite toy or something."

"That's a great idea. She might like to play with my dolls. They're packed away in a trunk in the attic." Though in truth, Hannah had no idea what this seven-year-old girl might treasure.

"I'll haul down the trunk." Matt's dark brown eyes bored into her. "You probably haven't thought where she'll stay, but the room I'm in faces the paddock. Maybe she'd like seeing the horses."

"Where would you go?"

A thought zipped through her. A crazy hope he'd ask to be a true husband and room with his wife.

"If it's all right with you, I'll take Martin's old room."

"Oh. Yes."

She forced a smile to her face, masking the disappoint-ment tumbling inside of her. She should've known Matt didn't want to change their sleeping arrangements. Well, fine. No matter how good she felt nestled in Matt's arms, no matter how good Matt's lips felt on hers, she didn't need a real husband; the business deal they had suited her perfectly.

Hannah shot up her chin. "Allie *should* have the nicer view."

Matt gave a nod, then glanced around him, as if getting his bearings. "I'll see to the trunk," he said, then veered toward the stairway leading to the attic.

To keep her mind off her husband, she'd focus on Allie's arrival. The move would be hard for the little girl. Along with missing her mother and grandmother, she'd lose her routine, her home, her security.

A huge responsibility. Still...

Something akin to joy bubbled up inside her. Having Allie here would provide a diversion. A diversion from the loss of Papa, from the emotional ups and downs of her and Matt's relationship. With Allie here, Hannah would have another chance to prove herself, more importantly, an opportunity to help a hurting child.

Lord, help me give this child what she needs.

Love, Allie needed love. With Papa gone and a husband in name only, Hannah had pent-up love to give. She'd make a cozy place for the child. Give Allie love like Papa had given her. Smiles of approval. Hugs and kisses. Time alone with her.

Why, with Allie here, Hannah might forge a family. A family she wouldn't get in this business-only relationship with Matt.

Eager to make preparations for Allie's arrival, she entered the guest room. Her gaze leapt from Matt's boots with fancy stitching propped in the corner, to his shaving mug and brush resting on the washstand, to the open door of the wardrobe where his shirts and pants hung. All proof a man occupied this room. That man was her husband. What would it be like to watch him shave? To see him shrug into a shirt? To look across the pillows at his sleeping face?

"Where do you want this?"

Heart in her throat, Hannah whirled toward Matt, then took a steadying breath, reminding herself he couldn't read her mind.

"At the foot of the bed," she said. Her voice sounded hoarse, unsteady even to her own ears.

Mesmerized by the rippling of Matt's muscles as he lowered the trunk to the floor, Hannah's mouth went dry.

He ambled about the room, gathering his clothes, his toiletries, his Bible, each movement masculine.

She'd once feared falling in love with Matt and having a real marriage, believing he would tie her down and treat her like a hothouse plant. But he had stepped aside, letting her make decisions on the ranch, encouraging her to handle the sale of her cattle. Her fear had been unwarranted. He'd been there for her, with the ranch, with her father's passing, yet their relationship hadn't moved beyond friends.

As much as she longed for love, to share every facet of her life, did she want that? Really? She'd lost her mother. She'd lost her father. Those she'd loved most. She couldn't bear to go through that again.

She tamped down such foolish thoughts. How could she lose a man who'd never been hers?

Arms full with his belongings, Matt stepped passed her, keeping his distance as he moved to his new quarters. She gulped. Right across the hall from her.

Determined to get back to the task at hand, Hannah knelt before the trunk, blew dust off the lid. Hand on the latch, she hesitated. More than possessions were stored in this trunk. Memories were stored here, too. Memories of Mama.

Matt strolled into the room. "I'm settled in," he said, then squatted beside her.

Close. Much too close. Yet for some reason she couldn't understand, she welcomed his presence. Welcomed the comfort of having him near when she opened this door to the past.

She lifted the lid, inhaling the sweet scent of roses wafting from a bar of soap nestled in a tatted handkerchief. Folded nearby was the baby quilt Mama had made for her from patterned snippets of pink and green.

"My mother made this quilt for me. It'll be perfect for Allie to wrap up in."

He smiled at her. "Nothing tomboy about that."

She laid the precious keepsake at the foot of the bed, then lifted out the tray. Several boxes filled the bottom of the trunk. Tucked inside the first, Hannah found Ruth wrapped in a cloth. She lifted the doll and inspected her sweet bisque face.

"Mama gave me Ruth on my sixth birthday. Far different than the pony you got."

"You remembered."

She recalled everything he'd said about himself. But she wouldn't tell him that.

"The doll's open-and-close blue eyes and wavy, brown hair were as close to mine as Mama could buy."

"You were a pretty little girl."

"You said I was gangly, remember?"

"That was later, when you were growing like a locoweed."

She plopped hands on hips. "Not sure I appreciate the comparison to a weed that sickens cattle."

"Is growing like a thistle better?"

"No." Giggling, she traced a finger along the kid leather body, jointed arms and legs, smooth and soft as velvet. "Mama and I gave tea parties for my dolls."

"Dolls? There's more?"

She gently laid Ruth aside, opened a pillowcase and pulled out the ragdoll. "I got Baby on my first birthday. Papa said I loved the soft floppy doll at first sight." Hannah's throat clogged. "Mama made Baby, stitched the pert nose, blue eyes, bowed lips. She had a knack with a needle and patience I could never match."

"I remember your mother's lilting accent, her ladylike ways. She was a Southern belle."

Hannah was nothing like her mother, but her heart gave a little flip that Matt remembered Mama. Not that he shouldn't.

"I was fifteen when your mother died." He touched her

hand, his eyes filled with compassion. "You were only nine, too little to lose your mother."

Tears brimmed in her eyes as she choked out the words, "After Mama died, I'd cuddle Baby close, wrap her arms around my chest. Pretend they were Mama's arms."

Matt tugged her close. "My arms are available," he said, offering her his handkerchief.

She swiped her eyes. "Hugging that doll brought me comfort, but still, at nine, I knew reality from make-believe."

At nineteen, she was old enough to realize the same. Matt might want to give her comfort, but he wasn't offering love.

Hannah slipped from Matt's arm and rose to her feet with both dolls. She propped them against the bed pillows. Perhaps they would console Allie, as they had Hannah all those years ago. As they still did. These dolls, the baby quilt, all bought or made by her mother, triggered warm memories. The effort Mama had taken to buy or make the perfect gift evidence of her love.

She returned to the trunk. To the stack of books she'd read many times over. *"Grimm's Fairy Tales, Bible Stories for Children, The Adventures of Tom Sawyer, Little Women, Jane Eyre."* She glanced at Matt. "Some of these are too advanced for Allie."

"Tom Sawyer was a favorite of mine."

Hannah stacked the books on the nightstand. "Perhaps come winter, we'll read it again."

Matt rose, leaned against the doorframe, glancing around the room. "Looks like a little girl already lives here. You've thought of everything."

"I'm no mother."

"You were a little girl once," he said with a grin. "Do

with Allie what you liked to do as a kid. Maybe have one of those tea parties. You'll figure it out."

Easy for him to say. She cocked her head at him. "So, I suppose that means you'll figure out how to be a father?"

As if jabbed by the horns of a steer, Matt lurched upright. "That job belongs to Jake."

"A man in his seventies can't keep up with a child. Besides, she'll need other people, too. As old as I was when I moved to Charleston, I missed being away from Papa, from everyone and everything familiar. I want to help Allie fit in, to be happy here."

Matt's brow furrowed. "I teased you about finishing school, but never thought how hard it was for you to move clear across the country. Leave the life you knew and loved." He took her hand. "That experience should help you reach out to Allie."

She stared down at their clasped hands, how perfectly her hand fit in his, then looked into his eyes. "We have a marriage of convenience. Allie may not fit our idea of convenience, but you and I are in this together."

As if to protest, he raised a hand.

"You hear?" she said, leaning close. "This isn't my job only."

"Yes, ma'am." He smirked. "Can't imagine Allie will be any harder to handle than her new ma."

She harrumphed.

"Okay, we'll do this together."

He stroked his lip, staring into space. Matt Walker, the problem solver. As if he could handle everything with logic. With action.

"You two can play with the dolls, draw pictures, bake cookies." He snorted. "Oh, I forgot. You'll have to ask Rosa to teach her that."

"You think you've got it all worked out. But what if Allie is more like me? Prefers to roam, ride and rope?"

"In that case, I'd say we're in deep trouble." He winked. "In way over our heads."

"I already feel in over my head, and she hasn't arrived."

He took a step closer. So close Hannah could feel the heat emanating from his body. "We may be in over our heads, but buck up, wife. I'm a mighty good swimmer."

She took a step back. Matt thought he had all the answers. This marriage had made sense, but with every passing day, the matrimonial waters grew more treacherous, the churning surf more unmanageable. Matt might be a good swimmer, but whether he knew it or not, she was on the verge of drowning.

If they weren't careful, they'd all go under.

In his room directly across the hall from Hannah's, Matt sprawled on the bed, arms behind his head, gazing out the window at the night sky. Moonlight streamed in, lighting the room enough to see. A shooting star streaked through the heavens, vanishing as quickly as it came. Then another. God was putting on quite a show. A show far better appreciated outdoors.

If only he could share the sight with Hannah, but he'd never consider knocking on her door.

He tugged on his boots then opened the door, fiddling with a button on his open shirt and walked into the dark hallway.

Right into soft curves. A gasp. *Hannah.*

"I'm sorry. I didn't see you there." He cleared his throat. "Can't sleep?"

"No, I hoped a glass of milk might help. What about you?"

"I'm on my way outside. To look for more shooting stars. Care to join me?"

She hesitated for a moment. "I would."

In the entry, he opened the wooden door and they stepped into the night. Another star streaked through the sky. Matt watched Hannah's upturned face, aglow in the moonlight. She looked young, at peace, even…happy.

Something akin to joy expanded then exploded in his chest. He might not be the reason for the contentment on his wife's face, but he'd brought her out here, given her this moment. Could he find ways to bring her many more such moments?

They stood there, soaking up the peace of the night. Soaking up the knowledge that God was in His Heavens. No matter what a mess they made of things on earth, God was in control, all the reassurance Matt needed.

"On a night like this, I feel God's presence everywhere, surrounding us, loving us, within us." Hannah sucked in a gulp of air, then turned to him. "Why didn't God save my father? I knew He could. I prayed and prayed He would, but He didn't."

The quiet question, spoken so softly, banged against his heart. The tortured uncertainty he heard in her voice sought an answer he didn't have. "I don't know. All I do know is Martin is at peace."

She turned to him, put a hand on her heart. "I feel that, too. I know my family is safe and happy in God's arms." She gazed up at him. "Thank you for bringing me out here to see the wonder of this night."

Hair flowing down her back, standing there in floor-length nightclothes and bare toes, she looked beautiful. Beautiful and oh, so vulnerable. An urge to protect her swept through him. To make certain she never faced such heartache again. Yet that was not in his power to do.

He encircled her in the cradle of his arms, gazing down at her upturned face. "Your beauty far surpasses this night."

Was that shimmer in her eyes tears?

Before he could ask, she lifted her face to his, closed her eyes, offering her lips.

"Oh, Hannah…dear, Hannah."

He kissed her with tenderness, brushing her sweet lips with his, then deepening the kiss, tightening his hold on her. She rose on tiptoes, pressing against him, kissing him back with a fervor that left him shaken. And had his heart galloping in his chest like a herd of wild mustangs.

Then she pulled away, fingertips pressed to her lips. "I… Good night," she said then fled inside.

As the door closed behind her, he stared up at the night sky, fighting for composure. How long could they go on this way?

Chapter Fourteen

$\mathbf{M}$att knew his wife. Knew the stiff smile on her face as she greeted Allie covered a passel of qualms. Well, he wasn't any surer of his role of temporary father. Nor could he guess how the child's presence would impact the strain between him and Hannah.

Jake stood beside his great-niece, his hand on Allie's shoulder, a proud smile on his face.

Slender, even wiry, Allie Solaro toed the ground, her dark hair falling around her face like a silk curtain, hiding her eyes. Clothed in cotton stockings and a frothy pink dress, the bow drooping like a saddle-weary drover, Allie would've looked downright citified, if not for the cowboy boots and hat Jake had bought her in Bliss.

Matt heaved a sigh of relief. No worry that this little lady would be a handful, like her temporary tomboy mom. More likely, she'd be scared of anything that moved.

"The Lazy P is your home for the summer, Allie," Hannah said.

Allie glanced at Jake, took in his reassuring nod. How well did the little girl know her great uncle? Yet she appeared to trust him and took the hand he offered.

Hannah rose to her feet. "You'll sleep in the main house."

Allie raised her gaze, her eyes misty, forlorn. "Can't I stay with Uncle Jake?"

"The bunkhouse is no place for a girl. Jake will take his meals with us so you'll see him often."

"That's right nice of you, Miz Hannah."

Matt clapped Jake on the shoulder. "Rosa's cooking will fatten you up."

"Ain't never had an ounce of fat on these bones. Reckon I'll enjoy Rosa's efforts to try."

"Let's see your room, shall we?" Hannah reached a hand to Allie. The little girl released her uncle's grip but didn't take Hannah's hand. "We'll get you settled in."

Eyes on their feet, as if answers for their circumstances could be found in the blades of grass, Allie and Hannah trudged toward the house.

The slender woman and child looked like a family. A lump rose in Matt's throat. A family wasn't what he and Hannah intended. Every day their marriage got more complicated, destroying the contentment he'd prized. In truth, contentment no longer satisfied. Now he yearned for companionship.

Marriage to Hannah was like riding a bronco without a saddle, every buck in their topsy-turvy existence flung him skyward, then landed him hard. He hung on, as if his very life depended on his grip, determined to tame the beast.

Allie glanced back at Jake, uncertainty in her eyes. Matt's heart went out to the little girl. And to the woman in charge of her. He vowed to do all he could to help, knowing full well that tomboy Hannah felt as lost as he did. Whether they wanted it or not, they were cobbling together a family.

Lord, help all of us give Allie love and security.

Beside Matt, Jake grappled with Allie's trunk, grimacing at the effort. "I'll haul in her things," Matt said, then heaved Allie's trunk to his shoulder and followed.

Inside Allie's room, he deposited the trunk under the window where Hannah indicated. "Girls tote a lot of stuff." He glanced at Hannah. "I'm mighty grateful Allie didn't bring as much as you did from Charleston."

"You still moaning about that measly trunk at the depot?"

"That trunk was twice the size of this one. As I recall you also had five, six pieces of luggage. Not that you wear many of those fancy dresses."

"Are you saying you're partial to dresses?"

"Reckon I'm partial to whatever you're wearing."

A blush bloomed in her cheeks. A chuckle burst from his throat. Hannah tried to stare him down, but failed.

She shot up her chin, then opened the lid of Allie's trunk. A brown bear nestled between stacks of clothes. "What's your bear's name, Allie?"

Lips pressed together, the little girl stepped away. She clearly had no intention of talking to Hannah.

With perseverance Matt admired, Hannah put on a bright smile, then showed Allie where to put her clothes. Once she'd stashed her belongings, he and Hannah gave Allie a tour of the large parlor and the dining room with a table that seated ten.

"Lots of room for you," Hannah said, then led Allie to the cozy kitchen.

Rosa sat at the table beside a plate of sugar cookies and a jug of milk.

Eyes on the snack, Allie moved closer.

"This is Rosa, Allie. She made the cookies." Hannah put her arm around the housekeeper. "She'll give you a snack while Matt and I handle chores."

8

Allie plopped into a chair. "Okay."

"When you're finished, you can come out to the barn. Rosa will show you where."

Allie sat beside Rosa nibbling on a cookie as Matt and Hannah stepped outside.

"Rosa's cookies should improve her outlook," Hannah said.

Matt grinned, holding up two cookies and offering one to Hannah. "Exactly why I nabbed a couple for us."

"Thanks. Not sure who needs them more," she said with a giggle, then promptly ate hers as they walked to the barn.

Inside the dim interior, Matt hauled a sack of feed, then dumped grain into the manger for the cows while Hannah fed the pigs. Matt joined her, propping a foot on the bottom rail of the pen.

"Allie's not happy about being here," Hannah said.

"Give her time."

"Time doesn't take care of everything. Love does."

"Love?"

She dusted her hands together, then sidestepped him as if he posed a threat. "I'm not saying we love her. We don't even know her, but if we're kind and gentle, she'll respond."

In a couple of steps, he moved in front of her, cutting off her retreat. "If I'm kinder, gentler, will you respond?"

Her uneasy gaze skittered away. "This isn't about us."

"Isn't it?" Matt's heart lurched then thundered in his chest, like a stampeding herd. Surely, she could hear the wild beat. "Really? Aren't we in need of affection, too?"

Those sky-blue eyes filled with disquiet. She flicked out her tongue and moistened her lips. "I'm afraid."

He took a step closer until the toe of his boots touched her skirt. "I would never hurt you. Never." Swallowing hard, he rested a hand on her arm. "My touch is gentle, nothing to fear."

The edgy look in her gaze eased. "I know," she said, then her eyelids drifted closed.

He lowered his head. Was inches away—

"Rosa said kittens are in here."

Matt and Hannah jumped apart like they'd been jolted by a cattle prod as Allie darted inside the barn, then raced past the cows watching her with large serene eyes.

"There they are!" Allie crouched across from the litter of striped kittens nestled beside their mother near the grain bin. Eyes barely open, the kittens mewed softly, jostling for position.

The next thing Matt knew Allie had claimed one of the litter as hers and named the kitten Tiger. "Can I keep it?"

Matt and Hannah's gazes met and they smiled. The kittens would help the little girl connect to a new place.

"The kitten needs to stay with his mama," Hannah said.

Matt squatted beside Allie. "You can visit every day."

Tears flooded Allie's eyes. "If Tiger didn't have a mommy, he'd be sad."

The child looked lost, dejected. A lump lodged in Matt's throat, but he had no idea what to do.

"Yes, he would. Now he'll have his mommy and you," Hannah said then opened her arms.

Allie stepped into the circle of those arms. "I can be Tiger's friend."

Hannah nodded. "And we can be your friends, too."

"Would my little friend like to see the horses?" Matt said.

"Yes!" Allie ran a gentle fingertip along the kitten's spine. "I'll play with you every day, Tiger, I promise."

With Allie tucked between them, Matt and Hannah walked toward the stable. The child flitted along beside them like a little pink bird. Yet inside she carried a heavy load.

They found Jake mucking out a stall. Between the roundup and losing Martin, they'd gotten behind with chores.

Jake leaned on the shovel. "Having fun, Allie?"

"Yes!" Her grin revealed a missing tooth. "I've come to see the horses."

Hannah bent to Allie's level. "I've got paperwork that needs my attention. I'll see you at supper, okay?"

"Okay," Allie said, then strolled along the stalls.

Matt turned to Jake. "How's Gertie getting along?"

"She's in pain, wearing a back brace. A widow from church is staying with her for now."

"Is her doc giving her anything for the pain?"

"Yep, but she says the upset stomach the medicine causes is worse than the pain."

"Sorry to hear that," Matt said, scanning the aisles for Allie. She was nowhere in sight. "Where did Allie go?"

A few frantic minutes later, Matt and Jake found the little girl climbing the gate to the pasture where seven bulls grazed.

His heart in his throat, Matt snatched her off the rail. A few minutes more and she could've been inside. Gotten herself killed. He hoisted the little girl to his shoulder. As he explained the importance of staying clear of the bulls, his cheek twitched. The minute he'd finished explaining the danger, she flapped her arms like a bird taking flight. Had she understood a word he'd said? Or even listened?

"I'm high," she crowed, then leaned down and peered over his head, smiling into his eyes.

As much as she'd scared him, he chuckled, unable to resist the little charmer.

Inside the stable, he swung her to her feet in front of Star's stall. "This is Star, Hannah's cow pony."

Allie gasped. "A cow has a pony?"

"No, that name means Star is skilled at moving cows."

"Where'd they move?"

With a glance at Jake, Matt nudged his hat back. Jake just grinned, was no help at all. "Ah, from one pasture to the next."

"But not to the bull's pasture," Allie said, eyes wide with alarm.

Apparently he'd gotten through to her after all. The tic in his cheek eased. "That's right. Not there."

"Can I get on?"

"Sure." Matt lifted Allie onto Star's back. She leaned over the horse's neck, burying her face in the mane. "I like her. Can I take a ride?"

Jake smiled. "Need some help?"

"If you'll lead Star around the paddock, Jake, I'll hold on to Allie."

From her perch on Star's back, the little sprite scowled down at him. "I won't fall off."

"Well, okay. I'll just walk beside you."

Matt held his breath as the threesome circled the enclosure, but Allie had no difficulty staying astride with her tight grip on Star's mane. "Want to help feed and water the horses?"

A smile lit her face. "Yes!"

Soon she was skipping along, carrying oats, toting buckets, slopping water on her dress and boots.

Goodness, Allie was one active, determined child. Strong, too.

By the time Rosa called them in to supper, Allie's face was smudged, her stockings had holes where the knees had been, her dress was filthy and had a rip in the sleeve.

And Allie's dark eyes carried a new spark.

That was good, wasn't it?

Still, one look at Allie's ruined dress and Hannah might not agree. Most likely would question his supervision.

He and Jake followed Allie as she skipped to the house. When had he felt more wrung out? Yet accomplished less?

Inside the kitchen, the aroma of chicken and noodles put a rumble in his stomach. The table was set. Dishes piled high. Ready for a hungry man.

Hannah blocked their progress toward the table, eyeing Allie's clothes. "What happened to you?"

Mute, hat in hand, Jake stared at Matt, as if Matt had deliberately destroyed the child's clothing.

Matt doffed his hat, and met Hannah's perplexed gaze. "She's...active," he said. His defense sounded weak, but what other reason could he give? "But she didn't get hurt. Not that she didn't try," he muttered.

Hannah's blue eyes twinkled with amusement. He had no idea why she found that funny, but at least she wasn't mad.

"Your ruined dress is my fault, Allie. I should have had you change clothes," Hannah said. "From now on, we'll remember not to wear your Sunday best when you're going out to play."

Play? Is that what Hannah called that frenzied race from one activity to another?

"Let me see those hands."

Allie held up hers, then frowned at Jake and Matt. "We're supposed to show our hands."

Matt held his up. Jake, too. Tarnation. The three of them looked like outlaws surrendering to the sheriff.

"Back outside. Wash up at the pump."

How had Hannah, in a matter of hours, managed to sound exactly like Matt's ma confronting her dirt-caked sons?

At the pump, they scrubbed up. With a shriek of laughter, Allie funneled the spray with her hands, shooting water at Matt and Jake, then stomped in the puddle, chortling.

From her behavior when she arrived, Matt had expected Allie to sit around morose and inconsolable. Perhaps time away from her elderly grandmother's quiet home felt like a holiday. He had no idea if the cookies or the kittens had changed Allie's attitude, but whatever had brought that smile to her face, he was mighty grateful.

Back inside, shiny-eyed with faces to match, Allie and Jake sat side by side. Matt joined Hannah across the table. Rosa took Martin's spot.

"Would you bless the food, Matt?" Hannah asked, her voice unsteady, no doubt missing her father saying grace.

Allie folded her hands and bowed her head, as they all did. Matt thanked God for the bounty before them and was about to say amen when something made him take a peek at the little girl.

Eyes dancing, she waggled her fingers at him.

A laugh scrambled up his throat and shot out as a strangled cough and a croaky, "Amen." Then he coughed again.

"You feeling okay, Matt?" Hannah asked.

"Feeling fine." He smiled across at Allie, sharing their secret.

She might be a handful, might exhaust him and risk her neck at every turn, but she added something this house needed badly. Laughter. A diversion from the sorrow of losing Martin, from the tension between him and Hannah.

He wasn't sure how he'd manage to work with that magpie's tendency to get into mischief. A ranch was a dangerous place. Surely, between Hannah, Jake, Rosa and him, they'd manage. Perhaps they needed a schedule. A schedule to make sure Allie was never on her own. Tonight, after Allie slept peacefully, he would suggest that very thing to Hannah.

Matt took a bite of chicken and noodles, his gaze roaming the table, the ragtag family gathered here. Four adults determined to give Allie a good summer. A safe summer.

Tonight Matt would share this first bedtime ritual. After Allie's long day, she'd surely be exhausted, eager for sleep.

Tomorrow, he'd put Allie to work mucking the barn. Garbed in suitable clothes, she'd expend some of her boundless energy.

Why, he might be getting the knack of this parenting thing.

Three hours later, Matt admitted he'd been an idiot. At bedtime, a new version of Allie appeared. A child determined not to sleep. She asked for more water, more stories, a snack for her, a snack for Ginger, as if a toy bear needed food.

At ten o'clock, Hannah declared the kitchen closed. "No more delays, Allie. It's late. You need your sleep."

Allie's face crumbled. She rolled to her stomach and sobbed into her pillow, her slender body shaking. "I…want my…grandma," she wailed between sobs.

He and Hannah exchanged a frantic look.

Tears flooding her eyes, Hannah scooped Allie up, cuddled her close, rocking back and forth. "Hush, sweet girl, don't cry. We'll take good care of you."

Matt sagged to the mattress, put his arm around Hannah who surely would be crying next. The three of them huddled there. Matt praying and cradling them in his arms with no idea what else to do.

The sobs subsided. Allie's breathing slowed, she slumped against Hannah.

"She's asleep," Hannah whispered, then tucked her into bed.

They walked into the hall, then looked back at the sleeping child. Peaceful and sweet.

Matt turned to Hannah. "That didn't go too badly."

She snorted. "I don't know how it could've gone worse."

"Tomorrow night will be easier." Or so he hoped. "You did a great job." He brushed his lips across her forehead.

As he turned to go to his room, she grabbed his hand. "Thanks for staying with me until she went to sleep."

"You said we were in this together and you were right. Sleep well," he said. "Unless you'd like me to tuck you in."

He shot Hannah a teasing grin. In the dim corridor, their eyes locked and held. The smile died on his lips. Heart racing like a horse nearing the finish line, he dropped his gaze to her mouth. He knew how full and soft her lips would feel beneath his. How sweet they'd taste.

Careful, Walker.

He might want to kiss her, hold her. But where would that lead? To the exact place it had in the past. To two people in the same house, yet worlds apart. He'd failed Amy. No matter how much he prayed, he couldn't seem to put that burden down. He wouldn't risk what he and Hannah had.

"I'll see you in the morning." Without a backward glance, he strode to his room.

Yet with Allie here, he couldn't run from the responsibility of helping care for the child. The cost of this growing longing for a real marriage was steep, a high price to pay. But, pay it he would as long as Hannah wanted him in her life. The day he knew she didn't, he'd set her free.

Hannah curled up in her bed, the pillow clutched in her arms, tears sliding down her face. She and Matt had been married for weeks. In that short span of time, they'd rounded up and sold cattle. They'd lost her father. They'd taken in a child in need of a temporary home.

All the work and grief and distractions didn't conceal the fact that their one-month anniversary had come and gone without fanfare. A sob escaped her throat. Nothing to celebrate about a loveless marriage. About the aching loneliness inside her.

As much as she tried to pretend otherwise, she was attracted to her husband. She admired Matt's strong grip on his faith. She admired his work ethic. She admired his commitment to this ranch. His commitment to her. Even as they tiptoed around each other, she knew he'd never forsake their bargain.

Yet underneath, she sensed Matt hid something. What, she didn't know. Whatever the reason, a barrier stood between them, a wall she wouldn't climb. She sighed. Why not be honest, at least with herself? Half of that barrier belonged to her.

When she'd proposed, she sought the freedom to keep the land and run the ranch. She'd feared Matt would try to take over, but he'd proved his trust in her by backing her up on the cattle sale. She had everything she wanted, or so she thought, but something was missing. Love was missing.

She'd lost her mother. She'd lost her father. No matter how lonely she felt, she didn't want to care about anyone that much again.

The kisses she and Matt had shared brought them closer, tethered them to one another with a stronger and stronger thread of connection. To risk love, knowing from experience she could lose it, would take courage. Courage she might find inside herself, if she believed Matt had gotten over Amy. Hannah couldn't risk loving a man who wouldn't love her back.

In the days ahead, she'd stay close to the house. Look

after Allie. Muck the stalls. Finish planting the garden. Keep so busy she wouldn't feel the hole in her heart.

A hole her mother and father left. A hole where love used to live. A hole Matt was unwilling to fill.

Chapter Fifteen

Matt couldn't take his eyes off Hannah as she scooped the last shovelful of manure from Star's stall and dumped it into the wheelbarrow. Even with splattered boots and britches, the smudge on her cheek, her braid swinging along her back, he found his wife captivating.

Determined to keep his mind on his work, not on his wife, he entered the empty stall, dropped a pitchfork of straw in the middle of the floor, then another and another. "Have at it, Allie," he said.

With a grin, Allie dragged a rake, spreading the straw around the floor. Donned in the same garb as Hannah, Allie's small hands swallowed up in too big gloves, the empty fingers sticking out at an angle and flapping as she moved, Allie looked cute as a bug's ear.

More importantly, she looked happy.

With her eyes on Allie, Hannah leaned against the wall, the proud smile on Hannah's face, the softness in her eyes evidence that she'd already taken the child into her heart.

He'd done the same. The last thing he'd expected. Or wanted. In September, Allie would return to Amarillo and leave a void he and Hannah could not fill. September was months away. No point in borrowing trouble.

Matt gripped the handles of the wheelbarrow and pushed it toward the garden plot south of the house. Weeks ago he'd plowed a small section that Rosa had planted with lettuce, cabbage, radishes and onions. The lettuce was up, the tops of the vegetables waved in the breeze. But Martin's illness had delayed planting the main garden.

A knot closed off Matt's throat. He missed those checker games, Martin's listening ear. But couldn't wish the man back. Not the way he'd suffered at the end.

Matt spread the load of manure onto the plowed red earth. Then he grabbed the spade propped against the gate and chopped the muck into the soil. As soon as he finished cultivating the garden, he'd hoe furrows and help Hannah and Allie plant sweet corn, beans, melon seeds.

Back in the barn, he pitched straw into another stall. As he straightened, he heard a giggle and turned. A clump of straw hit him in the face. Allie and Hannah, hands filled with ammunition, laughter rising from their lips, raced away.

Not to be bested, he scooped up a handful of straw. "You'll be sorry," he said and chased after them.

Eyes wide, they changed direction, darted around a post. He charged after them, grabbed Hannah by her throwing arm and rained down straw on her head. Shrieking, she yanked her arm out of his hands, stumbling as she did. He made a grab for her but off balance, they tumbled into the pile of fresh bedding.

Hannah's laughter echoed through the rafters, music to his soul. "You're not fast enough for me." He looked down at her nestled there in his arm.

"Maybe I wanted to get caught," she said, then her eyes grew wide, her cheeks flamed at the implication in her words.

"Hmm, that makes this all the more interesting." He

leaned on one elbow, smiling down at her, his face inches from hers.

"I…I merely meant I could outrace you if I'd wanted to."

Laughter burst out of him. "Yeah, and you can lift a trunk into a wagon bed, too."

Caught in the absurdity of her claim, Hannah grinned. Their gazes met and locked, the smile on her lips faded. He heard a soft sigh. Her indigo eyes, bluer than he'd ever seen them, softened with longing, then lowered to his lips.

With a whoop, Allie sprang toward them, her boots slipping on the straw. Matt freed his arms just as the little girl launched into the air. With both hands, he caught her in flight. She hung there midair, her eyes twinkling with mischief. Thunderation. If he'd been one second slower, she'd have conked her head on the boards.

With a sigh of contentment, oblivious to the risk she'd taken, Allie wiggled between them, then leaned pointed little elbows on Matt's chest. "You were going to kiss," she said, wrinkling her nose as if she found the notion disgusting.

No chance of kissing Hannah with this child around. One day Allie would understand and value the kiss between a man and woman. Assuming she lived that long.

Allie snaked out a hand and tossed straw in Matt's face. "I got you!"

He flicked the pieces away, then scooped the child under one arm and scrambled to his feet, offering Hannah a hand. "Ladies, we have work to do," he said, then put Allie down, giving her a stern look or trying to. "No time for games."

"Allie, remember this. Men don't like to lose."

Matt picked straw from his clothes and headed out the barn door to the sound of laughter. Hannah's laughter—

Allie joining in. He'd laughed at Hannah's claim she could outrace him, but apparently the last laugh was on him.

He chuckled. Nothing could make him happier than bringing joy to the two feisty females in his life. Well, perhaps one thing could. But, shared laughter was far safer than shared kisses.

Hannah leaned against the pen where the cows stood chewing cud. Instead of getting the milking done, what she'd come to do, she watched Allie pet the kittens. The contentment on the child's face no doubt mirrored her own.

Allie was filling that hole in Hannah's heart. The wonder of that notion slid through her. She inhaled sharply. How could she bear to lose that child when Gertie's back had healed and Allie returned to her grandmother?

Hannah tamped down the thought. She would enjoy these times, enjoy the fulfillment of nurturing a child.

Not that Hannah had ever considered motherhood. She'd spent most of her life resisting the typical roles of women, viewing household chores and frivolous pursuits as tedious and confining. The lure of the land, the excitement of a cattle drive, the fulfillment of seeing the ranch prosper gave her purpose.

But with Allie here, Hannah had seen that womanhood wasn't just fancy, confining clothes and dull domestic tasks. Womanhood could involve mothering a child, nurturing, protecting, teaching and loving a child, things mothers did every day.

She'd seen with Allie that motherhood was a high calling deserving of respect. Even menial tasks mothers performed were essential to a child's welfare. Those tasks might be tedious, as tedious as keeping financial records or keeping track of supplies or keeping the barns sanitary, but they were important.

The peeved look on Matt's face when Allie had unintentionally interrupted his kiss had made her smile. Then later, when he'd left the barn, a walking scarecrow, he'd triggered a fit of laughter. Laughter bubbled up again inside of her. She buried a smile in her arms, crossed atop her knees.

When had she had more fun? When had she wanted to open her heart more?

She dusted off her britches, grabbed the milk stool, then plopped down beside the cow, leaning her forehead against the cow's side. The first spray hit the pail with a ping.

Allie dashed over. "Why do cows make milk?"

"God made them for that purpose."

As the ranch was hers. Or did God want more for her? Was she afraid to examine the purpose He might have for her life?

The mother cat rubbed against her pant legs. "Will you get her bowl, Allie? Then play with the kittens until I'm finished."

Allie dashed off and returned with the dish, then wandered over to the kittens. Imagine, instant obedience. Perhaps Hannah was getting the knack of parenting.

The spray squirted into the dish, spraying the cat's head as she lapped up the milk with her pink tongue.

As Hannah milked, she hummed "Rock of Ages," Papa's favorite. Oh, how she missed him. His quiet strength. His steadfast love. His endless patience. She'd seen how much energy taking care of Allie required. Dealing with a tomboy daughter had surely taken a lot of effort. Hannah had been nine when Papa had taken over her care. With Rosa's help, but still, the burden fell to him. Never once had he made her feel like a nuisance.

Papa, I wish I could tell you how grateful I am for all you did for me. Your endless patience.

Patience was not Matt's or Hannah's strength, but they were showing improvement.

Finished milking the first cow, Hannah moved to the second.

A bloodcurdling scream froze her hand, raising goose bumps on her arms. She jerked to her feet. The cow stepped sideways as Hannah raced toward the sound. Her gaze darted to the kittens. No Allie. Where was Allie?

Chest heaving, Hannah sprinted toward the stable. "Allie!"

Inside the dim interior, her eyes took a moment to adjust. Then a movement in the straw, a moan.

"Allie!" She dashed to the spot, dropped to her knees beside the little girl, lying face down in the straw. "Allie, can you hear me?" Her shaking hands hovered over the child's head, her body. Dare she move her?

Allie lifted her head, shaking it as if dazed. "Oh, bright lights."

"What hurts?"

"My head."

"Can you turn over?"

She rolled onto her back. Her forehead was scraped, a lump already swelling.

"Can you see me?" Hannah said.

"Yeah."

A gust of air heaved out of Hannah. *Thank God.* She ran gentle fingers over the bump.

"Ouch."

"I'm sorry, Sweetie. Did you fall down?"

Allie pointed to the ladder that led up to the loft. "I fell off there."

Hannah gasped. "Off that ladder?"

"Yeah, I was at the top. I...I don't know what happened."

"It's okay. You're going to be fine." *Please God. Let her be fine.* "Tell me if this hurts." Hannah ran her hand over each arm and leg, over hands and fingers.

Tears spilled down her cheeks. "My whole self hurts."

The clatter of hooves. Matt led Thunder into the stable. "What the—?" He dropped the reins, ran toward them. "What happened? Is she hurt?"

With Matt there, Hannah's heartbeat slowed. He would know what to do. "She fell. Either off the ladder or from the loft."

Matt crouched on the other side of Allie, staring at the bump on her forehead. "You okay, Pumpkin?"

"I saw lights, like stars. Now I can see you."

"Nothing appears broken." Hannah didn't want to convey her fear to Allie so she tried to control her shaky voice and failed.

"Let's get her inside, get some ice on that bump." Matt slid his hands under Allie's torso and rose with her in his arms.

Hannah led Thunder into his stall, then hurried after them.

Allie's fall from that ladder had surely taken a year off Hannah's life. And had given her insight into Matt's cautious nature. All those times he'd warned Hannah against taking risks, he hadn't been trying to control her life, he'd merely wanted to protect her. Not that accidents wouldn't happen. Not that some risks weren't worth taking, but for the first time she understood her husband's vigilance.

In the kitchen, they gathered around Allie. Matt held cold compresses to the lump on her forehead and checked her pupils. Hannah swabbed her scrapes, thanking God that the child didn't appear seriously hurt.

"Can I have a cookie?" Allie asked.

"A cookie is good medicine," Hannah said.

Allie sat munching the treat, littering the tabletop with crumbs, looking happy, as if nothing had happened.

But something had happened. Something more than Allie's accident. She and Matt had shared their concern and affection for the child. Allie was bringing them closer. Something far riskier than any hazard on the ranch.

Matt met Hannah's gaze. "She'll be fine."

In that moment, Hannah knew she and Matt were on a collision course. The barrier between them was still solid and steep. When they hit that wall, someone was bound to get hurt.

Nothing held Allie's attention for long. To keep her in the house and quiet meant taking on a domestic chore Hannah avoided. Cooking.

At the kitchen table, Allie sat coloring on the back of a blank ledger sheet. The cow she'd drawn was pretty good for a seven-year-old city girl.

"Nice picture." Hannah smiled at Allie's upturned face. "Does our little artist want to make applesauce? I found wrinkly apples in the cellar."

Elbow on the table, chin in one hand, Allie shoved the curtain of hair out of her eyes with the other. "I want to make a pie."

"Ah, that sounds complicated." Especially with Rosa off visiting her cousin and with Hannah having no clue how to make a pie.

"I always make pies. Pies are easy. Pies make me happy."

For a moment, Hannah was tempted to say that pies made her very unhappy. But that sounded childish.

Allie pushed out of her chair and twirled across the floor. "Me and Grandma Gertie bake all the time. Mama likes pie best." Allie stopped her dance. "On Mama's birthday, me and Grandma maked a pie for her." Her face crumpled, tears welled in her eyes. "Mama never came."

Her own eyes stinging, Hannah looked away, unable to bear the pain of a mother's abandonment in Allie's eyes. Hannah had to ease that hurt. Fill that void Allie's mother left in her life. Even if that meant making a pie.

"When your mother comes back, Allie, you'll know exactly how to welcome her home. With a pie you made yourself. You'll make her proud."

The wide smile on Allie's face bloomed in Hannah's heart. She had to get this right. She couldn't let Allie down. "I saw a can of cherries in the cellar."

Somehow she and Allie would make a cherry pie. Within minutes she'd returned from the cellar with the cherries and found a recipe for basic pie crust in a cookbook. Flour, lard, a pinch of salt, water. Fewer ingredients meant fewer mistakes. Or so she hoped.

Once they'd washed their hands, they dumped the flour and salt into a bowl, spilling flour as they did. Lard came next.

"Grandma uses her fingers," Allie said, then dug right in.

No point in both of them getting into that mess.

"It's mixed," Allie said, then held up doughy fingers and wiggled them like attacking claws.

Hannah chuckled, then grabbed a spoon and scraped off what she could, then checked the recipe. "Water comes next. Cold water."

"Grandma Gertie puts ice in the water."

Hannah chipped a chunk of ice off the block in the icebox and dropped it into the small bowl Allie held. "Says to add three tablespoons of cold water or whatever is needed to make a soft dough."

As if Hannah knew what was meant by a soft dough. She belonged on horseback, not in front of a recipe.

But, Allie appeared fearless. She added the water, tossed the mixture with a fork. The peaceful look on the child's face was worth every knot in Hannah's stomach.

Allie declared the dough ready and divided the glob into two halves, patting them like a cherished pet. "Use the rolling pin to flatten the dough into circles," Allie said, then marched to the sink to wash her hands.

Hannah plopped one glob in the middle of the floury surface and shoved the rolling pin into the dough. The dough stuck to the wood like gummy glue.

"You forgot to flour it," Allie said.

To avoid Allie's shrewd eyes, Hannah kept her gaze on the pin as she scraped off the mess, then washed and dried the rolling pin.

With a fistful of flour, Allie dusted the rolling pin. "Now you can roll it," she said, handing the utensil to Hannah.

This time the dough didn't cling but took the shape of the pie plate.

"You're doing good." Allie shot her a big encouraging grin.

"Thank you," Hannah muttered, feeling more child than adult, then lifted the dough and dropped it into the plate. It landed off-center.

"You gotta pat it. Like you're tucking it into bed, Grandma always said."

"Oh…oh, okay. Well, why don't you do that?"

With a satisfied smile on her face, Allie patted the dough into the pan, then swiped her floury palms together, dispersing a cloud of white. She giggled. "I'm making it snow."

"Imagine that? In May. Have you ever seen snow, Allie?"

"No, but I've seen snow in storybooks. Snowmen, too," she said. "Grandma Gertie has."

Hannah opened the can of cherries then glanced at the recipe. "Let's see, we need—"

"You gotta do the other one." Allie pointed to a blob of dough. "One for the top. One for the bottom."

"Oh, of course."

The second attempt went more smoothly. With the crust made the worst part was over. The recipe said to mix the ingredients then cook the filling. Hannah added kindling to the embers in the firebox, then more wood. Soon the stovetop radiated heat.

With white palms leaving prints on everything she touched, Allie stood on a stool at the stove and dumped the juice into a saucepan, spattering dots of red on their clothes. "Whoops!"

"It'll wash." Or so Hannah hoped.

Hannah measured and added flour to thicken the juice, inadvertently puffing flour in Allie's face.

Allie coughed. "I can stir," she said, grabbing for the spoon. "How long does this take to cook?"

Hannah had no idea. "You look like a snowman, Allie."

With a mischievous look in her eyes, Allie lifted her hands and patted Hannah's cheeks. "You're a snowman, too," she said, giggling.

Hannah chuckled. "We sure have made a mess of this kitchen and of each other."

One glance around them, at the flour on the table, on the floor, the spatters of red on their clothes, and they both were giggling.

"Any chance I could get a cold glass of lemonade?"

Hannah and Allie turned toward the door. Matt stood

on the other side of the screen, taking in their silliness, a somber expression on face. Why, he looked unsettled, like an outsider observing a family he longed to be part of.

Matt doffed his hat and wiped the sweat off his face. He looked weary. Flushed from the heat. So handsome she couldn't move, couldn't tear her eyes away.

"Don't want to put you out," he said, then turned to go. "I'll get a drink at the pump."

His words heated Hannah's face and spurred her to action. "Wait!" She grabbed the pitcher from the icebox, poured him a glass, then strode to the door. "Don't you want to come in?"

"Too dirty to track inside."

With the lack of rain, the walk behind the plow had left him covered with a fine film of dust. But this was no snowman. The eyes he turned on her radiated heat. She swallowed hard, opened the door, handed him the lemonade, then stepped outside.

Matt drained the glass in one long gulp, his Adam's apple bobbing. "Working up the garden is thirsty work," he said, then swiped the back of his hand over his mouth.

One very appealing mouth. Hannah's went dry.

"You saved my life." He handed the empty glass back to her. "Thanks."

"You're welcome." And he was.

Stuck in the kitchen, making that pie, or trying to, she missed working with him. "Besides tilling the garden, have you had a busy day?"

"Fed the stock, the horses, rode out to check the herd. Calves are growing, getting friskier. The windmill's squeaking. First chance I get, I'll grease the gears."

The man worked tirelessly. "I should be helping you."

"No, you're looking after Allie. That's more important." He plopped his hat in place. "She doing okay?"

Allie raced to the door. "The pan's boiling over!"

"See you ladies later," Matt said, then marched off, a man on a mission. No doubt to put himself as far from them as he could get.

At the stove, Hannah slid the pan off to the side and stirred the mixture.

A frown on her face, Allie sighed. "I wanted to surprise Matt. Is it ruined?"

"We're lucky. Nothing stuck to the bottom and the filling's thickened," she said, then grabbed the cherries, ready to add them to the pan.

"I want to do it."

Hannah glanced at the red dotting her shirt. They'd be covered in red if Allie did it by herself. "Let's do it together."

They dumped the fruit into the pan, then Allie stirred it a few more times.

At the table, Hannah held the pan while Allie scrapped the filling into the crust, then lifted the top crust into place. She scrambled onto a chair, got a cup from the cupboard, then added a ladle of water. "Water sticks dough together. Grandma showed me." She plopped floury fingers into the water and moistened the inside edges of the crust. "Grandma said some bakers twist the edges, but she does it like this." Face solemn, Allie pressed the tines of a fork around the rim of the pie plate, careful not to miss a spot or overlap.

"Nice job, Allie." Hannah lifted the pie plate, ready to put it in the oven.

"Wait! We got to poke holes in the top or it'll explode."

"Explode?"

"Yep." The little girl poked the crust with her thumb. "Grandma told me that when Mama was a girl, one time she forgot the holes. Made a big mess in the oven."

With the four holes Allie had dug in the crust promising no explosion, Hannah popped the pie in the hot oven and checked the clock on the wall.

The messy kitchen wasn't quite as funny now. "Time to clean up," Hannah said.

"Ruth's calling me." An impish grin on her face, Allie raced off.

Hannah chuckled. Allie had outsmarted her. She should've helped, but Hannah had to admire her ingenuity. If not for the inconvenience she would cause Rosa, she'd want to get out of the chore, too.

Finally with the kitchen tidied, Hannah swiped a clean damp cloth over the smudges of flour and spatters on her shirtwaist. Why hadn't she thought to wear an apron? She'd change into the blue dress with sleeves to the elbow and a scooped neckline that would be cool in this heat.

Her breath caught. Her entire life all she ever wanted was to wear pants. She treasured the freedom of wearing pants, but was discovering she also liked feeling like a woman. Would she see approval of her appearance in Matt's eyes?

Chapter Sixteen

At noon, Matt slogged into the kitchen, hair wet from a dousing at the pump, the collar of his cotton shirt open at the neck, his sleeves rolled up, revealing tanned, muscled forearms.

The sight of him trapped the air in Hannah's lungs. Brawny, hardworking, all male, Matt dominated the kitchen. Everything else shriveled in importance.

Hannah's cheeks heated, and she felt conspicuous, out of her element. She stood frozen in place, wishing she'd donned pants.

His dark gaze traveled her blue dress from the scooped neck to the floor-length hem, then darted to her face. "You're prettier than a bushel of bluebonnets, Hannah. After working in the hot sun, looking at you in that dress—" he swallowed hard "—is refreshing."

She should've been out working with him, had no business in this kitchen. Had been more of a hindrance to Allie than a help. "Thank you, but I'm no debutante. I'm a rancher."

He tossed his Stetson on the hook. "I haven't forgotten," he said, his tone chilly, as if irked by the reminder.

Hannah pivoted toward the table where the pie sat in

the center. "Allie and I made a pie. Well, Allie did most of the work."

Allie bounced into the kitchen, waving the picture of the cow. Matt admired her drawing, then they gathered at the table with a plate of beef sandwiches Rosa had made before she'd left.

As they munched on sandwiches, Hannah couldn't take her eyes off Matt. How could he have this powerful hold on her?

As if avoiding her gaze, he leaned over and took a whiff of the pastry. "Can't think of the last time I had a piece of cherry pie."

Hannah cut Matt a large slice and a smaller one for her and Allie, then slid them on plates. The filling didn't run. The crust didn't fall apart. So far so good.

Not that she wanted to be a woman praised for her cooking. She'd done this to help Allie recapture happy times with her grandmother.

Matt dug his fork into the pie and took a large bite. His face scrunched up, one eyelid drooped low.

"What's wrong?"

He wiped his mouth with his napkin. "Nothing. I like cherry pie on the tart side."

"Tart?" Hannah took a bite, then spit it into her napkin. "Oh no! I must've forgotten the sugar."

Hannah sighed. This proved she wasn't cut out for the kitchen. As if she needed it.

"It's good—really," Matt said.

As if to verify his claim, he took another bite, much smaller than the first. This time he kept his face composed, though the effort must've cost him dearly. The cherry filling was sour enough to bring a pucker to a man-hating spinster.

She couldn't follow a simple recipe. She should've taken

the precaution of tasting the filling before putting it in the pie. "I can't cook."

"You can rope and deliver calves, drive cattle, handle the business end of the ranch. Makes a man wonder if he's needed," he muttered.

Why had his words stabbed at her: Hadn't he said what she'd wanted to hear—praise of her abilities on the ranch? But underneath she wanted a role no cowhand could step in and fill.

"It's easy to fix." Matt dumped a couple spoonfuls of sugar from the bowl on the table onto his slice.

Allie dumped sugar on her pie. "Look at me," she said then took a bite. The face she made had them all chuckling.

Not to be outdone, Hannah added sugar to her sliver, then took a bite. The tartness made her shiver and scrunch up her face.

Allie pointed at her, howling with laughter. "You look funny!"

Matt chucked Allie under the chin. "No funnier than you and I did."

Soon all three of them were trying to surpass one another's silly faces, winking eyes and shivering shoulders.

Hannah giggled, then met Matt's amused gaze. As they studied one another, the smile on his face faded. The intensity of his gaze bored into her. Something passed between them. Something personal. Meaningful.

"Can I have a cookie?" Allie asked.

Welcoming the interruption, Hannah took a breath, composing herself. She rose, put a plate of cookies on the table. "Rosa's cookies should get rid of that sour taste in your mouth."

Allie grabbed a cookie in each hand. "Cookies are almost as good as pie." Allie looked at Matt. "Hannah and me tried real hard, Matt. We wanted to surprise you."

"I know you did, Pumpkin. Thanks for going to all that trouble for me."

"It was fun." Her lips turned down. "Pie's no good without sugar."

Hannah scooped up all three plates and dumped the contents into the slop jar beneath the sink. Would the hogs reject her first attempt at baking?

To put distance between her and Matt, she cleared the table, swished soap in the dishpan and added boiling water from the teakettle.

Matt met her at the sink and laid a hand over hers. "It's okay, Hannah. Your skills aren't in the kitchen."

"I wanted this to work."

"Why?"

She shrugged then turned away.

"Tell me."

She pushed past him. How could she explain that by messing up that pie, she'd messed up the chance to connect with Allie's grief over her mother's abandonment? When Matt believed they'd made the pie for him?

He stepped closer. "You're avoiding me."

"Hardly."

"Thanks for making that pie for me." He leaned close and brushed his lips over hers. "My way of a thank you."

At his touch, she could barely stand, could barely think, barely breathe. "I don't cook for just anybody."

"That's good to hear."

"Only for tall, dark-eyed ranchers," she said as if the words had been pulled out of her.

"Could be a few of those around."

He stood inches away. Her fingertips slid through the hair at his nape. "With black curly hair?"

Why had she said that? What was wrong with her? This silly flirting wasn't who she was.

"Still might be a couple of those," he said, lowering his head, trapping the air in her lungs.

Losing herself in his eyes, she wobbled, then steadied herself with a hand on his chest. "With shoulders as wide as the great outdoors?"

Matt's eyes lit with something too personal. Too close. "After this," he said, his hand trailing her cheek, "sugarless pie will be a favorite of mine. Still, I have to wonder how you forgot the sugar."

"This fiasco was your fault."

"Mine?"

"When you came to the kitchen door asking for a drink, you and your rugged good looks and charm turned my brain into mush. And I forgot what I was doing."

A smile carved his face, softened every plane. "If it makes you feel any better, the rows in our garden aren't as straight as they ought to be."

He tugged her to him, his mouth claiming hers and reminding her exactly why this man kept her distracted. The feel of his lips on hers, the warmth of his arms, the strength of his grasp surrounded her, pulled her in.

Hannah circled her arms around his neck, and gave him all the sweetness the pie had been missing.

Then she pulled away. Matt had made her forget more than the sugar. He'd made her forget she wanted only one thing. To be taken seriously as a rancher.

Matt wore a dazed look on his face. "I, ah, almost forgot. I told Pa I'd ride over to the Circle W to lend him a hand," Matt said, then sped out the door.

As the screen door slapped shut behind him, Hannah collapsed into a chair and laid her head in her hands. Why not admit it? Matt Walker had a crazy power over her. She could no more have stopped her reaction to him, than she could stop a stampeding herd singlehandedly.

* * *

Matt could not blame his tension on the hard work, the scorching heat, the strong stench of mucking out Pa's stable. Those things were all part of ranch life in Texas.

He'd fled the Lazy P and been driven to the Circle W out of fear. Fear of what he and Hannah might cook up if he stayed with her. He'd come into the kitchen for dessert, and ended up with something far sweeter. Far more tempting, and oh, so bad for him.

Nothing wrong with kissing his wife. In an ordinary world. But their world was far from ordinary. Their marriage was a business arrangement. A solution for Hannah. A solution he'd agreed to, a solution he'd wanted, a solution he'd expected would protect his heart.

No more risk. No more heartache.

Trouble was, a kiss like that tempted a man to open up and let the risk and heartache in. He and Hannah teetered on the edge of a precipice. If they fell for each other, plunged over that sheer drop into a hotbed of emotion, they'd reap the consequences. Pay a terrible price.

He knew that from experience. No one could circle back and change the past. If he could, Matt had far worse regrets than that kiss. One long ago regret in particular.

Matt dumped a shovelful of manure into a wheelbarrow. If only he could discard all the rubbish inside him. The mistakes he'd made. He wouldn't think about all that now. He wouldn't. God had forgiven him. If only he could forgive himself.

The task of making certain he didn't let down another wife was his. And his alone.

To make matters worse, his plan to help his father, perhaps mend the discord between them, had backfired, adding another knot in his stomach. He couldn't blame the sour cherry pie or even his regret at kissing Hannah for this knot.

No, his problem stood across from him, leaning on his shovel, bossing him around. As only his father could do.

Matt lifted another shovelful out of the stall and into the wheelbarrow. "I'm doing the best I can, Pa." His arms ached, his back hurt, but the disquiet from earlier brimmed in his chest. "The best I can here, and at home."

"This family needs you." Robert raked straw over the stall beside him. "And you're over there—"

"With my wife. Helping her run her ranch."

Robert harrumphed. "Exactly. *Her* ranch. A man doesn't let a woman tell him what's his and what isn't. You ask me, your place is here. One day, you'll inherit this ranch."

The knot tightened. If Matt helped Hannah, he'd let Pa down. If he helped Pa, he'd let Hannah down. Why was his father putting him in this position?

Matt shoved his hat back and scrubbed the sweat from his brow with the back of his gloved hand. His gaze wandered out the stable door to the paddock beyond where the horses grazed, the peace of the scene in sharp contrast to the tension in the air.

"You should stay and run this ranch. The Circle W is your legacy, not the Lazy P."

"Pa, I can't live here. I'm married." Matt didn't understand what went on inside Pa's head, but he knew what needed saying. "But even if I could, your idea wouldn't work."

"Why not? Hannah can sell the Lazy P and the two of you could move in here."

"If I did, you wouldn't want me to run the ranch. You'd be trying to run me. I'm twenty-five, yet you're holding me back, keeping me from being the man you are."

"You're always over at that ranch," Pa said, flinging a

hand in the direction of the Lazy P, ignoring Matt's point. "Even before you married Hannah, you were there, every day."

"Martin was ill, Pa. He needed my help—"

"I needed your help!" Robert's voice vibrated the timbers of the stalls. He released a blast of breath. "Just go. You want to be there, not here, so go."

The frustration bottled up inside Matt flared. For a second, he considered doing that very thing. Then he looked over at his father. What he saw in Robert's face wasn't anger—

What he saw was hurt.

"Pa, I'm sorry. I never meant to hurt you by helping Martin."

"You didn't hurt me." But the furious way Robert raked at the straw told another story.

"Everything I know I've learned from you." Matt set the shovel aside. "I value your wisdom. I value your experience. I value your work ethic. But you won't accept that I'm capable, can manage on my own."

"Can't say you've done a good job managing everything in your life."

The words slammed into him, a barely veiled accusation he couldn't deny. He'd failed Amy. Pa knew that as well as Matt. Matt turned away, plunged the shovel through the debris, every muscle coiled. Why had he tried to talk to his father?

A hand on Matt's back slowed his frenzied shoveling. "I'm sorry, son. That was cruel." Tears welled in his eyes. "Amy's unhappiness wasn't your fault."

Matt pivoted to his father. "Of course it was!"

He took a steadying breath, determined to avoid talking about his first marriage and get to the trouble between him and his father. "I've made mistakes. But, this is my life you're trying to lead." He sighed. "Pa, you used to allow me to try my own way, and yes, sometimes to fail. That freedom is how men are made. You taught me that."

"This is my ranch. Things *should* run my way."

"Your way isn't working. We need to find a new way. *God's* way."

As if his knees had gone out from under him, Pa sank onto a bale of straw. "Surely God doesn't disapprove of a father expecting his son to claim his birthright."

"Cal and I won't turn our backs on the Circle W. We love this ranch. We grew up here. But we're both married. Married to women with ranches. But if you'd hand over some of the control, you might be surprised how much we'd choose to come to you for advice."

"Like you did Martin." Eyes damp, Pa glanced up at him.

"I'm sorry. I…" How could he explain his relationship with Martin without adding bricks to the wall between them?

"Martin was a good guy." With a sigh, Pa stood, faced Matt, defeat in his eyes and something else, too. An apology. "Truth is, overseeing you and Cal is wearing me out. You're right, I need to let go of the reins. Still, old habits die hard," he said. "I'll try to stop telling you boys what to do and how to do it."

For years Matt had believed the way to honor his father was by keeping his mouth shut, but his pent-up frustration had made him avoid Pa. That distance had hurt his father, especially when Matt had turned to Martin to fill Pa's shoes.

"What do you say? Want to play a game of checkers one evening?" Matt said.

"If you think you're man enough to beat me, come

ahead." No matter what Pa had said, the wide grin on Pa's face revealed his pleasure.

"I don't mind losing. As long as I get to play the game."

Matt and his father had taken the first step toward reconciliation. Not all that long ago, Matt wouldn't have believed they could spend a pleasant evening together.

Lord, help Pa and me heal our relationship.

He suspected progress between them would be two steps forward and one back. Whatever happened, Matt intended to keep taking steps in the right direction, here and at the Lazy P.

The trouble was, how would he know where those steps would lead him?

Chapter Seventeen

Hannah stepped into Bliss Christian Church, seeking peace for the havoc of her life. Every time she thought she had a handle on her existence, that peace was derailed faster than a train on poorly laid tracks.

With Allie's hand in hers and Matt at her side, Hannah entered the sanctuary, steeling herself for the first Sunday she'd attended services since Papa's funeral. To be here, where Papa's casket had sat, where Pastor Cummings had preached his funeral, took every bit of her willpower.

She and Matt introduced Allie to everyone they met, distracting Hannah from her sad memories. The parishioners greeted them warmly with hugs and smiles. Hannah had missed her church family, this quiet building, the stained glass window splashing a rainbow of color on the white walls.

Here in God's house, she'd find peace and strength. Here with Matt and Allie, she'd worship through prayer and hymns. And avoid the space at the end of their pew where Papa had always sat.

Leah stepped up to them, an expectant smile on her face. "Who is this sweet little girl?"

"Leah, this is Allie Solaro, Jake Hardy's great-niece. She's staying with us for the summer."

"Hi, Allie." Leah motioned to her parents ushering her well-groomed siblings into a pew, a pew they all but filled. "Now that school's out my brothers and sisters would enjoy a new playmate. Ask Hannah to bring you for a visit."

"Can we, Hannah?"

Why hadn't she thought Allie would want to play with children? She'd take the time to bring Allie to town this very week. "We'd love to come."

A visit would give Hannah a good opportunity to ask Leah's advice on handling Allie's ploys to delay bedtime. She and Matt might be too easy on the child, but they didn't want to risk making her homesick for her grandmother.

Hannah, Matt and Allie settled into their pew near the front. Allie craned her neck to gawk at the Montgomery family two rows behind them. Hannah named the children for Allie and gave their ages.

In the pew behind the Montgomerys sat a stranger, unusual in this town. A lovely woman, her dark hair swept up beneath a wide-brimmed hat, she was staring at Hannah. Or was it Matt? Hannah smiled at her. The woman smiled back. Upon closer inspection, she looked vaguely familiar, yet Hannah couldn't place her.

Bertram Bailey shot to his feet, tugged on his waistcoat and rattled off a page number in the hymnal. On Sundays, he led singing with the same energy he ran his store. Soon voices blended with the piano, filling the sanctuary with harmonious tribute to God.

At the conclusion of the last song, Pastor Cummings stood behind the pulpit. He smiled down at her, as if welcoming her back, then opened his Bible. "Today, I'm reading from the Book of James, Chapter Three." The words the pastor read warned believers to tame their tongues. He reminded them that gossip, lies and curses all came out of the same mouths as mercy, truths and blessings. "But the tongue can no man tame; it is an unruly evil, full of deadly poison."

Many chattered about other people's comings and goings in Bliss, but thankfully Hannah hadn't known anyone to try to ruin reputations or to deceive.

After the closing prayer the congregation rose, chatting as they headed toward Pastor Cummings shaking hands at the door.

The dark-haired stranger stepped into the aisle. Parishioners greeted her as they flowed past. She nodded and smiled, but had her eyes fixed on Matt.

As they reached her, the woman beamed. "Matthew, how good to see you."

Hannah glanced at her husband's face. His blank expression slowly transformed into a smile. "Julia? Julia Phillips?"

"You remembered," she said.

The quiet joy in her tone, as if his remembering mattered, sent a shiver down Hannah's spine. Who was this woman?

Matt cocked his head. "I haven't seen you in, goodness, six, seven years."

"Seven."

"What brings you back to town?"

Her expression flooded with sympathy as she rested a gloved hand on Matt's sleeve. "I heard about Amy." Her gaze landed on Hannah, then slid back to Matt. "I'm sorry for your loss."

"Thank you. Ah, Amy's been gone four years."

"Well, I just heard."

Matt glanced at Hannah. "Oh, forgive me. Julia, this

is my wife, Hannah. And this is Allie," he said motioning to the child.

"Your wife," Miss Phillips said blankly, as if she couldn't understand the term. "I didn't realize you'd remarried."

"We haven't been married long."

Miss Phillip's gaze landed on Allie. "She isn't your daughter?"

"Allie's the great-niece of a friend. We're enjoying her stay at the ranch."

"Oh, how nice." A smile on her lips, Miss Phillips leaned down, peered into Allie's eyes. "Aren't you the prettiest little girl? Why, you're the age of…" Her voice trailed off, then she straightened. "Matthew, I'm sure I'll see you around town. I'm glad to meet you, Hannah," she said, but her gaze remained on Allie.

"You're staying in Bliss?" Matt said.

She turned toward him. "Yes, I work at the Calico Café and rent a room overhead."

Hands fluttering like the plumes on her hat, Mrs. Cummings, the pastor's jovial wife, darted to them, then drew Miss Phillips into a one-armed hug. "In town only a week, and already Julia has volunteered to assist with Sunday school." She tugged the young woman against her ample frame. "You've blessed me more than I can say."

The pastor's wife gushed on to Miss Phillips as Hannah, Matt and Allie moved up the aisle, and spoke to the preacher and others. Matt and Allie headed for the buggy. Delayed by a member of the congregation who'd been ill when Papa died and wanted to offer his condolences, Hannah trailed behind.

She passed the newcomer. "Nice to meet you, Miss Phillips."

Miss Phillips bent close as if to give Hannah a friendly

embrace. "I didn't expect you," she said in a harsh whisper against Hannah's cheek. "That complicates things."

Goose bumps rose on Hannah's arms. Before Hannah could react, the woman sashayed off. But the chill remained. Hannah might not understand what Miss Phillips meant, but she understood a threat when she heard it. The peace she'd sought and found in worship had been destroyed.

On the way to the ranch, Hannah ran the encounter with Julia Phillips through her mind. The way she'd focused on Matt and Allie, all but eating them up with her eyes. That puzzling remark she'd made in private.

"Matt, how do you know Julia Phillips?"

"We go way back. Went to high school together."

"She was a friend of Amy's?"

The question seemed to puzzle him. "I wouldn't say a friend. More like a classmate." He glanced at Allie sitting between them. "I'll explain. Later."

Allie crossed her arms, a scowl on her face. "Kids never get to hear the good stuff."

Matt tugged the ribbon on Allie's hair. "Is that right?" Over Allie's head, he and Hannah shared a smile. "Well, does this rate as good stuff? I'd like to take you, Jake and Hannah fishing this evening."

"Whoopee! I've never been fishing." The smile back in place, Allie chattered away.

Hannah didn't hear a word the little girl said. Like a stuck phonograph, Miss Phillips' words kept running through her mind. The woman spoke in riddles.

During a break in the conversation, Hannah said, "Any idea why Miss Phillips moved back to Bliss? Surely not to offer condolences."

"I'm certain something else brought her here."

"Like what?"

He shrugged. "Hard to say. A job for one."

Pastor Cummings's sermon popped into Hannah's mind. If she wasn't careful, she'd be slandering a woman she'd just met.

But one thing she knew, she'd go along when Matt made his next trip to town.

At Matt's invitation to go fishing, Jake had agreed, returning a few minutes later with a bait bucket, tackle box and pole. "Ain't put a hook in the water in ages."

On the way to the creek, Jake rode in the lead, Hannah followed on Star and Matt with Allie perched in front of him brought up the rear.

The beauty of the Texas landscape stretched before him as far as his eye could see. Bluebonnets and Indian paintbrush dotted the countryside. Overhead, filmy clouds brushed across the blue sky. A mockingbird sang on a fence post nearby. Parrish cattle grazed in the pasture. A few lifted their large heads to stare as they passed, then returned to their mindless munching.

Near the fence, mustang grapevines grew over scrubby bushes. In midsummer he'd return to pick the small ripe black-skinned grapes Ma made into jam. No, he'd pick the grapes for his wife, not his mother, though most likely Rosa would be the one making the jam. He grinned. A good thing, if Hannah's attempt at a pie was any indication.

At the pecan grove, they hitched the horses to low limbs, then carrying fishing equipment and a bag of cookies, they walked to the stream. Allie dipped and skipped along, a human bobber if Matt ever saw one.

Alongside the creek, they found a comfy spot. Jake set down his gear, then baited Allie's hook. With the line swinging between them, he handed her the wooden pole he'd whittled from a tree limb years before.

"Be careful of that hook, Allie girl. It's sharp."

Matt knelt beside her. "If the bobber goes under, that means you've got a bite." He showed her how to grip the pole. "If you do, jerk back on the pole like this," he said, demonstrating the technique. "That'll set the hook in the fish's mouth."

"Does the hook hurt the fish?" Brows furrowed, Allie gnawed on a fingertip.

With a sweep of his hand, Matt turned to Jake. About time Jake took his uncle role.

"Don't rightly know," Jake muttered. "Reckon not much. They survive it just fine."

What Jake didn't say—any fish they caught would turn up in the frying pan.

With Matt on one side, Jake on the other, Allie settled on her haunches, waiting for a strike.

"Largest fish I ever caught was nineteen inches," Matt said. "Still remember that day."

"Largest fish I ever caught would've fed a bunkhouse full of drovers," Jake said, eyes on the bobber.

Hannah arched a brow. "Aren't you exaggerating a bit?"

"Been a lot of years since I wet a line. Memory's bound to fail a feller."

Matt chuckled. "Doesn't matter, Allie. Big or small, they all taste good."

The bobber dipped. "I got a fish!" Allie scrambled to her feet as the bobber moved across the water. "Help me!"

"Pull up on the pole, Allie, like Matt showed you," Jake said. "That's the way."

But whatever was on the other end of the line had some fight in him. Jake grabbed hold and helped his great-niece pull in an eight-inch bass that flopped on the creek bank.

"He's big!" Allie's eyes shone as she reached down to touch the scales, peer into the round eyes.

Matt patted her head. "Sure is."

Jake clutched the wiggling fish and removed the hook from its mouth, then strung the bass on a line tethered at the water's edge.

Hannah put an arm around Allie's shoulders. "You did it, Allie. You caught your first fish."

"Uncle Jake helped." She sobered. "Next time, I want to do it by myself."

Matt chucked Allie under the chin. "Nothing wrong with getting some help."

He sat beside Hannah on the grass. "Don't know if you're rubbing off on Allie or if that stubborn independence of hers comes naturally," he said with a chuckle.

"Either way, she's just fine."

"Yes, she is." Their eyes met, Hannah's warm, proud almost as if she were Allie's mom. Odd how quickly that child had become part of their life.

"Uncle Jake," Allie said. "Is Grandma going to die?"

In the process of putting a worm on the hook, Jake dropped the wiggly bait. "Gertie's doing fine, Allie."

"She's old."

"Well, that's true."

"You are, too. What if Mama doesn't come back? Where will I live if you and Grandma die?"

"No point worrying about what could be a long ways off. Why, I'm too stubborn to die anytime soon."

Allie didn't look convinced.

Matt's throat knotted, his gaze locked with Hannah's. He read the question in hers, the same question in his. At his nod, Hannah nodded, too. They could no more turn away from Allie, than they could forsake this ranch.

"You can live here, Allie," Matt said.

"You'll always have a home with Matt and me."

The little girl turned to them, a smile as wide as the

whole outdoors. "I can live here? Even if Uncle Jake doesn't?"

"We feel like we're your family, too."

"You're a fortunate little girl to have two homes and lots of folks who care about you," Jake said, swiping at his eyes.

"Mama loves me, too," Allie said, in a tone that forbade anyone to disagree.

"She's your mama," Jake said. "How could she not?"

Matt hadn't lost a parent, not to death or desertion, but he knew the pain of a severed relationship. He suspected Hannah had felt as abandoned as Allie when Melanie Parrish had died.

He tucked Hannah close. "You'll always have me, too," he said.

She glanced away, as if their marriage of convenience didn't bring her comfort. Did she feel as he had with his father until recently, that their relationship of father and son was in name only? That possibility bothered him. Yet they were managing, walking that line, doing the best they could.

As Jake dug into the bait bucket in search of another worm, Matt rose and took Hannah's hand. "We'll watch from over here," he called, then led Hannah to a felled log near the water. "This should be far enough away we can't be overheard."

"You're going to tell me about Julia."

"Yes." He sighed. "It's not a pretty story. Julia got pregnant out of wedlock. Caused quite a stir in town."

"Who was the father?"

"Don't know. I suspect he left town and she didn't see the point in naming him. Some folks treated her badly. You know, walked passed her, didn't speak, as if she wasn't there. Her parents weren't much better. Amy and I would talk to her. Ask how she was feeling, stuff like that."

"She was appreciative."

"Yes. Not that we spent much time with her. She dropped out of school, but I'd see her in town now and again when I came for church, for school. To visit Amy."

At the mention of Amy's name, Hannah's eyes clouded. He suspected Hannah believed he still loved his wife. The truth would shock her.

She frowned. "What happened to her baby? Did she put it up for adoption?"

"The baby died a couple hours after birth."

"Oh, no."

"Losing that baby hit Julia hard. She was always crying. Her family moved away not long afterward, taking her with them. Said they wanted to start over. As I recall, they left town about a week before Amy and I got married."

"She must've been sorry to miss the ceremony."

Matt shrugged. "I don't think so. She avoided all the wedding talk. Not easy, when the wedding was Amy's prime topic of conversation. Probably reminded Julia of all she'd lost."

"That's sad. I feel sorry for her. But, she said the oddest thing to me at church."

"What?"

"She said, 'I didn't expect you. That complicates things.' Almost like she believed I interfered with her plan to have you."

He shook his head. "That's crazy talk. Are you sure you heard her right? The Julia I knew was never mean or conniving."

"I heard her right."

"Well, no telling what she meant. Hope she can find some happiness here. Reckon with a town named Bliss, she should."

Not that he'd found any truth to the town's claim.

Still, across the way, Allie and Jake were having fun, no doubt reassured by the promise of a home for Allie. He and his pa were moving along the trail—perhaps a bumpy trail—toward accord. He and Hannah shared the goals on the ranch and affection for Allie. The future looked good.

Julia might be odd, but she wouldn't bring them harm.

Chapter Eighteen

On Monday morning, Hannah pulled up in front of the Montgomery house, then wound the reins around the hitching post. She'd promised Allie a visit with Leah's siblings. Allie was practically popping out of her skin with excitement. She clambered off the buggy seat, her upper lip beaded with perspiration, a smile wide on her face. Hannah welcomed a day away from responsibilities at the ranch, too.

Yet uncertainties niggled inside her. What if some section of barbed wire didn't hold? Or the windmill broke down? Or they didn't get the rain they desperately needed?

She tamped down all the qualms running through her mind, grabbed a handkerchief and patted her damp face. Ten o'clock and already the heat rolled in waves that took her breath away. The black buttoned-up mourning dress stuck to her skin and drew the sun's rays.

"Hello!" Leah motioned from the porch. "I've got lemonade waiting."

Within minutes, the five children downed their cold drinks, then scampered around the shady yard in a game of hide-and-seek, oblivious to the sweltering temperature.

On the porch, Hannah removed her hat, then lolled in

the wicker rocker, sipping from a tall glass, totally at ease as she and Leah watched the children and talked about the weather.

"So." Leah arched a brow, her eyes twinkling. "How's married life?"

Heat that had nothing to do with the temperature flooded her cheeks. Why hadn't she thought to bring her fan? "Uh, fine."

Leah chuckled. "That blush on your face tells me your marriage is better than fine. I'd say you're a happily married woman, Hannah Walker. Not that I expected anything else with that man you married." Leah grinned. "Wouldn't surprise me if you announced you're expecting."

Hannah choked on the lemonade she'd swallowed, then went into a fit of coughing.

"You okay?"

"Fine." Leah would faint dead away if she knew Matt and Hannah didn't share a room. Hadn't shared more than a few kisses.

Leah propped her chin in her hands. "Tell me. What's it like to be Mrs. Matt Walker? What's he like?"

"He's kind and ah, gentle."

Leah nodded once, twice, obviously wanting more.

"And, well...funny. He makes me feel safe. Special."

"Spoken like a woman in love." Leah sighed, then her smile faded. "I was afraid losing your father would make things difficult for you both."

"Matt's been very considerate." She'd appreciated the care he'd taken with her, the sympathy he'd extended. "He mourns Papa, too."

"He sounds wonderful."

Though the talk about wedded bliss had Hannah as edgy as an untamed horse being broken to saddle, she recalled the straggly bluebonnets Matt had brought her as a peace offering.

The way he'd tugged her to him after Papa died, insisting it was all right to cry.

His attempt to sweeten the mess she'd made of her first pie.

He'd perceived her needs and gave generously of himself, trying to meet them; unlike some men she'd witnessed who were long on orders and short on tenderness.

"I envy you, Hannah. No one in this town comes close to being suitable." She sighed. "I want what you have. A husband who makes me feel special."

Special.

Matt did make Hannah feel special, but always with the nagging reminder that they had married for business, not for love. Matt had made it clear he'd never love again.

That was fine. Just fine. She took a sip of lemonade, but the drink soured on her tongue.

"What about Zack?" she said, directing the conversation back to Leah.

Leah's lips turned down. "He's written me only twice. He came to Bliss for your wedding and your father's funeral, but never to see me." She sighed. "I felt a spark between us, but obviously that spark fizzled."

"His law practice may keep him too busy to come."

"Maybe. But, if you care for someone, nothing keeps you apart."

Hannah slid two fingers down her glass, wiping away the moisture in their path. How could she and Matt spend day after day together, as close as these two fingers, yet still be so far apart. Separated by something Hannah couldn't quite name.

Well, she no longer clung to the silly schoolgirl fantasy, but wouldn't ruin Leah's expectations for marriage.

"Anyway, let's talk about something else," Leah said. "Something fun like the kids. How's temporary motherhood?"

"Allie's a great little girl, but she resists bedtime. Most nights it takes us an hour or more to get her to settle down."

Leah chuckled. "Lots of children use one excuse after another to delay bedtime."

"You don't think anything's wrong? The first night she cried for her grandmother. Maybe she's afraid. Or feels deserted by her family."

"If she's not still upset, crying or having nightmares, I suspect she's got you and Matt wrapped around her pinkie," Leah said, wagging her little finger. "Have you tried giving her a glass of water, leaving on a kerosene night-light, then just leaving the room?"

"She clings to us for one more story, one more drink, one more hug."

"This is what we do with my brothers and sisters. After one story, one drink, one kiss, we say 'sleep tight' then leave. If Allie calls, ignore her. If she comes out, take her back to bed. Use a firm tone. Refuse to let her run the household."

After Hannah's mother died, Papa had stayed with her at bedtime until she'd fallen asleep. Was it cruel to expect more of Allie? To expect her to sleep in a strange house? Without her family?

"Thanks for the suggestions," Hannah said, then rose and hugged her friend.

"Yeah, all this wisdom about raising kids, yet I can't find a man who wants to spend his life with me and give me some."

"You will. You're pretty, smart, feminine as they come. And only nineteen." She clapped her hands together. "Oh, why don't you invite Zack to the Fourth of July picnic? It's the perfect occasion to see if there's still a spark."

Leah's face brightened. "You know, Hannah Walker, you may not know much about children, but you're shrewd about matters of the heart."

Hannah ran a finger around the high neck of her collar. If Leah realized the absurdity of her claim, she'd be aghast. "We'd better be going." She settled her straw hat in place, then slid her hatpin in the crown. "I promised Allie dinner at the café."

She called Allie's name, but getting the little girl to leave her new friends and into the buggy took ten minutes.

Leah leaned close to Hannah. "Yep, she has you wrapped tight. Nothing wrong with that, as long as she doesn't cut off your circulation. If you get my meaning," she said with a wink.

"What?"

Leah chuckled. "You're hopeless. By cut off your circulation, I mean with Matt, your time together. Don't let Allie keep you two apart."

If anything Allie brought them together when Hannah knew full well keeping them apart was a good thing. Keeping them from more of those confusing kisses. But Hannah merely gave Leah a nod, untied the reins, about to climb in the buggy.

Matt rode up on Thunder. "Hi, ladies." He tipped his hat to Leah, standing off to the side, watching their every move. Then swung down and strode toward the buggy. "You having fun, Allie?"

The smile on Allie's face said she was delighted to see him. Exactly what Leah would expect from Hannah, especially after everything she'd told Leah earlier. She would have to act lovey-dovey. A part she'd played before.

"Hi, Sweetheart," Hannah cooed, gazing at him with what she hoped were adoring eyes.

At her welcome, Matt jerked his head, ever so slightly, then gave a big smile and her arm a gentle squeeze. "Hello, wife."

"What a nice surprise. I didn't expect to see you in town."

"I promised Pastor Cummings I'd fix the railing on the church steps this afternoon. On my way through town, Martin's lawyer called to me. Wants you to stop in and sign a paper before you leave today."

"Thanks for bringing me the message."

"I'll see you at home," he said, his tone eager.

And grinding on every one of Hannah's nerves. "Do you want to join Allie and me for dinner at the café?"

"No time. You two have fun." He leaned down and kissed her cheek, staring into her eyes. "Don't stay away too long."

In a few strides, he swung into the saddle, tipped his hat to Leah, then rode off.

A dreamy look on her face, a sigh on her lips, Leah clasped her hands in front of her bosom. "Oh, you are the luckiest woman alive."

"I am." Hannah gave her brightest smile, then climbed into the buggy and flicked the reins.

Lucky hardly described her life. She'd come to town to give Allie friends to play with and forget her duties at the ranch. Forget Matt. Or try to. Instead his interruption had forced her into performing the second act in a three-act play. When would the curtain go down and expose the real Walker marriage?

On the square, the bench sitters were doing an admirable job of keeping their fingers on the town's pulse. Hannah ushered Allie to the gentlemen and introduced her.

"Howdy-do, young lady," Mr. Cooper said. "Nice to meet ya."

"Thank you."

"Ain't it a hot one for May? Hot enough to wither a fence post."

Mr. Brand nodded. "'Cept for our lips a'flapping, there ain't a puff of breeze."

Mr. Seller turned speculative eyes on Hannah. "Heard you was running the ranch yerself. One of your peeved cowpokes said he and yer foreman quit afore they'd work for a woman."

Mr. Cooper nodded. "Reckon ya got Matt to see everything gits done."

As if Hannah were merely a figurehead with no involvement in the operation of the ranch. She wouldn't grace the comment with a response. "We're off to the café."

"Git yerself a piece of the pecan pie. Nothin' better in that diner," Mr. Brand said. "Well, 'cept Miss Phillips. She's a real looker."

Hannah ushered Allie toward the Calico Café, steeling herself for an encounter with Julia. Inside she glimpsed the waitress out of the corner of her eye, and saw when Julia fixed her eyes on Allie.

"Come on, Allie. Let's take a table by the window," Hannah said, steering her across the room and into a seat. "Oh, look, at the pretty posies on the table. I love flowers, don't you?"

"Well, hello. Welcome to the Calico Café." Julia held out menus. "Here's one for you, Sweetie Pie."

"Hi." Allie took the menu in her hand. "I remember you."

"I could never forget *you*." Julia smiled down at Allie, who smiled right back. "Why, your smile is brighter than a sunbeam in summer."

Allie giggled, tucking her hair behind her ear, obviously delighted by the attention.

They ordered drinks. "Allie, did you look at the menu? See what you want?" Hannah said.

"Be right back for your order." Julia patted Allie on the head.

With Julia gone, Hannah folded her arms on the table and leaned toward Allie. "Did you have fun with the Montgomery children?"

"We played hide-and-seek. Abe's nice. He saw me hiding behind a bush, but found me last." She giggled. "Anna's the boss of everybody, but she let me pick the first game." Allie inhaled. "Pete's speedy, runs like the wind." Her brow furrowed. "Susie's a crybaby. She's only six." Allie puffed out her chest as if a year made her far older. "Leah's pretty, but not as fun cause she's a grown-up."

After only a couple of hours in their company, Allie's descriptions were both accurate and amusing. "So grownups aren't much fun, huh?"

Julia returned with Allie's milk and Hannah's ice water. She plunked Hannah's drink in front of her, then bent toward Allie. "Here you go, Sweetie. Careful not to spill on your pretty dress."

"Thank you."

Julia crouched beside Allie, bringing herself to the child's level. "Aren't you a polite little girl. What grade are you in school?"

"Second," Allie said. "I can read good. Add and subtract."

"I loved to read when I was your age. What are your favorite stories?"

"I like books about animals." Allie's face lit. "We've got baby kittens at the ranch."

Hannah cleared her throat. "We probably should order." But Julia ignored the not so subtle hint.

"Oh, how sweet. What do the kittens look like?"

"Like tigers, only littler."

"Have you given them names?"

"I tried, but I keep getting them mixed up." Allie grinned. "So I call all of them Tiger."

"Aren't you smart. You won't get the name wrong."

Giggling, Allie leaned on her elbows, gazing up at Julia, obviously taken with the interloper. Hannah had looked forward to having a meal with only the two of them, expecting the outing would give her and Allie a chance to bond.

Instead Julia had commandeered the table the way a pirate seized a ship at sea, making Hannah the outsider. Or trying to.

"Do you have a special doll?" Julia asked.

"I like Ruth best. She's Hannah's doll. She sleeps with me cause she doesn't have a bed."

Hannah set her menu aside. "I'd like the special."

Julia didn't glance her way. "When I was little I loved dolls," she said. "Especially with open and close eyes."

"Julia, food's waiting to be served." Mrs. Shields stood at the kitchen door, a frown on her face.

"Oh, goodness." Julia smiled at Allie. "Be right back, Sweetie."

Throughout the meal, Julia hovered nearby, refilling Allie's glass of milk, praising Allie for her fine table manners, buying Allie a red lollipop from the stash for sale on the front counter.

Hannah wrung the napkin in her lap. Nothing wrong with all that attention, not really. Yet Julia had wheedled her way into what should've been Hannah's special time with Allie. Why, the woman might as well have taken a seat and joined them at the table.

Then she remembered Papa after Mama and the baby died. He'd stare at the empty cradle near the fireplace, then quickly look away with tears in his eyes. For three months that cradle stayed there, then one day the cradle was gone. Hannah knew Mama and the baby who should've filled the cradle were never far from Papa's mind. How could she resent a wounded woman for connecting with Allie?

But how could she trust Miss Phillips after that weird comment she made outside of church yesterday?

Finished with the meal, Hannah and Allie were leaving the restaurant when Julia met them near the door. "Come back and see me, Allie."

"Thank you for the lollipop, Miss Phillips."

"You're welcome, Sweetie." She touched the bow in Allie's shiny dark hair. "I feel like we're friends. Call me Julia."

"Okay," Allie said, "Bye, Julia."

"I'll have a lollipop waiting for you."

To ask Allie to call a virtual stranger by her first name tightened every muscle in Hannah's body. As she helped Allie into the buggy, she glanced back toward the café.

Julia stood at the door watching them. Then she called to Allie and waved.

With a flick of the reins, Hannah started the buggy for home. She couldn't get there fast enough.

Mrs. Shields was an excellent cook, but today, the food in Hannah's stomach churned. Why had Julia Phillips taken such a consuming interest in a child she didn't know?

Chapter Nineteen

Matt folded his arms across the top rail of the fence. "The way Allie went right to sleep last night, I'd say the day in town yesterday must've done her good."

With her desire to get back to work, to get back to normal, Hannah had shrugged off her worries about Julia Phillips. But Matt's comment brought the woman's strange behavior to mind. Her stomach rolled, and not from the noon meal they'd just eaten.

"Are you troubled about something?" Matt tipped back the brim of his hat to get a better look at her.

"No, just concerned about this cow."

From their side of the fence, Hannah and Matt inspected the cow and her calf. One of the heifer's corneas was cloudy, her eyeball red, inflamed and weepy. She swung her head, bellowed, obviously in a nasty mood.

Hannah couldn't blame her. "Pinkeye."

"Yep, she's losing weight. Probably not up to looking for feed and water. Should know in a month, maybe two, if she's on the mend or will lose her sight in that eye. Or worse."

"I've seen pinkeye before," Hannah said. "We'll need

to be vigilant. Find and isolate infected cattle so this thing doesn't spread."

"The cow's other eye looks good. Something may have irritated that eyeball. If that's the case, this won't spread." He laid a hand over hers. "In the meantime, stay clear of her. Never seen a more cantankerous female."

With her elbow, she gave him a light teasing jab. "Keep giving orders if you want to see a doubly cantankerous female."

A lopsided grin on his face, he leaned close, studying her. "Better cantankerous than injured. Please, stay out of that pen. This gal's hurting and isn't partial to company."

With a noncommittal nod, Hannah turned away. When would Matt believe she could handle cattle? Even cantankerous cattle?

"Not much we can do for the cow. But if she doesn't eat well, her calf will suffer," she said.

"Once I'm back from greasing the windmill, we'll see that the calf gets nourishment."

Hannah had trained calves to drink milk from a bucket. Not hard to do.

A buggy drove under the Lazy P arch, interrupting the conversation. Visitors during the week were rare. Hannah watched the buggy's progress, trying to make out the driver's face.

"Oh, Julia Phillips," Matt said. "Wonder why she's here."

"Me, too," Hannah said. "Me, too."

Julia pulled into the barnyard. Matt crossed to the buggy, spoke to Julia, then offered his hand, helping her down.

Hannah clenched her jaw so tight her teeth hurt. Julia had fawned over Allie at the café, now she was here at the Lazy P, touching Matt.

Dressed in ruffles and lace, a jaunty hat and gloves,

feminine and beautiful, the woman could turn any man's head. But if that flirty smile she gave Matt meant anything, the only man's head she seemed intent on turning was Matt's.

Hannah's gaze dropped to her attire, smudged britches, rumpled shirt, dusty boots. She considered ducking into the barn. But wouldn't leave Julia alone with Matt. Hannah marched to the two of them.

Julia laid a dainty gloved hand on Matt's arm and gazed up at him with eyes filled with adoration. "Thank you, Matt. You're such a gentleman."

Matt's kindness to Julia all those years ago didn't explain this flirtatious behavior. With a married man.

Hers.

"What brings you here?" Hannah said.

Julia pressed a gloved hand to her nose. "Working hard today, Hannah?" Julia's smile held an edge, but then she turned to Matt. "Your wife defines helpmate to a T. You must be proud of her."

"I am."

Matt's tone was strong, his words certain. Still, he hadn't rebuked Julia for belittling Hannah, which was exactly what she was doing.

Inside Hannah, temptation reared its ugly head. She'd like to toss this woman, fancy finery and all, into a pile of manure. Even that fine perfume Julia swathed herself in wouldn't cover that stench.

To keep from doing that very thing, Hannah fixed a smile to her face. "You haven't said why you're here."

"Why, I've come to see Allie," Julia said, her voice filled with anticipation.

As if the child had heard her name, Allie raced out the barn door from a visit with the kittens, then skidded to a stop in front of Julia. "Hi!" Allie said, eyes aglow, obviously delighted to see the intruder.

"Hello, Sweet Girl." Julia bent down and patted Allie's cheek. "I brought you a gift."

She reached into the buggy and brought out a doll-sized four-poster mahogany bed with a lacy canopy and coverlet, much like Aunt Mary Esther's bed in Charleston. That fancy doll bed had to cost a considerable sum of money.

"I was passing the Dry Goods Store this morning and saw this in the window and thought of you. Ruth deserves her own special bed, don't you think?"

"The gift is too much," Hannah said. "Really, you didn't have to do that."

"I know I didn't." Julia turned to gaze at Matt. "But this little girl is so sweet I couldn't resist."

"Well, thank you, Julia," Matt said. "That's mighty kind."

"Want to meet Ruth, Julia?"

"Oh, yes, I'd love to."

Without hesitation, Allie took the hand Julia offered and they strolled toward the house.

Hannah folded her arms across her chest as she turned to Matt. "That woman infuriates me."

"She is a nuisance."

"Nuisance? She's trouble. She practically drools over you."

"If you believe Julia means something to me, you're dead wrong."

Hannah snorted. "Like you didn't notice her feminine curves and fancy clothes."

He wagged his brows. "Your clothes appeal to me more. Must be the woman wearing them."

Julia Phillips was everything Hannah wasn't. She held

out her callused work-reddened hands. "Look at my hands. Have you seen Julia's? They're dainty, dimpled—"

"Your hands are capable of branding cattle, handling a horse, tucking a child into bed." He chuckled. "Even baking a pie."

"No doubt Julia Phillips wouldn't forget the sugar when she makes her perfect pie."

As if he found the conversation amusing, Matt merely grinned at her.

No wonder. Like an idiot she'd listed Julia's assets, as if he hadn't already noticed. Matt had attempted to ease her mind about that woman with all this silly banter. Not that the ploy worked. Julia set her teeth on edge, but when it came to seeing trouble of the female kind, men were gullible.

"Be on guard with Julia."

"You're overreacting. Julia's lonely. Lost a child. She's obviously smitten with Allie, but—"

"That doesn't concern you?"

"Who wouldn't be? Allie's a delight."

"No one else in town makes a huge fuss over Allie like Julia does. She buys Allie gifts, comes for a visit. Uninvited. Compliments her for everything but breathing."

"I don't see the harm in that."

A hundred different possibilities for harm marched through Hannah's mind. Julia treated Matt and Allie as if she believed they belonged to her. Why couldn't Matt see Julia's behavior was odd? The bargain she and Matt had signed might one day be sealed with affection. But with Julia around, the possibility of fondness between them seemed doomed to failure.

"Well, that windmill won't grease itself. Jake's going with me to ride fence and save my hide if I fall."

"Don't you dare fall," she said.

With a chuckle, he leaned down and gave her a peck on the cheek.

"A kiss doesn't mask the truth, Matt Walker. Julia Phillips is up to no good."

He chucked her under the chin. "Jealous?"

"Don't be ridiculous. If you've changed your mind about our marriage and want Julia Phillips, be my guest." Even as she uttered the words her stomach lurched.

The gaze he turned on her exuded anger, hurt. "Those vows we took were for as long as we both shall live," he said, tone steely, eyes hardening into glittering coal.

She meant to keep those vows. Wanted him to keep them, too. Till death do us part. But she remained silent.

He trotted toward his horse. Long-legged, wide shouldered, brawny armed, one gorgeous work-honed package encasing a good heart, a committed will, a strong faith.

Hannah's jaw dropped. Was it possible? Was she starting to fall in love with her husband? Had feelings for Matt made her see a problem with Julia where none existed? Had jealousy distorted her perceptions as Matt had intimated?

Why not admit it? Matt was becoming the center of her world. Just by entering a room, he made her pulse race. He made her laugh. He made her feel safe.

Tears filled her eyes. She'd believed the worst thing imaginable was to marry a man she didn't love. Now she knew that caring about a man who'd never love her in return was far worse.

With every breath in her, she'd fight those unwanted feelings. From now on, she'd handle the work on the ranch and tiptoe around her husband.

She couldn't keep kissing him, couldn't keep walking

into the circle of his arms, couldn't keep playing this newlywed game. A game she'd lose.

Just as she'd lost everyone she'd loved most.

Matt and Jake rode out to grease the windmill. Not that the job required two men, but Jake had suggested he go along and ride fence. Probably feared Matt would fall off that tower, something he had no intention of doing. Still Matt was glad for the company.

"I appreciate you and Hannah taking Allie in," Jake said.

"Allie's a great kid. We're both fond of her. Not sure how we'll manage when she goes back home."

"Thought you and Hannah might be eager to see her go, being newlyweds and all."

What did a man say to that? Better to keep his mouth nailed shut.

Jake sighed. "Gertie's losing steam. My sis and I are getting old."

"When we said Allie would have a home here, we meant it."

The cowpoke released a gust. "Not that I'm trying to play God. A feller don't know what the future holds." He motioned across the way to some buzzards circling overhead. "But I can't pretend otherwise. Dying is natural, part of living, the cycle of life we see every day on this ranch. Cows die. Calves are born. We ain't got a say in any of it."

"Do you believe stuff just happens?"

"Not sure what you mean."

"Do you think accidents just happen? Or is God numbering our days?"

"Can't rightly say, but God's got the power to change the outcome. He allows what He allows. Ain't gonna question His wisdom." Jake tugged at his frayed cuff. "Even if my sis lives to be old as Methuselah, not sure that little imp will be happy with Gertie after the excitement of the ranch. Not sure how much longer Gertie can keep up with a child."

Matt chuckled. "That's a job, for sure. We'd need to talk to the women first, of course. But, I'm guessing Hannah and Gertie will want Allie to stay where she'll be happier."

Jake smiled, deepening the lines in his craggy face. "Gotta say, Matt, you've relieved my mind."

Up ahead the windmill rose into the sky. Beside it, cattle waded in the earthen tank. Jake rode off to look for breaks in the barbed wire fence.

Matt swung down, grabbed the grease pot and climbed the forty-foot windmill tower. His gaze settled on the herd grazing in the distance. A mighty fine view. Not his favorite perch but nothing compared to the peril of getting close to his wife.

Why, earlier, Hannah had practically handed Julia Phillips over to him. Blast it all, they were married. Married meant unavailable. Period.

As much as Matt didn't trust his feelings, knew he dared not rely on his judgment, he couldn't keep his distance with Hannah. Couldn't stop wanting to hold her in his arms. Couldn't stop wanting to kiss her. Not that his feisty wife gave him many openings.

He hooked his arm around the metal, holding the bail of the pot in that hand, then put the mill out of gear and greased the mechanism.

Matt knew his way around a ranch. Knew his way around horses. Knew his way around cattle. Much about the land, the weather, the animals was unpredictable. But nowhere near as changeable as women.

Women were baffling puzzles. Not surprising when he'd grown up in a household of men. His sensible Ma hardly counted. With Ma, he didn't need to be a mind reader. She spoke freely in language a man understood.

If only he could interpret his wife's words and actions as easily. Even Allie played that game upon occasion. He had no idea how to soothe his wife.

He had even less idea how to decipher Julia's conduct. Hannah saw Julia as a threat. Julia had flirted with him, but how could the woman be a threat when he had no interest in her? Still, with Julia butting into their lives, the added strain could sever the fragile thread of his and Hannah's connection.

One thing he knew. He'd stay clear of Julia. Not that he found the woman attractive or a menace, but she might misread the slightest kindness for something more.

His hand slipped and he wobbled, then tightened his grip. Better keep his attention on the chore at hand and off his wife, lest he break his fool neck.

He put the windmill in gear, then climbed down the tower. On the ground, he gazed up at the mill spinning without a sound. With a nod of satisfaction, he untied Thunder and swung into the saddle.

Jake rode up. "Fence is solid in this section."

"Nice to hear." Matt glanced at Jake. Never married, but still a man with wisdom. "Jake, you understand women?"

Hooting like a barn owl, Jake slapped his knee. "Only thing more unpredictable than a longhorn is a woman. Reckon the reason I never got hitched." He grinned at Matt. "Still, who needs to understand something so pretty to look at?"

Matt chuckled. "You've got a point."

"If it's all right with you, I'll ride on to the south pasture. Check that fence while I'm at it."

"Good idea. See you back at the house," Matt said, then rode for home.

He would check on that heifer and calf he'd wrestled to the corral. And on his wife. He might not understand women, but he agreed with Jake. Just looking at his pretty wife was worth every bit of his confusion.

Chapter Twenty

An hour spent watching Julia rope Allie in with compliments and gifts had Hannah cranked tighter than an overwound clock. Not able to take it any longer, Hannah had walked out to the stables and cleaned tack. Finished with the chore, she found Julia's rig was gone. Finally, the woman had left. Left Hannah's mind churning with possibilities. Possibilities that threatened Hannah's wobbly world. Julia's obsession with Allie and Matt put the life Hannah had built in peril.

Hannah had to do something to work out all her pent-up frustration or she'd burst. She strode to the corral, turning her gaze on the calf. The poor thing was unsteady on his legs, clearly in need of more nourishment. To train a calf to drink from a bucket was a sloppy task, but hungry calves learned fast.

The only obstacle—his cantankerous mother.

The heifer stood in the far end of the corral, turned away from the bright rays of the sun, her backside to Hannah. She wasn't eating. Wasn't producing sufficient milk.

Across the way, the calf moseyed toward the barn door. Why, in a couple of minutes, Hannah could have that calf inside.

Matt had asked her to stay clear of the heifer, but that calf could die while Matt was forty feet in the air, greasing the windmill. Jake had ridden with him to check fence. If he found breaks in the fence, they would repair the barbed wire. No telling when they'd return.

With Allie in the house with Rosa, Hannah had an opportunity to save that calf.

She moved to the section of the fence nearest the barn and farthest from the heifer. If she descended the rails real easy like, then moved slow and steady, she could guide the calf into the barn before the cow knew what happened.

With her eyes on the heifer, Hannah eased over the top rail and lowered herself into the corral. The sick cow showed no awareness of Hannah's presence. Hannah edged toward the calf, was steps away. Soon she'd have him drinking from a pail.

A bellow. Hannah whipped toward the sound. The cow charged. She shouted, flinging out her arms, waving wildly. The heifer kept coming and coming fast.

Hannah dashed toward the fence. She slapped her hands on the top rail, rising up to leap the rail. Just then the cow plowed into her hip, loosening her grip on the wood. With a shriek, she tumbled back into the corral.

Roaring with rage, the cow lowered her head, slinging slobber. Hannah rolled to the edge of the fence, curled into a ball, throwing her arms over her head.

Lord, help me!

The eeriest sense of doom shook Matt to the core. Something was wrong. He kneed Thunder. Under him, the stallion shot off, racing for home. The barnyard came into view, nothing appeared amiss. No buggy. Julia was gone.

Near the barn, he pulled back on the reins, slowing his

horse when a flash of blue tumbled into the corral with that heifer.

"Hannah!" *God, help her. Help me.*

Strength surged through him. He dismounted at a run, flung himself over the fence, screaming like a wild man, waving his hat. The enraged heifer whirled toward him.

Behind Matt, Hannah huddled, quiet. Was she hurt? His throat closed. Was she dead?

Red eye weeping, the heifer pawed the ground, shaking her head, eyeing him. Her calf bawled. The cow swung toward her offspring, then trotted to the calf's side.

Before that cow changed her mind, Matt scooped Hannah into his arms, plopped her over his shoulder and raced for the fence. A few feet more and they'd be safely on the other side.

The cow roared, hurtling after him, hooves flinging clods of muck. Matt tore open the gate and shot through, fastening it behind them just as the heifer's wide body crashed against the wood. The gate vibrated on its hinges, but held. The animal butted the frame once more, then again returned to the calf.

Matt knelt and lowered Hannah to the ground. "Are you okay?" he said.

"I'm fine." She jumped to her feet, dusted herself off, then rubbed her side. "The heifer barely grazed me with one of her hooves. Must not see well enough to take good aim."

She behaved as if nothing had happened. As if she hadn't put her life at risk. Matt's face flushed with anger. "You might not have been as fortunate with the next stomp!"

"Why are you so upset?"

"What if I hadn't arrived when I did? In a battle between you and that heifer, the heifer wins."

His throat closed. And he would bury another wife.
Thank God not today.

"I'm grateful you did," Hannah said, then turned back to the corral as if nothing had happened.

A wave of helplessness crashed over him, washing away every pretense he'd clung to, revealing the ugly truth. Hannah would never turn to him for help. He'd never be an equal partner with a woman who couldn't trust. A woman who took terrible risks to prove she didn't need him.

How could he keep such a woman safe? Whether she recognized it or not, he'd saved her life today. But what about the next day? The day after that? He couldn't go on like this.

Hannah's side ached, but she had no difficulty breathing, which told her she had no broken ribs. She'd be sore for a few days. Bruised. But nothing to slow her down. Things could've been far worse. *Thank You, God, that Matt came along when he did.*

Across from her, her husband paced the room like an angry bull about to charge. She'd upset him with what he saw as a reckless act. She'd apologize. Try to mend that fence standing between them.

"Please, sit. I'm fine," she said.

"You are not fine."

"Well, I will be fine. In a day or two."

Matt released a shuddering breath and halted in front of her. "Why did you enter the corral alone? What were you trying to prove?"

"Nothing. The calf needed nourishment. That's all. I'm a rancher, Matt. It's my job to take care of livestock."

"It's also your job to use common sense."

She shifted her position, trying to ease the ache in her side. "I thought I could handle it. I'm sorry."

Matt knelt. "You and I aren't in a contest to see who's the better cowboy, Hannah. If I hadn't shown up when I did, you could've been seriously injured, maybe…killed."

Had she been trying to prove something? "I'm grateful you did, Matt, more than I can say. I don't know what would've happened if you hadn't come along."

"Does that mean you'll think twice before taking such a risk?"

If she didn't keep her independence, she might start relying on him. Counting on him. A huge lump lodged in her throat. She'd rather face a crazed cow than make such a promise.

"I…I can't promise. You know ranching. Dangerous situations come up every day. Anyway," she said, smoothing a hand over her lap. "I'm fine now and the calf will be, too. Life can get back to normal."

He rose, crossed to the open window, putting his back to her, staring out at the vast pastures. The clock ticked on the wall. The notes of a song drifted in. Rosa must be working in the garden.

Matt released a long breath and turned toward her. "Any man worth his salt would protect a woman. I can't protect you."

Why *had* she taken that risk in the corral?

"You're a bullheaded woman, Hannah Parrish."

To hear her husband call her by her maiden name sent a chill slithering along her spine.

He gave a wan smile. "I like that about you. I really do. Still, I've lost one wife," he said so softly, she strained to hear him. "I can't lose another. I can't live like this."

"I promise," she said, putting up her right hand. "I'll ask for help before going in the corral like that again."

"That's not it." A shade dropped over his features, trapping the air in her lungs. "I've made a decision. I'm moving back to the Circle W in the morning."

His words ricocheted through her like a bullet, banging against her heart, her lungs, her very soul. "What? Why?"

"I'm giving you what you want. Your freedom. You no longer need my help to run your ranch. Well, you may need my help, but you'll never admit it. We're not partners, Hannah. You're a solo act."

Her throat knotted. "The ranch is *ours*."

"No, it's yours. You've proven yourself. The ranch hands understand they work for you now. Our deal has been fulfilled. It's time for me to leave."

The rigid set of his jaw, the stony look in his eyes belonged to a man who'd had enough. Enough of this farce of a marriage. Enough of her.

On booted heel, he pivoted to go.

Stifling a groan, Hannah struggled to her feet. "Wait!"

Rosa appeared in the doorway, brow furrowed, hands knotted in her apron, blocking Matt's path. "Allie gone. I look in house. In barn. In stable. I no find her."

Hannah's gaze flew to Matt. "What? That's impossible."

When had she seen Allie last? With her injury and their argument, they hadn't checked on the child.

"When did you last see her, Rosa?" Matt asked, his tone steady, every muscle alert. He looked strong, capable, ready to take action.

Tears brimmed in Rosa's eyes. "She play dolly with Miss Julia. I weed garden, see Miss Julia leave in buggy. I come inside, Allie gone."

"She can't have gone far," Matt said. "I'll ask Jake and one of the Lazy P hands to search the ranch. We'll find her." He turned to Rosa. "Stay close to the house, in case Allie comes back." He met Hannah's gaze. "Any idea where she'd be?"

"The only place I can think of is the Montgomery's."

"That's an hour on foot, a long walk for a child." He plowed his hand through his hair. "Still, I can't think of anywhere else she'd go."

"Unless… Unless she went with Julia."

"Why would Allie do that?" Matt said.

Hannah's mind traveled back to that day at church, to the words Julia had spoken. Was Allie a lure? A lure to snare Matt? Hannah's heart hitched. "What if she didn't have a choice?" she said, forcing the words past the knot in her throat.

Hannah knew then that she couldn't handle this alone. Not without Matt, a man who cared about Allie as much as she, and not without God. "We need to pray." Tears welled in her eyes. "Will you? Please."

With a nod, Matt took her hands in his. In his grip, she felt a sense of calm, of togetherness. These might be their last moments as husband and wife, but at least they were joined in purpose—to find Allie.

Matt bowed his head. "Lord, show us where Allie is. Keep her safe until we find her. Amen."

"Amen."

They strode out the door toward the stable. Matt turned his gaze on Hannah. "Why do you think Julia's involved?"

"Something she said to me that day at church."

"What exactly did she say?"

Hannah shivered. "She said, 'I didn't expect you. You complicate things.'"

Matt's features flattened, contorted. He looked riled, even dangerous. "Let's ride for town."

Hannah and Matt rode hard into town. Outside the Calico Café, they drew their horses to a halt, kicking up dust.

The town's bench sitters sat out front, eyeing them. Matt swung from the saddle, and then helped Hannah down.

The ache in her side a painful reminder that the risk she'd taken had driven Matt away. She'd deal with all that later. For now, all that mattered was Allie.

"Howdy-do, folks," Mr. Brand said then gave a wheezy cough. "Appears you're in a mighty big hurry."

"We're looking for Julia Phillips," Matt said, ushering Hannah toward the door.

"Miz Phillips sure took a shine to that little girl living at your place," Mr. Brand said. "Got her that fancy dolly bed."

Matt paused and turned around. "You knew about that?"

Mr. Seller nodded. "Yep, saw Miz Phillips leaving the store with it. Said she'd bought it for her little girl."

At his words, Hannah's veins iced. She worked her mouth until the words came out, "Did you just say *her* little girl?"

Mr. Sellers nodded. "Strange, ain't it?" He turned to Mr. Brand. "Must've been one of them there slips of the tongue."

"At my age, I have them slips all the time. Why, I…"

But Matt and Hannah didn't wait to hear the rest. They dashed inside the deserted café. The noon crowd had gone. Evening diners hadn't yet arrived.

Carolyn Shields stood at the front scrubbing the counter. Strands of her salt-and-pepper hair had pulled loose from her bun, giving the tidy woman a disheveled appearance. "What can I get you folks?"

"Is Julia Phillips here?" Hannah asked.

"This is Julia's day off." Mrs. Shields shrugged. "I don't know where she is."

"Mind if we knock on her door?" Matt said.

"Not at all. I'll show the way."

They clomped up the stairs, trailing the widow. Mrs.

Shields stopped in front of a door, slightly ajar. "Looks like she forgot to lock up."

They followed her inside. A breeze filtered in through the open windows. The fragrance Julia wore hung in the warm air. The room was tidy, the bed made.

"What on earth?" Mrs. Shields plopped fisted hands on her hips. "I didn't know Julia was getting married. An employee should tell me such things."

Hannah shot Matt a puzzled frown.

Matt shook his head. "Julia's not getting married."

"Then what's that for?" Mrs. Shields pointed toward the far wall.

A wedding dress and veil hung from a hook.

Fingers of fear settled around Hannah's heart and squeezed.

"Well, looky there," Mrs. Shields said. "Can't imagine what she'd do with all those little girl dresses."

On an upholstered chair in the corner, as if on display, small dresses had been fanned out across the seat and back. Dresses that would fit Allie. These clothes—were they bought to earn Allie's love? Or to clothe Allie after Julia abducted the child and fled town?

"This is scaring me."

Matt put an arm around Hannah's shoulders. "We'll get to the bottom of it."

Carolyn Shields walked to a writing table under the window, leaned over, perusing something. She turned toward them. "There's more. Take a look."

She and Matt joined her. Laid atop the desk was a lithographed wedding certificate with Esther and Naomi gathering wheat in the field, a pleased Boaz looking on.

Hannah's gaze moved up the document.

Matthew Aaron Walker and *Julia Katherine Phillips* joined together in Holy Matrimony on the___day in the month of *June,* in the year of our Lord *Eighteen hundred eighty-eight.*

To see her husband's and Julia's name on that wedding certificate with only the day of the week left blank chilled Hannah to the bone, left her shivering.

Matt stood behind her, rested a hand on Hannah's shoulder. "This is crazy. What's she thinking?"

"I'd say Julia Phillips has set her cap for you." Mrs. Shields frowned. "But, aren't you two already married?"

"Apparently that's a complication Julia didn't foresee," Matt said.

Hannah locked her gaze with Matt's. For the first time, in his eyes, Hannah saw fear. Her stomach tumbled. How far would Julia go to get what she wanted?

"We need to find Julia." Matt strode to the door. "Now."

"Where?"

"I have no idea. But God does."

As they headed out, Hannah whispered a frantic prayer, "Lord, help us find Julia."

The One who ruled the Universe, the One who overcame evil with good would intervene. For surely Julia Phillips was evil.

Chapter Twenty-One

Matt and Hannah strode to their horses. The overcast sky promised rain, something they needed badly, yet Matt hoped the rain would hold off until they found Allie. A storm would only hinder them, eat up valuable time.

Where would they search? Matt's mind traipsed back through the years, searching for clues to Julia's whereabouts. He hadn't gone three feet when a possibility hit him.

He reeled to Hannah. "I know where Julia has Allie."

"Where?"

"Years ago, Julia confided to Amy that she and the father of her baby rendezvoused in the line shack on the far edge of the Circle W. The shack's out of the way, could hold supplies. Has a path of sorts leading to it. A path a buggy could manage."

"Makes sense. We'll find her," Hannah said, her voice strong with resolve.

"Before we leave town, let's stop at the jail. Tell the sheriff what's going on and give him the location of the line shack."

Within minutes they'd spoken to Sheriff Spencer and rode side by side for the Circle W, hoping they were wrong about Julia and would find Allie safe and sound inside the line shack.

A terrible heaviness pressed against Matt's lungs. Once again he'd failed the people in his care. He'd not taken Hannah's warnings about Julia seriously and put an innocent child at risk.

"We have to find her," he said. "I can't live with letting Allie down, too."

"What do you mean—*too?*"

Might as well reveal what kind of man she'd married. "I'm to blame for Amy's death. Me. Her husband." His shoulders slumped. "The man who should have protected her."

"Amy fell from her horse during a race. Why are you to blame?"

In one long shaky breath, Matt released some of the pent-up pain he'd carried since that day. "What you don't know is I challenged Amy to that race. She died before my eyes." His voice broke. "I've gone over and over that day a thousand times. If only I'd taken a different route, nowhere near the gopher colony. If only I'd suggested a walk along the creek, not a race. If only…"

He couldn't finish. Couldn't tell her all of it.

"Sometimes things just happen and there's nothing we can do." Hannah's eyes brimmed with tears. "Like Mama dying. Like Papa. Like Amy. We don't understand why, only God does. You shouldn't feel guilty."

"But I do." He tore his gaze away. He couldn't bear to look at her. Couldn't bear to see her reaction to the truth. He sucked in a gulp of air. "Oh, Lord, forgive me, a part of me was…" He closed his eyes. "Grateful."

"Grateful?"

He forced the admission over the lump in his throat, "Her death released me from a difficult marriage."

"You and Amy weren't happy?" Hannah said, her tone, her expression bewildered.

"We loved each other, but things got complicated. She didn't like living at the ranch. Didn't like the long hours I spent away from her."

"She knew all that when she married you."

"Maybe she didn't know she'd hate ranch life. She withdrew more and more." He sighed. "Our love got lost in a battle we both were determined to win." Weary of the regrets eating away at him, he groaned. "I never had a chance to make things right."

"Oh, Matt, I understand regrets." She sighed. "The day before Mama died she tried to pull me into her lap. I don't remember why but I wiggled away." A sob escaped her lips.

He wanted to stop, to pull her into his arms, but they had to keep going. Had to find Allie.

"The next day…Mama was gone. I'd never have the chance to sit on her lap again. I wanted to relive that day. But I couldn't. All we can do is ask forgiveness, then let it go," she said, sweet forgiveness in her eyes. "I can see guilt holds you in chains. Prevents you from living. In a way, you're killing yourself, too. Amy would want you to be happy."

Could that be true? Moments ticked by. Matt thought about all the years he'd carried that guilt. Guilt hadn't changed anything. Anything but him.

"I do want to be happy. Maybe I'll find contentment when I return to the Circle W."

She stiffened. "Alone."

"I have to, Hannah."

"No, you don't." She nailed him with her gaze. "Admit it. You're running."

"Maybe I am. But what do you expect me to do?" He scrubbed a hand over his face. "Living with you in the same house, a bedroom apart, is sheer torture. *That's* what's killing me." He leaned toward her. "You tell me to take a risk and find happiness. What will it take for you to do the same?"

Her gaze dropped away. Silence.

More evidence he'd made the right decision about leaving. He clicked to Thunder and shot ahead, leaving Hannah, his past, what he'd once thought was his future, behind.

What mattered was finding Allie.

Despite the pain carving her features, Hannah kept up the pace. To leave this strong, feisty woman would be hard. She was like no woman he'd ever known. Yet he'd release her from a marriage she no longer needed, having proved she could run her ranch without him as a buffer. She might want him at her side, but her silence earlier proved she didn't want a real marriage.

In the distance thunder rumbled, the sky grew dark, matching his dark concern for Allie and the dismal prospect of life without Hannah. The wind kicked up, setting the branches of the trees swaying. Overhead the ceiling of clouds turned turbulent.

As turbulent as the eyes Hannah turned on Matt. "Do you…do you think Allie's safe?"

"Yes, I do. The clothes Julia bought her, the belief that Allie's her child imply Julia won't bring Allie harm."

"What's stopping her from taking Allie and fleeing town? Getting far from Bliss? Someplace where we'd never find her?"

"And leave that wedding dress behind?"

"Don't you mean leave *you* behind?"

Was that jealousy in Hannah's voice?

"If Julia sees Allie and me as her family, she'll stay put. For now."

No matter what he'd just said to Hannah, Matt wasn't sure about Allie's safety. Julia's belief that Allie was her daughter, along with the evidence they'd found in her room—the little girl clothing, the wedding gown and veil, the marriage certificate filled out with his and Julia's names—not only implicated her in Allie's disappearance, but proved Julia wasn't in her right mind. Somehow she'd functioned rationally in Bliss, held a job, attended church, taught Sunday school. How she'd managed that he didn't know, but those delusions of hers made Julia dangerous.

If she harmed or frightened that child—

Matt couldn't allow himself to consider the possibility.

"The sheriff promised to check out the line shack once he'd finished processing the prisoner in his jail."

Not that Matt intended to wait for the law.

A drop of rain fell on his hand, then raindrops spattered, leaving craters in the dust. Matt spurred Thunder on. Beside him, Hannah did the same.

The line shack came into view. A horse hitched to a buggy stood at the rail out front, his tail swatting at the rain like this was an ordinary day.

"Looks like the rig Julia drove earlier," he said. "Reckon she's holed up inside with Allie."

"I'm praying she'll give Allie up without trouble."

"Me too. But with or without trouble, we'll be leaving with Allie."

The front door swung open. Julia stood in the entrance, wearing a confident smile and a fancy pink dress. "I've been expecting you," she said in a chirpy voice, as if they'd come to pay a social call.

"And here we are," Matt said, forcing his tone to remain light, when he wanted to push past her and see with his own eyes that Allie was unharmed.

The rain came, harder now. Before Hannah could dismount, Matt strode to her side. He helped her down, then took the reins from her hands and looked her straight in the eyes. "Trust me," he whispered.

She held his gaze for a moment, then nodded.

He gave her a parting smile, then flung the leather around the hitching post.

"Aren't you cute as a button, Hannah?" Julia said with a smirk. "Why, it's hard to tell if you're a man or a woman."

Matt recognized the spark of temper in Hannah's eyes and shot her a steely look, a warning not to raise Julia's ire.

Hannah gave the slightest nod, then smiled at Julia. "Pretty dress."

"I wore it just for this occasion." Julia flashed a flirty smile at Matt, then sashayed inside.

He and Hannah followed her in. Holding his smile firmly in place, he closed the door behind them, then scanned the room. A cozy spot if not for the cobwebs and the faint odor of rodent excrement barely discernible under the fresh scent of rain. A stove sat in the middle of the floor, obviously lit by the steam coming from a tea-kettle. Two cots lined the walls. One empty.

Matt's gaze darted to the bed beneath the single window. Covered with cobwebs and coursing with rain, the small pane let in meager light. Still, it was enough to see Allie curled on her side, asleep, her chest rising and falling. Matt released the breath he hadn't realized he'd been holding. Proof he'd been less certain about Allie's welfare than he'd let on to Hannah.

"You've made a cozy place here, Julia."

"I had to." She heaved a sigh. "Hannah can't keep an eye on the child."

"I can see that." He glanced toward Hannah, then back to Julia. "So did you and Allie make plans?"

"I invited Allie and she came willingly. Allie loves spending time with me."

Apparently, Allie had fallen for Julia's ploy. No doubt Julia had offered candy or a toy or some adventure.

With an eye on Julia, Hannah edged toward the cot, no doubt to position herself near Allie. He'd never been prouder of his wife.

"Leave my daughter be!" Her face contorted in anger, Julia slashed a hand at Hannah. "You're not responsible." She smiled up at Matt. "You can count on me. I'll never allow Allie out of my sight."

If the situation weren't so grave, Matt would've argued the point. Allie Solaro was not an easy child to corral.

"Hannah's not worthy of you, Matt. I'll be a good wife. Just wait and see," Julia said, then laid a hand on Matt's chest.

A hand Matt covered with his own. "You're a lovely woman, Julia. What man wouldn't appreciate a wife like you?"

Unable to tear her eyes away, Hannah watched as her husband cupped Julia's jaw with his hand, gazing down at the woman with admiration in his eyes.

Julia snuggled against him, laying her head against his broad chest, wrapping her arms around him. "I love you, Matthew. I've loved you for years."

A woman who would speak those words to a married man in front of his wife had a skewed view of reality. Hannah's hands fisted. *And* whether she knew it or not, took her life in her hands.

"That's mighty good to hear. I feel the same, Julia," Matt said wrapping her in his arms, murmuring endearments in her ear.

Hannah's heart tumbled in her chest. Matt had told her

to trust him. She knew he was performing, pretending to adore Julia. But, to see him hold another woman in his arms, to hear him all but declare his love for her, slashed at every inch of Hannah like a serrated blade of a knife.

A desire rose up inside of her. To grab Julia by that fancy collar, snatch her from Matt's arms and toss her out the door and onto her backside in the mud. Exactly what the woman deserved.

Hannah's breath caught. She wasn't reacting like a woman content with a marriage of convenience. She was reacting like a woman in love with her husband. Who longed to hear words of love directed to her.

As if the floor shifted beneath her feet, Hannah fought for balance, for composure. Was it possible? Was it possible she had fallen in love with her husband?

Matt was mouthing make-believe endearments, performing like an actor in a play, a play with high stakes. Hannah knew no matter what he'd said, Matt felt nothing for Julia. Tears stung her eyes. And he felt nothing for her. He might want her, but he hadn't mentioned love. Every particle of her being wanted to run, to hide out, to wrap herself in that armor of fear. But she didn't have the luxury. They had Allie to protect.

As soon as they got the little girl safely home, Matt would move out as he'd planned, leaving behind the pretense of a marriage. Of love.

One glance at Allie curled on the cot, vulnerable, in need of protection, stiffened Hannah's spine. Twice before, Hannah had played a role. To protect Allie, she would play a part again. Only this time, instead of pretending to be the blissful bride, Hannah would pretend not to care, not to feel anything, while her husband held another woman in his arms.

"He's mine, Hannah." Julia cackled. "Not yours."

Had Julia read her mind? Hannah forced up the corners of her lips. Her face felt rigid, as if the effort to smile would crack her skin. "Matt and I married to save the ranch." Hannah's voice caught, but she forged on, "To give my father peace before he died. We never had a real marriage."

Their marriage was a farce. Something she'd thought she wanted, had even proposed, but now that arrangement left her empty. Now that marriage cost her far more than she could give.

Julia chortled. "I have the man I love." Eyes glittering, she glanced at Allie. "I have my child."

The crazy conversation swirling around Allie hadn't disturbed the little girl. She slept soundly. *Too* soundly. Nothing looked amiss but Allie was a light sleeper. The only explanation was that Julia had drugged Allie with something.

Had she given her too much?

A maniacal expression in her eyes, Julia celebrated her victory with a chuckle. "I will soon be Mrs. Matthew Walker." She tilted her face to Matt. "As soon as I heard Amy died, I came." She pulled away, the frenzied glow in her eyes hardened into icy shards. "Why didn't you wait for me?"

"I didn't know where you were, Julia," Matt said, cupping her jaw in his palm. "I didn't know if you were married or single."

Tears flooded Julia's eyes. "If my baby girl had survived, you'd have married me. We'd have been happy, the three of us."

"I'm sorry your baby died. You've been through a hard time."

"I missed my chance. Then. Now I have a second chance. A second chance with you and Allie." She touched

Matt's cheek. "We'll go to my room at the café. Pack Allie's and my things, then leave for Louisiana tomorrow."

"What if Allie doesn't want to go?" Hannah said.

"She'll go. A little laudanum and she'll sleep like a baby on the train."

For the briefest moment Matt's dark eyes blazed with rage, then as if donning a mask, his expression softened. "Whatever you say, Julia. You deserve to be happy."

Julia rose on tiptoe and kissed Matt's cheek. "We'll get married in my church. Live in a mansion surrounded by live oaks dripping Spanish moss. You and Allie will love living there."

"You have it all planned out," Matt said.

"I've thought of nothing else for weeks." She giggled. "Amy talked on and on about your wedding until I wanted to slap her senseless. Now I understand. I can't get the image of our wedding out of my mind."

Lightning flashed, illuminating the dingy shack. Thunder rumbled. Rain hammered the tin roof, the din almost deafening.

Julia's brow furrowed. "Except *she's* still your wife." She pivoted to Hannah. "Well, that's easy enough to fix." She chuckled, the sound devoid of humor.

As if on a Sunday stroll, she stepped to the stove, opened the door handle with her skirts, then grabbed the unlit end of a small log from the fire with both hands. She whirled toward Hannah, carrying the log upright like a torch. With each step Julia took, the burning end flamed brighter.

"It'll appear like an accident," she said softly.

Icy fingers danced along Hannah's spine. *God, save us!*

With quick, silent steps, Matt edged behind Julia, clasped her shoulders, stopping her in her tracks. "We don't want to hurt anyone," he said firmly. "Give me that log."

Julia spun toward him, waving the torch toward his torso. "You're a liar! You don't love me. All you want is Allie!"

The flames lapped at his sleeve, the cotton flared. Hannah shrieked. *God, help him.* Matt wrestled the wood from Julia's hands, then slapped at his shirt, losing his grip on the wood.

The log tumbled to the floor, blazing brighter as it rolled across the planks. Hannah jerked a blanket off the empty cot and dropped the wool over the flames and stomped them with booted feet, smothering the blaze.

Red-faced, Julia screeched, heading toward Hannah. "I can't let you live!"

Matt grabbed Julia's arms and dragged her kicking and screaming toward the door.

Away from Allie. Away from Hannah.

Julia's features contorted with hatred. "What are you doing?" She jerked against Matt's hold on her, lunging toward Hannah, flailing her arms. "You're hurting me!"

Matt lowered his face to hers. "Julia, you're in big trouble. Settle down."

"Let go of me!" Julia hissed. She twisted in his arms, raised cupped palms and scrapped her nails down his cheeks.

Blood oozed from the welts. *Oh, Matt.*

Breathing heavy, Matt rammed Julia against him, pinning her arms to her sides. She fought him, shrieking like a banshee, but wrapped in those strong arms, she didn't have a chance of escape.

The door banged open. Sheriff Spencer stood in the doorway, expression fierce, gun drawn, rain dripping from his hat, from his slicker. "What's going on here?"

Snarling like a vicious animal, Julia lunged against Matt's hands, kicked at his shins. "I hate you!"

"Appears the lady's not in the mood for reason. Still, won't be needing this." The sheriff holstered his gun, then whipped shackles from his belt and snapped the cuffs to Julia's wrists. "Sorry, ma'am, but I can't trust you to mind your manners," he said, then let his gaze scan the shack. "The child okay?"

"Julia gave her laudanum," Matt said. "Her breathing is regular. She should come around soon."

"You or the missus hurt?" He scowled. "Looks like you've got a burn."

"We're fine."

"Now," Hannah said. "I'll see to Matt's burn."

With a nod, the lawman led Julia toward the door.

"The rig belongs to the livery," Matt said.

"I'll drive it to town. Mind getting Miss Phillips inside the buggy while I tie my horse to the back?" he said, then turned Julia over to Matt.

On shaky limbs, Hannah stepped to the doorway. She wanted to fall into Matt's arms, to thank him for everything he'd done to protect them, including pretending to love Julia. One thing she knew. Matt would never knowingly put anyone in danger. Yet, he felt responsible for Amy's death and carried a load of guilt.

Matt lifted Julia onto the seat, then cuffed her hands to the rod supporting the roof. She slumped against the cushion, her hair already matted to her head by the deluge, never once taking her eyes off Matt.

Sheriff Spencer untied the reins, then clambered aboard. "Will need a statement soon as you can get to town."

Matt nodded. "Ask Doc Atkins to look at Julia. Maybe he'll know how to help her."

"I'll ask him to stop by the jail."

At the mention of jail, Julia swayed toward Matt. "Don't

let him take me! You love me. Why are you pretending you don't?"

"I'm sorry, Julia." Matt took a step back. "Sorrier than I can say."

With a shake of his head, Sheriff Spencer clicked to the horse. The mare started forward with a weeping, wet and bedraggled Julia on board. Julia twisted back as far as the cuffs would allow, staring at Matt. As if he somehow held the answers.

He watched her go, solemn, resolved. Silent.

The nightmare was over. An icy dose of reality hit Hannah. As soon as they returned to the ranch, Matt would leave and return to his land. And she'd be left feeling as bereft as Julia.

How could she say goodbye to him? How could she let him go?

She loved him.

The truth swished through her, trapped the air in her lungs. She loved her husband. The way he teased her. The way he supported her. Oh, and the way he kissed her.

Tears stung her eyes. Too late. She was always too late.

Or was she? They had one last evening together. She had one last chance. One last chance to try again.

As disturbed and misguided as Julia had been, she'd gone after what she wanted.

Perhaps, just perhaps, Hannah would take the biggest risk of her life and fight for her marriage.

Would she fail as Julia had? If so, the pain she carried from that tussle with the heifer would be nothing compared to the pain in her heart.

Chapter Twenty-Two

Allie came first, before Hannah, before Matt, before this last chance to save their marriage. Hannah shifted her gaze to her little charge. Allie had come through the ordeal with Julia, without any lasting physical effects. Thank God.

Now tucked on the parlor sofa between Hannah and Matt, her thin arms wrapped around her bent knees, Allie chewed on her lower lip. Then, gazing up at Hannah, finally, the story unfurled, one quiet word at a time. "I cried to go home, but Julia said no. She said we would ride on a train, go far away. She said it would be fun, but…" Tears filled her eyes. "I didn't want to go. I want to stay here. With you and Matt and Star. So I ran outside. She ran faster and caught me. She held my nose. I had to drink yucky medicine." She wrinkled her nose at the memory. "I was scared, Hannah."

Over Allie's head, Hannah met Matt's dark stormy eyes. Hannah wanted to wring Julia's neck. Beside them Jake and Rosa's lips thinned, their nostrils flared. From the look on their faces, Hannah would have some help.

Matt tugged Allie close. She released her knees and curled against him with a sigh. "I'm sorry, Pumpkin," he said. "Julia shouldn't have done that."

"Why did she say, 'You're my little girl. You're my little girl?' Over and over. I'm not."

Hannah trailed her fingers through Allie's hair. "Julia's confused, that's all. Don't worry, Sweetie. You'll never see her again."

"Good. She's not nice." Allie held up a forearm with bruised spots where Julia's fingertips had pressed into her skin. "She hurt me."

"You were very brave, Allie," Matt said.

Jake's jaw tightened. He knelt beside the sofa. "Shame on her. Want me to kiss those spots?"

Allie giggled. "They don't hurt now, Uncle Jake. Unless I poke them."

Eyes luminous with unshed tears, Rosa bustled around the room, plumping the pillow behind Allie's head, giving her a blanket. "I sorry. I not see you go with Julia."

"Did Julia hide you?" Jake asked.

They'd all wondered how Julia managed to conceal Allie.

"Julia told me to hide on the buggy floor. She said it was a…game." Allie's face crumpled. "When I was on the floor under the blanket, I prayed. Really, really quiet." Allie smiled at Matt. "And God sent you and Hannah."

Tears of gratitude and praise slid down Hannah's cheeks. *Lord, please help this child recover from this trauma. Keep her safe for all her days. Help Julia find the help she needs. We're all wrung out.*

Allie yawned, proof the hour had gotten late. "Matt, will you read me a bedtime story?" Allie asked. "Please."

"Of course," Matt said. "Tonight I will."

The unspoken message—tomorrow Matt would be gone. The truth pressed against Hannah's lungs.

Allie chattered a while longer, then began to nod off.

"See you tomorrow, Allie," Jake said, then gave his

great-niece a kiss on the forehead and trudged for the bunkhouse.

Rosa gave Allie a hug with a promise of fresh-baked cookies in the morning and anything Allie wanted for supper, then left for her quarters off the kitchen.

Matt hoisted the child into his arms. She nestled her head in the crook of his shoulder as Matt led the way toward her bedroom. Why, the three of them looked like a family. Allie could have been their daughter.

Up ahead, Hannah caught a glimpse of Matt's belongings stowed in a neat pile outside the door to his room. She realized then, tomorrow this perfect little bubble would burst. Matt was leaving. Her family, if she could call it that, was dissolving. Soon Allie would go to live with her grandmother. In the morning, Matt would be gone.

Inside Allie's room, Matt tucked the little girl in, then they sat on either side of her on the bed. Struggling to keep tears at bay, Hannah watched Matt read the story about a lost duckling finding the way home. She loved this little girl. How could she bear to lose her?

An answer gripped her, giving her the first ray of hope for the future. She'd invite Jake's sister to move here. Gertie, Allie and Jake would be Hannah's family.

Finished, Matt closed the book, got to his feet and kissed Allie good-night.

"Night." The little girl's mouth stretched wide in another yawn that ended with a hiccup.

"Sleep tight, Allie." Hannah leaned over and gave her a hug and kiss.

Matt helped Hannah to her feet. The solid warmth of his grip slid through her, felt right, like home. The soreness in Hannah's body from the tussle with the heifer had eased, but the ache inside her had grown until she felt like her heart would burst.

She bit her lip. That pain was partly her own doing. She'd stubbornly refused to seek Matt's help with the heifer, adding the last straw that had shoved him to quit their marriage.

As if by an unspoken agreement, she and Matt strolled to the porch, the place they'd spent many evenings, talking and studying the night sky. The thunderstorm earlier had ended the drought and moved on, leaving stars twinkling above and the earth with a fresh scent, washed clean, revived after an arid season.

Hannah had experienced the bleakness of an arid season and would know one again when the man she loved left. She needed the refreshment of God's gentle shower of blessings, the certainty of the direction God had for her. If Matt was her future, how could she plead with a man determined to go?

She'd need courage. Courage to fight for her marriage.

Lord, help me to take a different kind of risk. A risk with my heart.

Hannah dropped onto the settee, leaving room for Matt. Instead of joining her, he took the chair across from her.

She forced a smile to her lips and worked a sentence to her throat. "How's the burn?"

That would hardly convince him to stay. Still, fear of rejection kept her mute.

"Doc gave me a salve that's helped ease the sting."

"What did he say about Julia?"

"He believes she's delusional. He says as long as she's in town, she's a threat to Allie, you, even me. Doc gave her a sedative and she's locked up in a cell. Unless we file a complaint, at some point, the sheriff will have to let her go."

"How long can they hold her?"

"The sheriff wired her brother. He can hold her until her brother arrives to take her home."

"That's good to hear. I promised Allie she'd never see Julia again."

"And she won't."

A lump knotted in Hannah's throat. Banalities. They were making small talk instead of discussing the real issue hanging between them like a dark ominous cloud.

"We've got a lot to be grateful for." Tears sprang to her eyes. "God protected that precious child. God answered our prayers to find her safe."

"I've thanked Him for that." Matt shook his head. "Never thought I'd be glad to see a child drugged but I'm grateful Allie slept through Julia's attack." His brow furrowed. "No matter what, I wouldn't have let you and Allie down."

"You've never let anyone down, Matt. Not my father. Not Allie. Not me."

"I'm not a man you should depend on, Hannah. Stop making me out to be something I'm not."

"Oh, Matt." She leaned forward. "Why can't you forgive yourself? What happened to Amy wasn't your fault."

He lurched to his feet. Tall, powerful, all cowboy. From his stance, he had his defenses firmly in place. "We can't change the past."

"Can't we?" Hannah rose, lifted a hand toward him.

"No, we can't. I didn't protect Amy. Just like I couldn't protect Allie from falling into Julia's clutches." He shook his head. "I'm not the man for you."

"You're the best kind of man," she said softly, laying a hand on his arm. She waited for him to meet her eyes. "You're a man who has loved and lost. Most of all, a man who risks everything he has for others." She cupped his cheek. "Risks everything that is, but his heart."

He didn't speak, but shifted his gaze to some spot over her shoulder. The drained expression on his face suggested he'd traveled a long, weary road. "I...I can't do that, Hannah. What if..." He let out a gust. "What if something happens? What if I'm not here when you need me?"

"And what if a tornado hits tomorrow? Or a nor'easter? Or the sky falls?" She sighed. "You can't live life worrying, Matt. All you can do is put your faith in God and let Him take the reins."

He harrumphed. "Says the woman who never lets anyone take the reins."

She grinned. "I'm good at giving advice, not necessarily good at taking it."

"Care to explain why you can't give up those reins?"

"I've learned to handle every aspect of my life on my own."

"You're a competent rancher. I should've trusted you more."

"I should've trusted myself less. And God more."

"Like you just told me to do," he said, arching a brow.

"Exactly. You know, for two risk takers, we're both running scared." She fiddled with his collar. "Take a chance, Matt. On us."

He took a step back. "It's getting late. You've had a rough day and need sleep. I need to finish packing."

"You're still leaving?"

"Has anything changed, Hannah?"

"I have."

"I can't—"

She put up a palm. "Hear me out. Seeing you with Julia today made me think. About a lot. Like why I can't give God the reins." She sighed. "When Mama died, I was too young to understand what happened. To me, she died because she was delicate like a rose, not suited for life on a Texas ranch. I needed to be sturdy like Indian paintbrush and bluebonnets that thrive here, like my papa. I had to

take care of things. Take care of myself. Not rely on anyone."

"Losing your mother had to be hard on a little kid."

"I used that independence as armor to protect my heart.
I see now that my need to handle everything myself, instead of relying on you, trusting you, comes from fear.
Fear of needing another human being, of loving another
human being. Then, losing him."

"You weren't the only one who wore that armor. I let
what happened with Amy stand between us."

"And what good did that armor do? For either of us? I
lost Papa anyway." She choked back a sob. "Now I'm losing you."

Matt shifted on his feet. "Hannah, we had a marriage
of convenience. We both know that. I'm giving you what
you wanted." His gaze softened. "Your independence."

"I want that independence. With you." Tears brimming
in her eyes, she stepped closer until she was inches away.
"When Papa was dying, God planted the idea in my mind
to propose to you. I didn't trust His plan for my life. I didn't
trust that God had given me a far better gift than a solution
to my problem. He'd given me the man of my dreams."

He arched a brow. "Me?"

She laughed. "Who else could tame this filly?" She
sobered. "If I could design a man especially for me, you
would be that man. You love the land and the way of life
I cherish. You have a work ethic that never stops and a
heart as big as Texas. And kiss like…well…" Heat flooded
her cheeks.

A smile curved his face. He touched her cheek with cal-
loused fingers. "Ah, my strong-willed wife."

"Not strong when it comes to you, Matt Walker." She
took a deep breath and swallowed hard. "I tried, oh, how

I tried not to, but I've fallen in love with you. With all my heart. The question is—can you take a risk and love me?"

A grin quirked up Matt's face. "Love a woman who insists on carrying her own trunk? Love a woman who delivers a calf in jeopardy? Love a woman who races breakneck over Texas to save a little girl?" He tugged her to him. "Yes, Hannah Walker, I love you. I love every side of you. Debutante, filly, cowpoke, doesn't matter to me."

Hannah arched a brow and shot him a saucy grin. "Even if I can outwork, outride and outshoot you?"

"Even if."

"Then you'll stay?"

"Forever."

Life hadn't been easy for Hannah. Yet she never lost her strong faith. Her determination to save the Lazy P and her way of life. How could he have ever thought of leaving her? Feminine and fragile one minute, strong and capable the next, Hannah challenged him, made him want to be a better man, a better person, a better husband.

He brushed his lips across her cheek. "I love that cute way you have of raising your eyebrows when you're amused. That endearing habit of lowering your eyelashes when embarrassed. The way you can put me in my place with just a look."

She laughed. "Why, you're a romantic, Matt Walker. I love you lock, stock and barrel."

She curved into his arms, a perfect fit, and a perfect mate. Matt's heart filled with an almost painful bliss. After years of living with the guilt of Amy's heartrending loss, lonely even when surrounded by family and friends, he'd been given a second chance. A new beginning with the woman he loved. The woman who loved him in return.

The sorrowing years were over. The joyful years just beginning.

He lifted his hands to her face and showed her that truth, the deepest feelings of his heart with his kiss. A long, tender kiss filled with certainty that God had brought them together for a real marriage.

"Mercy, this marriage of convenience is most definitely in trouble." She raised her face to his, an invitation in her eyes. "Trouble we both are prepared to handle."

"No trouble at all." He grinned, hugging her to him. "I'm not letting you go, wife."

"Well, in that case, how will we get the work done?"

"Maybe you should take life a little easy and let me carry the weight for a while."

She tilted her head, considering. "Okay, but only until my ribs are healed. Then I'll go back to carrying my own weight."

"I have no doubt that my feisty wife can handle the heavy things, the tough things, even the imperfect things." His dimple winked. "The reason she married me."

She snuggled closer until their hearts beat as one. "We'll hang a W beside the P and make the ranch ours."

"Our land," he said, "our home."

"Yes," she whispered as the night birds called and the moon caressed the landscape. "Forever."

* * * * *

Dear Reader,

I grew up watching TV Westerns and hunky cowboy heroes like Wyatt Earp, *Cheyenne* and *Bonanza*'s Little Joe Cartwright. Something about the Old West drew me. Perhaps the rugged individualism of the cowboy, the danger of man pitted against man, nature or beast and the sheer wildness of the setting fueled my imagination.

I'm excited to have my first Western on the shelves. I hope you enjoyed *The Bride Wore Spurs* as much as I enjoyed writing the story!

God bless you.

Janet Dean

Questions for Discussion

1. Hannah and Matt's decision to marry had nothing to do with love. What circumstances motivated Hannah to propose to Matt?

2. How did Matt arrive at the conclusion he should marry Hannah? What circumstances motivated him to accept a marriage of convenience?

3. What concerns did Matt and Hannah share? What interests did they have in common?

4. Matt and Hannah had good reasons for entering a marriage of convenience, but what else motivated them underneath? How did this keep them from falling in love?

5. Hannah kept the truth about her loveless marriage from everyone except her father and Rosa, including her best friend Leah. Why?

6. Hannah was wounded by the loss of her mother. How did Hannah feel after her mother died? How did this impact her?

7. Matt was wounded by the loss of his first wife. How did Matt feel after Amy died? What added to his grief?

8. How did Hannah's strengths, her fearlessness and self-reliance, impact her relationship with Matt?

9. How did Matt's need to protect and lead impact his relationship with Hannah?

10. Matt tried to honor his father as Scripture instructs. When he finally talked to his father, what happened?

11. How did seven-year-old Allie's arrival impact Matt and Hannah and their relationship?

12. How did Julia Phillips' arrival in town add more stress between Matt and Hannah?

13. Matt and Hannah both felt led by God to marry. Yet Hannah didn't trust that God's plan might include falling in love with her husband. Matt's guilt over failing Amy made him feel undeserving of a second chance at love. What were they forgetting about God?

14. The crisis of Allie's disappearance and Julia's delusion broke down the barriers between Matt and Hannah, enabling them to finally declare their love. How can something negative, even bad, produce something positive, even good?

COMING NEXT MONTH
from Love Inspired® Historical
AVAILABLE MAY 7, 2013

THE COWBOY'S CONVENIENT PROPOSAL
Cowboys of Eden Valley
Linda Ford
Ward Walker thinks he's doing Grace Henderson a favor when he rescues her from a saloon, but she's been hurt too many times to trust the handsome cowboy. Can Ward convince her that he loves her despite her past?

THE MARRIAGE BARTER
Orphan Train
Christine Johnson
Recently widowed Charlotte Miller will do anything to keep the orphan placed with her—even marry the bounty hunter who's threatening to take her child away.

HILL COUNTRY CATTLEMAN
Brides of Simpson Creek
Laurie Kingery
Escaping a romantic scandal in England, beautiful aristocrat Violet Brookfield arrives in Texas and falls for rugged cowboy Raleigh Masterson. But is love enough to bridge the distance between their two worlds?

THE PRODIGAL SON RETURNS
Jan Drexler
As an FBI agent, Bram Lapp denied his Amish roots for twelve years, but an assignment forces him back into the Plain world where he meets Ellie Miller. Could Bram be the young widow's second chance at love?

Look for these and other Love Inspired books wherever books are sold, including most bookstores, supermarkets, discount stores and drugstores.

LIHCNM0413

REQUEST YOUR FREE BOOKS!

2 FREE INSPIRATIONAL NOVELS
PLUS 2
FREE
MYSTERY GIFTS

Love Inspired

HISTORICAL
INSPIRATIONAL HISTORICAL ROMANCE

YES! Please send me 2 FREE Love Inspired® Historical novels and my 2 FREE mystery gifts (gifts are worth about $10). After receiving them, if I don't wish to receive any more books, I can return the shipping statement marked "cancel." If I don't cancel, I will receive 4 brand-new novels every month and be billed just $4.49 per book in the U.S. or $4.99 per book in Canada. That's a saving of at least 22% off the cover price. It's quite a bargain! Shipping and handling is just 50¢ per book in the U.S. and 75¢ per book in Canada.* I understand that accepting the 2 free books and gifts places me under no obligation to buy anything. I can always return a shipment and cancel at any time. Even if I never buy another book, the two free books and gifts are mine to keep forever.

102/302 IDN FVXK

Name	(PLEASE PRINT)

Address	Apt. #

City	State/Prov.	Zip/Postal Code

Signature (if under 18, a parent or guardian must sign)

Mail to the **Harlequin®** Reader Service:
IN U.S.A.: P.O. Box 1867, Buffalo, NY 14240-1867
IN CANADA: P.O. Box 609, Fort Erie, Ontario L2A 5X3

Want to try two free books from another series?
Call 1-800-873-8635 or visit www.ReaderService.com.

* Terms and prices subject to change without notice. Prices do not include applicable taxes. Sales tax applicable in N.Y. Canadian residents will be charged applicable taxes. Offer not valid in Quebec. This offer is limited to one order per household. Not valid for current subscribers to Love Inspired Historical books. All orders subject to credit approval. Credit or debit balances in a customer's account(s) may be offset by any other outstanding balance owed by or to the customer. Please allow 4 to 6 weeks for delivery. Offer available while quantities last.

Your Privacy—The Harlequin® Reader Service is committed to protecting your privacy. Our Privacy Policy is available online at www.ReaderService.com or upon request from the Harlequin Reader Service.

We make a portion of our mailing list available to reputable third parties that offer products we believe may interest you. If you prefer that we not exchange your name with third parties, or if you wish to clarify or modify your communication preferences, please visit us at www.ReaderService.com/consumerschoice or write to us at Harlequin Reader Service Preference Service, P.O. Box 9062, Buffalo, NY 14269. Include your complete name and address.

LIH13

Charlotte Miller has already lost her husband…she's terrified at the thought of giving up her little girl. The orphan Sasha is the daughter Charlotte has always wanted. But only married women are permitted to take in orphans. And the only eligible bachelor in town is Wyatt Reed—the tracker hired to take the orphans away!

Read on for a sneak preview of
THE MARRIAGE BARTER by Christine Johnson,
the second story in the ORPHAN TRAIN *series.*

"I won't lose my daughter. I'll do anything to keep her."

He flinched and looked away. "I'm sorry. I tried my best."

"I know." She boldly grasped his arm, forcing his gaze back to her. "Thank you." The time had come. "Will you help me again?"

Confusion clouded his expression. "How?"

She opened her bag and pulled out the wallet. "Charles left me some money. Whatever Mr. Baxter paid you, I'll pay double."

He pulled back. "It's not that simple."

"Of course it is."

"No, it's not. The Orphan Salvation Society has an agreement with Greenville. If the judge rules that the children must go to Greenville, then I have no choice but to take them."

Charlotte shook her head. He didn't understand. "I'm not talking about all the children. I'm talking about Sasha."

Instead of walking away or shouting at her, he spoke firmly. "There's nothing I can do to help you keep Sasha."

"Yes, there is."

He stared at her. "No, there's not."

"You can marry me." The words exploded down the street like gunfire.

He didn't blink. Not one muscle flinched except that tick below his eye. Dear Lord, he must think her mad.

"For money," she added, lifting the wallet. "I'll pay you double, triple. I'll give you all I have." Tears threatened, but she refused to let them surface. "I don't want anything from you. You don't even have to live here. I just need to be married long enough to legally adopt Sasha. Once the adoption goes through, you can move on." She shoved the wallet at him.

He held up his hands and backed away.

"Please help me." The words came out strangled, and for a moment she feared he didn't understand. She held out the wallet again. "Please."

Don't miss THE MARRIAGE BARTER
by Christine Johnson, available May 2013 from
Love Inspired Historical.

Love Inspired HISTORICAL

In the fan-favorite miniseries
Cowboys of Eden Valley

LINDA FORD

presents

The Cowboy's Convenient Proposal

Second Chance Ranch

She is a woman in need of protection. But trust is the one thing feisty Grace "Red" Henderson is sure she'll never give any man again—not even the cowboy who rescued her. Still, Ward Walker longs to protect the wary beauty and her little sister—in all the ways he couldn't safeguard his own family.

Red desperately wants to put her tarnished past behind her. Little by little, Ward is persuading her to take a chance on Eden Valley, and on him. Yet turning his practical proposal into a real marriage means a leap of faith for both…toward a future filled with the promise of love.

Available May 2013

www.LoveInspiredBooks.com

LIH82963

Will You Marry Me?

Bold widow Johanna Yoder stuns Roland Byler when she asks him to be her husband. To Johanna, it seems very sensible that they marry. She has two children, he has a son. Why shouldn't their families become one? But the widower has never forgotten his long-ago love for her; it was his foolish mistake that split them apart. This could be a fresh start for both of them—until she reveals she wants a marriage of convenience only. It's up to Roland to woo the stubborn Johanna and convince her to accept him as her groom in her home and in her heart.

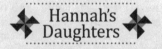

Hannah's
Daughters

Johanna's Bridegroom

by

Emma Miller

Available May 2013